Life of Tagore

Probhat Kumar Mukherji

Translated by
Sisirkumar Ghosh

HIND POCKET BOOKS
An imprint of Penguin Random House

HIND POCKET BOOKS

USA | Canada | UK | Ireland | Australia
New Zealand | India | South Africa | China | Singapore

Hind Pocket Books is part of the Penguin Random House group of companies whose addresses can be found at www.hindpocketbooks.com

Published by Penguin Random House India Pvt. Ltd
4th Floor, Capital Tower 1, MG Road,
Gurugram 122 002, Haryana, India

Penguin Random House India

First published in Hind Pocket Books by Penguin Random House India 1976
This edition published in 2022

10 9 8 7 6 5 4 3 2

ISBN 9789353493776

Printed at Repro India Limited

CONTENTS

PREFACE

This is a simple and condensed edition of my four-volume *Rabindrajibani* in Bengali. Obviously, I have worked within a deliberately limited field. There has not been much of an attempt to relate the life of the poet and the life of the person. Though there must be a relation—if not exact equation— between the two, I have refrained from trespassing into that dangerous borderland. This is not an interpretation of his creative life, which the reader should find elsewhere.

Rabindranath lived a varied and crowded life, with his ever-widening interests. Whether and how far he was able to harmonise these different interests and involvements, in life and art, is another question. But there can be little doubt that both the quantity and quality of his contacts with the life of the time, the peoples and of a world fellowship, which became increasingly the cry of his heart, are impressive. I have merely tried to provide a plain chronicle of an outstanding career which, a strange mixture, at once evokes admiration and raises ever-new questions. Its relevance can never cease.

In my work I was greatly assisted by my young colleagues, Shri Dilipkumar Dutt and Shri Prabir-kumar Debnath, of Rabindra Bhavan, Santiniketan. As for the translator, I would have been lost without him. To all of them my blessings.

P. K. M.

TRANSLATOR'S NOTE

Tagore is no longer the Colossus, or the Sentinel, as the Mahatma called him. There has been a sharp decline in interest and understanding, and some of the recent writers have been both rude and ignorant. History has no doubt its own ways of revising reputations. Generation gap does the rest. But the poet is always our contemporary, holding fast against the ruins of mutability.

Events across the eastern borders have witnessed a rare resurrection. His one-time swadeshi song Amar sonar Bangla (O my golden Bengal) has been the rallying cry, the national anthem of one of the most remarkable risings in modern history. The poet speaks for Man, beyond religion, beyond politics. (Pace T. S. Eliot). Tagore was more than a Bengali poet. A prophet of the Universal Man, viswamanab, not to know him is to declare oneself insensitive. But—it must be made clear—in this little Life or chronology we have not concerned ourselves with literary assessment. We did not set out to use biography to illuminate creative activity—a risky, if sometimes rewarding, game. On his part Tagore himself was chary of historical determinism and claimed autonomy for the aesthetic activity. The chief concern in the following pages has been mostly a narration of the main events, great and small, of a career remarkable by every known standard, a creative, colourful, growing, paradoxical person, at once lyrical and heroic, committed and transcendental, labouring in the cause of rural welfare and dreaming of a world fellowship of artists and thinkers, the meeting of the East and the West. The puzzle will not easily cease. As Soren Kierkegaard's secretary had said, anyone who wished to deal with S.K.'s life must take care of not turning his finger—it is so full of contradictions—so difficult to get to the bottom of that man of moods. Dr. P. K. Mukherji's superb sanity has preserved him from probing too deep into the puzzle, and he has pointed to the heights as well as the abysses, the flat-lands no less. The reader is free to draw his conclusion.

To watch the shifting scene is to recognise that the age of miracles is perhaps never over. This is the gift of genius, that it makes the impossible happen. If ordinary men had to go through half the activity that the poet easily took in his stride they would be dead or suffer nervous breakdown. But this poet's outer activities were no less versatile and bewildering than his inner. Through events, commonplace and dramatic, we have but tried to follow his footsteps. In the process large areas of modern Indian history and some of Western may come into a single focus. Whether there is a pattern in the process it is not for us to say. Tagore himself did not claim to have pierced the veil.

If this deliberately short account helps new readers to a better appreciation of what the poet as person was like and arouses interest to know more, that will be reward enough for the chronicler. As with the larger, four-volume biography, this small chronicle too may act as a mini source-book, or lead the curious to the source itself. If the work helps in making known to a larger reading public at least the facts about the poet's outer life the labour that has gone into its making will not be in vain.

S.G.

1

The Water Falls, the Leaf Trembles

RABINDRANATH WAS BORN in 1861. The years preceding his birth had covered a variety of events and innovations in the cultural life of Bengal, such as the foundations of the Calcutta University, the propagation of Brahmoism by Debendranath, the movement for widow re-marriage and women's education sponsored by Vidyasagar, the protest in the columns of the Hindu Patriot by Harish Mukherji against the atrocities of the indigo planters; the Santhal rebellion on the Bengal borders, the death of the poet Iswar Gupta and the emergence of Madhusudan Dutt and Dinabandhu Mitra on the literary scene, the publication of Somprakash, and the stirrings of the first Bengali theatre. Each of these movements was a precursor of the modern era and helped to wean Bengal from an obsessive mediaeval mentality, or attachment to the past. Rabindranath's birth coincided with the dawn of this age.

The family into which he was born, had already shed—not without a price—many of the old Hindu conventions. Early in life, in 1843, his father Debendranath had been converted to Brahmoism. In this free-thinking age, when orthodoxy has lost its edge or is fast disappearing, it is difficult to imagine what an ordeal it must have been then, especially for a youth born into wealth and an aristocratic patrimony, to break away from an all-powerful, sacerdotal social system. In the words of Rabindranath, "Even before my birth, our family had weighed anchor and moved far away along the stream of heterodoxy." His father's conversion had radically altered the family mores, and rituals and religious observances grew less and less frequent. Debendranath had handled the periodic fiestas and other ceremonies—'thirteen in twelve months', as the Bengali phrase puts it— usually observed in the more well-to-do Hindu household. To Rabindranath "even their memory was remote. . . . When I came on the scene. . .the new age had just declared itself."

Let me give a few illustrations of what the spirit of the modern age meant in those days. In etiquette and dress, the menfolk were quasi-Moghul; up to the middle of the last century this was the hallmark of aristocracy. Into this nearly static world flowed a steady trickle of the latest in *haute couture.* Debendranath's father, Dwarkanath, was as rich as he was respected, as much an epicure as an aesthete. European paintings, Italian statuettes, Western furniture—chairs, tables, sofas, coaches, etc.—were all introduced during his lifetime. Debendranath's own children and sons-in-law were not entirely indifferent to Western ways and manners. Organs, pianos, the flute and the violin were freely used in family gatherings; even into the prayer hall of the Adi Brahmo Samaj the English pipe-organ had found its way. Rabindranath's boyhood days were passed in this melange of East and West, a legacy to which his own life and thought would give a new turn across the years.

Satyendranath Tagore, Debendranath's second son, was the first Indian member of the coveted Indian Civil Service. He returned from England a keen supporter of many Western ideas. One of these was the education of girls. When, in 1866, he came home from his headquarters in the Bombay Presidency the spectacle of his wife "a young matron, getting down from an open carriage, like a Memsahib, caused laments loud and long, impossible to describe." Another brother, Jyotirindranath, used to ride to the Maidan with his young wife by his side. People inside and outside the family cried shame. It is as well to remember that up to this time ladies of the Tagore family used to be taken to the river Hooghly in closed palanquins and it was these, along with the *purdanashin* occupants inside, that were dipped into the holy water. A good part of Rabindranath's formative years were spent with these two brothers and the new outlook which they championed and fashioned could not but have influenced him.

Among the literary lights of the age were Madhusudan Dutt, Dinabandhu Mitra, and Bankim-chandra Chatterji. Michael's blank verse had struck a new note and given Bengali poetry a strength, ease and spontaneity it did not have before. The new medium influenced not only thought and expression but also the vision. The language in which Dinabandhu wrote his plays was genuine, homely speech, his characters spoke in the idiom of the folk and their plots were based on the intimate joys and sorrows, the life and problems of everyday human experience. So long, the Bengali drama had been content with either adaptations from English or Indian myths and histories of old. Dinabandhu's *Neeladarpan* (Mirror of Indigo) was a landmark in the history of the Bengali stage and literature. At this point of transition appeared Bankim. His brilliant style, the rich variety of plots, and characterisation were all new. In him the opposing tendencies of the East and the West had come together, a blend of cold logic, utilitarianism and conservatism. In Rabindranath we have more of a marriage of true minds, though not without tensions of its own.

A few words about the Tagores. One of the early forebears, Jagannath Kushari, had married into a Peerali Brahmin family. The land he had received as dowry in a Khulna village (now in Bangladesh), became his home. For marrying into an outcaste group, Jagannath was naturally ostracised. During the Muslim period in Bengal, there were many such cases of outcaste groups among the Bengali Hindus. Jagannath's father-in-law belonged to one of these.

After a few generations one Panchanan and his uncle left their village home due to some family broil. In search of a fortune they came by boat to Calcutta, then a cluster of villages, where British merchants had already started commercial activities. In those days a job could be had for the asking.

The Kusharis settled down at Govindpur village in Harijan quarters. No Brahmin had lived there so far; and the local folk gave them a glad welcome. In Khulna they had been outside the pale. Here they were nothing short of *Thakur Masai!* To these simple people the Brahmin was a *thakur*, a deity. Panchanan worked as a sort of stevedore for the merchants, who put him down in their ledger books as Panchanan 'Tagore'. *Thakur* in English had become 'Tagore' (Tagoure). Thus the Kusharis were transformed and after a time they themselves came to use the surname.

How the successors of Panchanan Tagore built up their fortune in Calcutta during the transition period between the fall of the Nawabs of Bengal and the rise of the astute mercantile class need not be described in detail.

One of the descendants, Nilmoni Thakur, later got a job in the Orissa Collectorate, under the East India Company, where he made his pile. Afterwards he built a house in Pathuria Ghat (Stony Stairs), on the banks of the Bhagirathi-Ganga now known as the Hooghly. But wealth is often a source of trouble. Soon a dispute broke out, between him and his brother Darpanarayan, who too had not been slow in amassing wealth. Luckily the two brothers settled their differences amicably. In consideration of a lakh of rupees Nilmoni handed over the house and other properties to his brother and left Pathuria Ghat for good, taking with him the idol of the family deity.

In nearby Jorasanko, to the east of Chitpur Road, he purchased a plot of land and built a house. This was towards the end of Warren Hastings' administration (1784). The locality, not too far away from the river, was then known as Machua Bazar or Fishermen's Mart.

Dwarakanath (1794-1846), the poet's grandfather, was born in this branch of the family. The wealth, prestige and influence of the Tagore family stem from him.

Known to be rich, shrewd and learned, he came in time to be one of the city's leading business magnates. Indians, Englishmen, officials and business folk, all held him in high esteem and looked forward to his garden parties with their splendid dinners, drinks, music and dance. His earnings were fabulous but so were his expenses. "Prince" Dwarakanath was a friend of Raja Rammohun Roy. But he did not, on that account, think it necessary to go back upon Hindu customs and manners; nor did he oppose his friend in deference to the clamour of public opinion. If it suited his purpose he followed the ways of old; if not, he did not mind a little heterodoxy. His was a free spirit with a dash of opportunism such as often found among men of affairs.

Dwarakanath's eldest son Debendranath was made of different stuff. Early in life he had a spiritual experience and entered the Brahmo fold of Rammohun Roy. One day, he chanced upon a stray slip of paper on which was printed the first verse of Isha Upanishad: 'All that is in this world is enveloped by God. Enjoy that through renunciation. Do not covet the wealth of others.' A new light dawned upon Debendranath's troubled mind and it became the mantra or guiding insight of his life.

In the meantime Dwarakanath had passed away in England. The entire responsibility of the *zamindari* and business interests of the family devolved upon young Debendranath. A sizeable portion of the property had to be sold in order to clear off the heavy debts left by his lavish father. Debendranath was determined to settle, fairly and squarely, all the liabilities, and he did not listen to the relatives who counselled chicanery. Some of the debts, they argued, could not be easily proved in a court of law. But Debendranath was a righteous soul; he treated even his father's promise of charity—well over a lakh of rupees—as virtual debt, and in instalments spread over years he paid the amount with interest to date. It was because of his rectitude, that he came to be called Maharshi, the Great Sage.

In his autobiography Debendranath has recorded his inner and outer struggles. Its style and sincerity make it a Bengali classic. He also compiled an anthology of excerpts from the Indian scriptures, *Brahmo Dharma*, with whose help he gave an exposition of his own religious faith. The book not only provides an excellent selection of Hindu thought but may well serve as an introduction to universal religion.

The seventh of Paus (21 December, 1843), the day on which Debendranath had been converted to the Brahmo fold and found his true faith, was ever looked upon as a sacred day, and is even now observed at Santiniketan. To Rabindranath too the memory of this day carried its own sanctity and he cherished it to the end of his life. The book *Brahmo Dharma* was always by his side, the source and support of his spiritual life.

Debendranath had a large family, fifteen children in all. Rabindranath was the fourteenth and, since a younger brother died shortly after, also the youngest child. He was born in the Jorasanko Mansion where, eighty years after, he breathed his last. To this day his countrymen, and many from all over the world, visit the place twice a year, on the day of his birth (25th Vaishakh or May 8) and the day (22nd Shravana or August 7) on which he passed away.

At the time of Rabindranath's birth, his father was fortyfive. The eldest son, Dwijendranath, was twenty-one; the next Satyendranath, about to leave for England to compete for the Indian Civil Service, was nineteen; the next Hemendranath, seventeen; Jyotirindranath was thirteen. The others need not be mentioned here, since it was the influence of these four that counted.

The married daughters of Debendranath, along with their husbands, lived with him, as permanent members of the family. For marrying into a family of Peerali Brahmins—on top of it Brahmos—the Hindus had ostracised them and they had no alternative but to seek refuge in the sprawling ancestral home. It was among this heterogeneous crowd, of relatives and dependants of all denominations, maids, servants, attendants and liveried retainers that Rabindranath's early years were spent.

As in most affluent families the children were left to the tender mercies of the maids and the servants. Rabindranath's mother, Sarada Devi, the mistress of this huge household, had most of her time taken up with house-keeping. The Master was often away in the Himalayas or out on river trips. The daughters and the daughters-in-law were busy looking after their own darlings. Also, after the birth of her last child, Sarada Devi's health had broken down. As it is, young Rabindranath received scant attention from the ladies of the family. Most of his time was spent in the servants' quarters. Often, he would remain confined to a room and gaze on the pond under the window. A large banyan tree stood at the eastern bank near the wall, a coconut grove on the south. Like his own Amal in *Dak*

Ghar (Post Office) the boy would gaze and gaze. He was not allowed to move out; the servants spoke harshly if he ever strayed out of bounds, as this added to their responsibility.

The family mansion had been put up by Nilmoni Thakur after he had separated from his brother. Later on Dwarakanath had raised, just by its side, a palace of his own, where he used to entertain his European guests. Even after him it remained the aesthetic and cultural centre of a new movement in Bengal, for the brothers Gaganendranath and Abanindranath lived there. Today there are no traces of the old palace. On its site has risen a new structure: Rabindra Bharati or the new Tagore University.

Across the years, with the growing need of expansion, the family residence had been added to bit by bit. It had many rooms and staircases scattered everywhere. It was like Ariadne's maze. For Rabindranath these half-familiar nooks and corners and the roof overhead breathed a sense of wonder and mystery. The boy, imaginative as he was, had an enormous fund of fantasy. In one of his later poems a child asks :

> No one knows
> Where my king's palace is
> Would it be anywhere, if they but knew
> Where it is ?

Elsewhere he has said, "J remember how now and then, in the mornings specially, my mind would be filled with a strange joy. It looked to me as if this universe was wrapped in some deep mystery . . . With a little stick I would dig up earth in our farmhouse and wonder if some strange discovery would not come my way. On the veranda in the south I heaped up a little dust and sowed some custard-apple seeds. I watered them at all hours and loved to imagine what a strange thing it would be when these would at last begin to sprout." Further quotation is unnecessary. *Chelebela* (My Boyhood Days), which he wrote in his advanced and reminiscent years, has been widely read in the original as well in the English and Hindi renderings.

Keen business instincts, honesty, sobriety and economy helped Debendranath to recover the family's lost fortune. In his hands the zamindari yielded a considerable income, and the family did not have to struggle for its livelihood.

The Tagores lived in an exciting ambience of culture, music and amateur theatricals. But in those days the gap between the old and the young was wide and quite unbridgeable. The young were not permitted in the soirees or *jalsas* (musicals) arranged by and for the adult members of the family. Yet their echoes must have reached the young folk and fired their hearts and imaginations. His eldest brother, Dwijendranath, was then writing *Swapna Prayana* (Dream Journey), parts of which he used to read out to his friends. Rabindranath, an eavesdropper, remembered huge chunks out of it. The influence of his brother's poem on his early works is there for all to see.

Even as a child Rabindranath had a most musical voice. He once said that he could not think any period of his life without music. Srikantha Sinha, an uncle of Lord Satyendra Prasanna Sinha of Raipur (Birbhum), was a devoted follower of Debendranath. On his visits to

Calcutta he used to put up with the Tagores; passionately fond of music, Srikantha was either humming a tune or playing on the sitar most of the time. "He did not teach us music," the poet wrote later, "he made a gift of it. We did not know when or how it had become ours." Bishnu Chakravorty, a celebrated musician of the day, was in the employ of the Tagore family and the boys had their early lessons from him. During special occasions and in the family prayer hall every morning and evening they heard him sing the religious airs from *Brahma Sangit*. When the children had grown up a little, Jadu Bhatta, an unusually gifted *ustad* (musical teacher or composer) was appointed to teach them classical music. But Rabindranath was from the beginning allergic to routine and rigid training of any sort; he used to pick up odds and ends just as he pleased. That way he managed to learn a good deal from listening to the tunes and songs hummed by the valets, maid-servants, beggars, boatmen, the wandering minstrels, and the *bauls* (street singers of Bengal).

Rabindranath's life was spent mostly in the servants' quarters, as was then the vogue in aristocratic families. One of these servants, lsvara, or Brajesvara, had been at some period a village schoolmaster, and, probably on that account, had been put in charge of the boys. At night the young folk gathered round the dim glow of oil lamps and listened to lsvara recite the age-old stories from the *Ramayana* and the *Mahabharata*. Dinner over, they all huddled into a spacious bedstead—the practice of having a separate cot for every child was yet to come. Some elderly maid-servant or a female relation would sit at the end of the bed and recount tales of long ago. And so, one by one, the little ones would drop off to sleep.

His earliest lessons began in the traditional way, with the Bengali primer *Varna Parichaya*. Crossing over the hurdles of spelling, when on the very first page, he came upon the phrase *Jal parey, pata narey*, (the water falls, the leaf trembles) to our young poet it seemed as if he was reading the original verse of the world's first poet. Even after the book was closed and kept aside, the phrase echoed and re-echoed in the child-heart *Jal parey, pata narey*, (the water falls, the leaf trembles).

In the early stages the children were taught at home privately. The tutor in charge was one Madhab Pandit. One day when the bigger boys, in fresh linen, were leaving for school, little Robi suddenly let off a loud and uncontrollable wail. He too would go with them. Madhab Pandit gave him a smart slap and told him tartly, "Now you are crying to go to school. But a day will come when you will cry more bitterly to be out of it." "Never have I heard a prophecy more completely come true," was the poet's subsequent comment.

Passion for schooling soon got the young learner into the Oriental Seminary. But he had not been there long when the guardians removed the whole lot to the Normal School, supposed to be modelled on English schools. In keeping with its progressive theory of education in which instruction blended with delight, before the classes began, all the children had to assemble in a hall and had to recite, a refinement of torture, an English poem in chorus. Readers of *My Boyhood Days* will recall how outlandish the poem sounded in the mouth of uncomprehending lads religiously going through an abracadabra. His school days, were far from happy, indeed they were a long agony.

2

A Mind is Moulded

AT ELEVEN HE was taken to a suburb of Calcutta and for the first time escaped the city. Calcutta in 1873 was in the grip of dengue fever. The Tagores decided to shift to a garden house in Peneti or Panihati. This had no little influence on the boy Robi, so long confined to the high-walled palace in the alleys of Jorasanko. The river flowed nearby and through the foliage of the green trees near the servants' outhouse one could see country boats in full sail drifting midstream. Even in his old age the image stayed with the poet and he used it in many of his poems.

Back from Panihati the boys had to go through the old drudgery, to the same Normal School. By now Rabindranath had come to dislike the school much as Madhab Pandit had predicted.

Lessons in the school apart, special and elaborate arrangements were made to supplement the boys' education, to turn them into prodigies of learning. In this educational adventure one of his elder brothers, Hemendranath, showed an uncanny interest. He wished to fill the mind of these boys with universal knowledge, to make polymaths of them. But in all this (it is worth noting) the medium of instruction was Bengali. Thus they had a thorough grounding in their mother tongue.

Even otherwise the boys had a crowded and Spartan programme : the day began with wrestling under the tutelage of a wrestler, blind of one eye ; their young bodies smeared with yellow dust. Next came, according to strict schedule, lessons in mathematics, history, geography, etc., from private tutors. After school hours it was the drawing teacher's turn; this was followed by gymnastics. The evenings were devoted to English but by then the young scholars had started to doze, eyelids heavy with sleep. If the elder brother, Dwijendranath happened to pass by and noticed the nodding heads he would mercifully let the young scholars off. Then, all thoughts of sleep left aside, little Robi would dash towards the inner apartments, to the undisputed kingdom where his mother reigned.

On Sunday morning came the science teacher. Fond of demonstrations with scientific instruments, the boy felt most happy. Rabindra's life-long interest in science had its roots in these early days. The Bengali books which he had to read were all on scientific subjects. But oddly enough, the book chosen to teach him the use of Bengali was Michael's epic, *Meghnadabadh*. The boy reacted rather violently against this pedagogic use of literature and the poem obsessed him long after and even in his teens he slashed the poem in a longish article in *Bharati* (1877).

This was never reprinted, and Tagore later thought it was very immature.

The boys were soon removed from the Normal School and admitted to Bengali Academy. The idea was that they should have a good grounding in speaking and writing English, the dream of young India, both before and after Independence. The hope was fed by the fact that the school was run by an Anglo-Indian. Here the poet made friends with a boy well up in magical tricks and sleights of hand. In a short story, *Magician*, written in the last year of his life, he immortalised the character, though of course the facts as given in *Reminiscences* have been considerably touched up.

Even at that early age Rabindranath was a voracious reader; but he seemed more interested in books outside the prescribed syllabus. In Dwijendranath's rich and sprawling library there was, among other things, an anthology of Vaishnava lyrics, together with back numbers of such serious journals as *Abodhbandhu* and *Vividharthasangraha*. A serialised translation of the well-known French novel *Paul et Virginie*—the pathetic story of a youth and a girl marooned in an island in the Pacific— had appeared in *Abodhbandhu*. The young reader was filled with grief at the sad story. His own juvenile work, *Banaphul* (The Wild Flower) showed clear traces of the novel, especially on its scenic side.

About *Vividarthasangraha* we have the poet's own words: "I spent the long afternoons during the holidays poring over that thick square volume spread across the chest, reading about the marvellous tales of the arctic Norwhale, the amusing judgment of the Kazi, and the novel about Krishna Kumari." Biharilal Chakravarty was the poet of the day. His poems were a regular feature of *Abodhbandhu*.

As these were entirely new in style and diction, the boy was thrilled to the core. To his palace-ridden mind the idyllic picture, drawn by Biharilal, of a tumbledown leafy cottage, where one "slept like a king" appeared altogether entrancing.

In the meantime appeared Bankim's *Bangadarshart* (1872). This ushered in a new era in Bengali language and literature. Rabindranath was then only a boy of eleven, and he would read it greedily from cover to cover. Apart from these contemporary writings, what attracted the boy most was the lilting rhythm of Jayadeva's *Geetagovinda* and the Vaishnava lyrics. The affinities are easily explained.

In spite of its iconoclastic spirit, the Adi Brahma Samaj had not totally dispensed with all the traditional Brahmanic rituals, but kept up a few of them, such as the sacred-thread ceremony of the Brahmanic type; but these were shorn of idolatorous touches by Debendranath. In the sacred-thread ceremony of Rabindranath the reformed ritual was observed with eclat. The ceremonies in connection with the elder sons of the family, had been conducted in conformity with orthodox Hindu ways.

At the time Rabindranath was little more than eleven, the age when one could not hope to understand the deeper meaning of the sacred formula of initiation, the *Gayatri Mantra*. Yet the boy showed an unusual eagerness to recite it. Its magical incantation profoundly influenced his spiritual outlook. Even at the end of his life he looked back, nostalgically and gratefully, to the morning of his initiation. In *The Religion of Man* he has said, "I was at the time only twelve. But as I brooded on this mystic verse it dawned on me that my soul and the spirit of the universe were identical. ... I can still remember the joy and the thrill of illumination which this thought brought to me."

He was now the little 'Brahmin'. But what bothered him was how to attend school—and a Eurasian school at that—with a tonsured head ? The gods must have taken pity on him and release came from unexpected quarters. His father one day sent for him: he was going to the Himalayas, would Robi care to join ? Care to join ? "To express what I felt I would have needed to rend the sky with a mighty 'yes'. The Bengal Academy and the Himalayas—oh, the difference !" He jumped at the idea and soon after father and son left on a long trek together.

Debendranath wanted to draw his younger son closer to him. He probably foresaw in him some latent uncommon qualities, and he took him out of noisy Calcutta to the serene solitude of the Himalayas. On the first lap of the journey father and son spent a few quiet days at Santiniketan. This was Rabindranath's first contact with Santiniketan. In 1873 Bolpur was but an inconspicuous village. Here about a mile and a half from the railway station,. Debendranath had bought a piece of land (later the nucleus of Visva Bharati) in 1863 and put up a one-storeyed house. The house was called Santiniketan or Abode of Peace. Later on the name spread to the whole area.

Years after Debendranath founded an ashram (hermitage) and still later built a temple (Brahma Mandir) made of steel and glass, a unique structure. A little way off could be seen the embankments of the neighbouring village lake, surrounded by a cluster of palm trees. The lake is still there, quartered and sliced to suit Santiniketan's needs of water supply, but not a single palm tree survives.

It was here that Robi came to know his father more closely. Debendranath used to spend most of his time away from Calcutta. Between the father and the children there hardly existed any close tie. The familiarity between parents and children, common in our days, was then not in vogue. This was specially so in aristocratic families. There was a considerable distance between the generations—the distance of respect, and the natural distance between the old and the young. In the wide expanse of Bolpur, Rabindranath had many opportunities of coming nearer to his father and studying his ways. He had a number of small duties to perform, such as looking after his father's cash and accounts, winding up his watch, etc. He had also absolute freedom of movement, a freedom which he never knew in Calcutta and which, we may be sure, he must have utilised to the full.

In the solitude of Santiniketan, poetry came to him naturally. One cannot be sure when he first started wooing the muse. But this much is known that here, sitting under a coconut tree, the little lad had dashed off a pretty poetic play, *Prithviraj Parajaya*, the Defeat of Prithviraj. The manuscript has been lost. This is perhaps not such a great loss, for *Rudra Chanda*, written some years later may, be but another version of the same.

Debendranath left Bolpur after a while and reached Amritsar in the Punjab. Father and son were frequent visitors to the Golden Temple. Debendranath was particularly fond of the devotional singing and would liberally reward the musicians. The memory remained vivid in Rabindranath's mind till the end. The Sikh mode of worship and the continuous reading of the sacred text, the *Granth Sahib*, must have impressed the Maharshi; and he tried to adopt it for his own *mandir* at Santiniketan in a modified form. Brahma Sangit and the reading of Brahmo scriptures, morning and evening, was introduced in the daily service. This practice continued for several decades.

From Amritsar they went to Dalhousie, a small hill station in Himachal Pradesh. The house where they stayed on the peaks of Bakrota is still there; the snow-capped Himalayan ranges shining white in the distance, the pine forest all around, the deep gorges and narrow footpaths cutting across the hilly tract opened up a new world. The little boy roamed over the hillside, all alone, without let or hindrance. His father gave him unlimited freedom which he had never enjoyed before. But back in the bungalow, his father took good care to give him regular lessons in Bengali, Sanskrit and English. With the help of books the mystery of the heavenly bodies was explained to the boy; under the open night-sky his father would point out the stars and their positions. The little boy would then write down, in Bengali, the lessons he had learnt.

The interest in astronomy thus created, remained with him till the end; and he read widely on the subject. Young as he was, he managed to get up an article based on his studies and his father's lessons. In an abridged form this was published, anonymously, in the *Tattvabodhini Patrika*. This was perhaps his first literary work to appear in print but on a scientific subject.

After four months in the Himalayas, Rabindranath was sent back to Calcutta. But he did not return to the same old place in the same old way. In the large ancestral house he had so far lived like an exile. Now, travel-wise, he took his rightful place in the family circle. The servant-infested outer apartments were not enough for him and he now came to occupy a place of importance in the largely feminine group that used to sit in his mother's apartments. It is pleasing to imagine the little boy holding forth about his experience in the forest fastness at the foothills of the mighty Himalayas, forever sacred to the Indian imagination. He also came to receive, in increasing measure, much affection and pampering from the youngest and sweetest of his sisters-in-law, Kadambari Devi. Of her more later.

His guardians had not forgotten about his schooling and the unwilling lad had to join Bengal Academy again. After the Himalayan experience the school looked even more like a prison-house. The budding poet's mind was also crossed by new fancies and aspiration. These he expressed in *Abhilash* (Desire). The poem was published in the *Tattvabodhini Patrika*. But the mark of anonymity remained. The Bengal Academy, it was obvious, formed no part of the young poet's scheme.

Madhab Pandit's prediction was turning to be too true; Rabindranath began to play truant from his school. It was finally decided to withdraw him and educate him privately. A graduate Jnanchandra, was appointed house tutor. A talented young person, he devised a rather novel method for his extraordinary charge. The bold teacher used to read with him Kalidasa's *Kumarasambhava* and Shakespeare's *Macbeth*, in the original. Wonderful new worlds opened before the boy's vision. Not content with this Jnanchandra made him render both classics into Bengali. This was 'discipline of letters' with a vengeance. Portions of these translations were published, anonymously again, in the *Bharati*. In *Jeebansmritl* (Reminiscences) the poet has related how he had once been taken to Pandit Isvarchandra Vidyasagar and had to read out his renderings of *Macbeth* before him. And how, though the heart beat wildly, he had returned home in a glow of excitement.

Many of the poems written at this period were published anonymously and possess but historical interest. One was incorporated in his brother Jyotirindranath's play *Sarojini*.

The first poem to be printed in his own name was *Hindu Melar Upahar* (The Gift of the Hindu Mela). It came out in the bilingual *Amrita Bazar Patrika* (1875). This particular Hindu Mela was held at Parsibagan on the Upper Circular Road (now Acharya Prafulla Chandra Road) and was presided over by the veteran patriot, Rajnarayan Basu. The poem was written in imitation of Hemchandra Bandopadhyaya. "Blow, bugle, blow" a poem which, at the time many knew by heart and few care to read today.

His first verse narrative, *Banaphul* (The Wild Flower) was composed during this period when he was studying at home after return from the Himalayas. It was printed, serially in *Jnanankur* and *Pratibimba*. The publication in book form owed everything to the enthusiasm of his elder brother, Somendranath. The volume was never reprinted, though of course it has now found its way into his Collected Works. Besides *Banaphul*, the periodical *Jnanankur* published a few more of his 'Poeac<???> Effusions'. The description is just. Listen to the precious lines:

> Come, my maiden gay, heartless beauty,
> What do I tell thee, over and over again ?
> The wound has rocked the abyss of my soul,
> My heart and mind, oh how they burn !

His first prose writing, a critical essay, came out with a good deal of fanfare in the same journal. Seriously, ever so pompously, he discussed the characteristics of narrative verse, the lyric and the epic; and then proceeded to analyse three contemporary poems (now dead and forgotten), *Bhubanmohini Pratibha, Abasar Sarojini* and *Dukha Sangini*. He tried to show that all these poems were totally lacking in true poetic feeling and other lyrical qualities. His nephew, Satyaprasad, later warned him that a University graduate was writing a rejoinder to his attack. This filled the young author, a truant, with panic. A graduate at his heels !

The private studies soon languished as Jnanchandra resigned his post. He wanted to study law. The boys were now admitted to St. Xavier's School. Smartly dressed, every morning they would get into a landau and drive to school. But very often, on some pretext or other, Robi would manage to stay behind. So the days passed. Meanwhile (March 1875) his mother had died. For want of an able mistress the whole household fell in a heap. Thanks to the indulgent sisters and sisters-in-law, Robi's attendance at school suffered even more than before. He spent the leisure merrily going through Bengali books and journals that came his way. Their number was legion. In particular he devoted himself to a study of the Vaishnava lyrics. At the end of the academic year, as was only to be expected, he failed to secure promotion to the next higher class. It was probably due to this that he left school. He had read up to the Preparatory Entrance class or the Fifth Year as it was called then.

Once more private arrangements had to be made. But Robi was not amenable to routine activity. He was interested only in taking part in all kinds of exciting and interesting discussions which were going on all the time at the Jorasanko Mansion. Excited by these, he also dashed off poems and songs aplenty. The main stimulus came from the *Sanjibani Sabha*. The Hindu Mela had now converted itself into an annual cultural conference. To free the country was beyond the means of the literary idealists, who could but talk and talk. What the country needed was a desperate remedy, a revolution. For this purpose a secret society, *Sanjibani Sabha*, was founded by the firebrand members of the Mela. Rajnarayan Basu, Jyotirindranath and others were its leading lights. Members had to sign a nihilist declaration with their own blood. A code language was used by its members. For some strange reason the Society was called *Hamchupamuhaf* ! This was modelled after Mazzini's *Carbonari Society* of Italy. "Even a tyro like me," Rabindranath wrote in his later days, "was a member of the society. We lived in a world where blew the hot winds of every impracticable notion. It seemed as if we were borne on the wings of unclouded enthusiasm.

We were lost to all sense of modesty, fear or doubt. Our chief occupation was to warm ourselves in the fire of enthusiasm." At this Society the youthful patriot sang lustily :

> Linked in one resolve are a thousand hearts,
> To the same purpose offered a thousand lives.

This song which became very popular in Bengal has been wrongly attributed to Rabindranath.

At the tenth anniversary of the Hindu Mela, Rabindranath read another fiery poem. The new Viceroy, Lord Lytton held at this time a grand durbar in old forlorn Delhi, where Victoria, so long known as 'Queen' was declared 'The Empress of India' (Jan. 1, 1877). The country was then passing through a crisis, famine was raging. Young Rabindranath's poem was a bitter attack on the celebration (Feb. 1877). But it could not be printed. The Press Act aimed against journals and newspapers printed in the vernacular had already come into force. But soon a way out was found. With some changes, it was put into the mouth of a mediaeval hero in Jyotirindranath's play, *Swapnamoyee* (The Dream Lady). To rouse the nation against the Mughals and the Pathans was not an accountable offence.

In later life Tagore took a sober view of the whole affair and wrote, amusingly : "During Lord Lytton's administration I had written some defamatory verse about the Delhi Durbar. The British Government was mortally afraid of Russia but it little feared the effusions of a youthful poet."

It was at the Hindu Mela that Rabindranath was first

introduced to the rising Bengali poet, Nabinchandra Sen, whose *Palasir Yuddha* (Battle of Plassey) had just come out (1875). The heroic speech of the dying Mohanlal was on everybody's lips. In his *Autobiography* Nabinchandra has left a delightful account of his first meeting with young Rabindranath, whom even then he recognised as the coming poet.

3

A Litterateur in the Making

LITERATURE AND THE arts, their creation and Tagore family. A literary group had gathered round Dwijendranath and Jyotirindranath. This was not a regularly constituted club or society, but more informal. It was attended not only by well-known literary figures like Akshoy Chaudhury and Biharilal Chakravorty, but by mediocrities and sycophants. Akshoy set before the young poet the high standard of literary criticism in the West. It was from him that Rabindranath first came to know how vast and comprehensive were the canons of European literary criticism. It was Akshoy who first told him about the 'modern' English poets—that is, those that were looked upon as modern in the 'seventies. The influence of Akshoy's *Udasini* (an adaptation of Goldsmith's *Hermit*) on Rabindra's *Banaphul* is obvious.

At this time the elders were planning to bring out a journal. There were a good many among the brothers and sisters who could, or at any rate would, write. Friends of the family were also free to contribute. In the seventies there were not many Bengali journals. Even *Bangadarshan* had to be discontinued after a run of four years. It is true it had just reappeared. There was, however, hardly any other journal of the calibre of the old *Aryadarshan* and *Bandhab* (Dacca). At last with Dwijendranath as editor the first issue of *Bharati* came out in July 1877 (Shravan 1284 B. S.).

The new journal found in the sixteen-year-old Rabindranath a most prolific Contibutor. In *Jnanankur* his prose writing had opened, as we know, with literary criticism. It was the same with *Bharati*. And the object to be pilloried this time was *Meghnadabadh*, an ancient grudge. The impertinence of youthful genius had clouded his judgement and he chose rather easy way to fame by tearing the immortal epic to tatters. In later life he subjected his own earlier critcism to a similar treatment. In a later essay *Literary Creation* (1908), he made ample amends for the earlier intemperate attack and pointed out the real value of Madhusudan's great work. Yet impulsive and impertinent as it was, the Bharati article cannot be entirely ignored.

Bhikharini, a short story, appeared in the first issue of *Bharati*. A serialised novel, *Karuna*, also came out. It had all the romantic flame of the age and was on par with the effusive poems he was then in the habit of writing.

The story element was quite wanting. These were never reprinted, even though an eminent critic like Chandranath Basu had praised them liberally.

But at least one of his juvenilia has worn exceedingly well: *Bhanu Singher Padavali*, written when the author was but sixteen. It was written in what is called Brajabuli dialect, an artificial language used by Vaishnava poets. Bankim had made some experiments in this medium. But Rabindranath's imitation was so successful as to mislead people. The poet himself blandly informed a friend that the manuscript had been discovered in the library of the Adi Brahmo Samaj. The unsuspecting friend swallowed the story, as did many others, including a research scholar in Germany.

In his *Reminiscences* the poet has told us how the poem came to be written: "Rejoicing in the greateful shade of the cloudy midday rest hour, I lay prone in the bedroom and wrote on a slate *Gahana-Kusuma Kunjamajhe:*

> Deep in the bower filled with flowers
> Vibrating with the music of the flute,
> Casting off all fear and shame,
> Come, dear one, come.

The single phrase gave him the necessary self-confidence and he dashed off any number of verses.

We have seen that the boy was inordinately fond of Vaishnava lyrics: their language, rhythm, and sensibility, every thing about these seemed enchanting. As yet he had no interest in the philosophy of Vaishnavism. For a boy of his age the philosophy was indeed a little too profound. He read the lyrics more for the sake of poetry. But many of his poems are so close to their ideas and imagery that to many Rabindranath looks a Vaishnava in disguise.

Among his different works that appeared in *Bharati*, the poetic drama, *Kavi-Kahini* (The Poet's Tale) deserves special mention. This was his first published work. But he never reprinted it. Years after he wrote, "It is the product of that period of life when the writer had little experience of the world and tended to magnify the shadows cast by one's own dim subjectivity. My . . . mind had nothing in it but hot vapour." A harsh but not inaccurate evaluation.

Five years had gone by since the trip to the Himalayas. All efforts to educate the boy had failed. He was now seventeen. His guardians felt worried. Robi was such a problem ! At last it was decided to send him over to England to qualify himself for the bar. In those days when boys of well-to-do families failed to make good at home or showed little interest in matters educational, they were as a rule sent abroad. It was the one unfailing panacea. The prodigals spent lavishly during their sojourn in England; and after acquiring English etiquette and attending the proper number of dinners, were called to the Bar and returned home as legal luminaries. But Rabindranath, it was felt, had not picked up enough English. Would the English trip do him any good ? It was suggested that before sailing he should spend some months with his civilian brother at Ahmedabad and brush up his English.

Almost a Mughul palace in miniature, Sahi-bag, the Judge's House at Ahmedabad, on the banks of the

Sabarmati, was an imposing structure. His brother's family was then in England and during the midday Satyendranath would be away in the Court. In the lonely house Rabindranath spent long hours in the library, reading, with the help of a dictionary, the English classics. Where the passages did not make sense his literary instinct helped to make them out.

He continued to write critical essays for the *Bharati*—on Dante, Petrarch, Goethe, and the English poets. His was a lonely life in a lonely house. "On moonlight nights pacing round and round the extensive terrace overlooking the river," he was touched by poetic fancies; melodies floated in the air to which he tried to supply the words. His first bunch of songs to be set to music by himself was composed here: 'Behold the silent night rapt in the light of the moon', and 'O my rose-maiden', etc. The other poems he wrote were mostly adaptations from Sanskrit, English and even Marathi *abhanga* of Tukaram the saint.

Opportunities for practising spoken English were meagre at Ahmedabad. So he was sent to Bombay to stay with Satyendranath's friend, Atmaram Pandurang. For its anglicised ways the Pandurang family had quite a reputation. One of its girls, Anna Turhkhar, was in the van of progress. Rabindranath was placed in her charge, and he was careful to let her know that the pupil, for all his lack of English, was a maker of music and a dreamer of dreams. He would sometimes read to her English versions of his own *Kavi-Kahini*. Whatever may have been his mature attitude to this poem, there is no doubt that, at eighteen, he had a soft corner for it. Anna was of course deeply attracted to the handsome, romantic, refined pupil and poet. She once asked him to coin a new name for her, a delicate and dangerous compliment. The gallant poet did not fail to oblige her.

"O my Nalini*, open your eyes. Have you not woken up yet ?" he wrote in a dedicatory poem. She often heard Rabindranath sing Bengali airs. Maybe their melody—or was it the poet's voice— cast a spell on her. "Your voice can bring me back from death's kingdom," she once whispered to him. The rest is silence (though the anecdotal hounds would not have it so).

Looking back, in his old age the poet wrote about her: "I have never been able to forget her. Nor did I ever look upon her passion in any frivolous fashion. Since then my life has moved through the light and shade of diverse experience, the Lord has brought many strange things to pass. But I can honestly say that at no time have I looked down upon love, be of what kind it may." Some of the poems in *Saishab Sangit* (Boyhood Melodies) seem to suggest this youthful attachment. Later, recollecting in tranquility, he wrote: "In course of men's life there comes now and then from some unknown world, the messenger of the Beloved, and the heart overflows. She comes unbidden, but the day comes when no cry or call can lure her back anymore."

Satyendranath was leaving for England on furlough. His wife and children were already there. Rabindranath accompanied him. Getting down at Brindisi, they took the overland route and passing through the Swiss tunnels reached Paris. The city was then the venue of an international exhibition. France had just overthrown

* Nalini=lotus

the monarchy and asked the world to be present at the opening of this new era in her national life. Rabindranath paid a fleeting visit to the exhibition.

Reaching England, the brothers went straight to Brighton where Satyendranath's family was staying. The family reunion, after six months, made everybody happy. Rabindranath was particularly glad to meet his nephew, Suren, and niece, Indira.

At Brighton he was admitted to a public school. It did not take the townsfolk long to get introduced to this strikingly handsome bright young lad from India. Invitations to dance and dinner were frequent. Rabindranath was quick to learn dancing and picked up a few English songs as well. The Brighton days were gay indeed. But he had to leave Brighton soon and move up to London.

Taraknath Palit, a rising barrister of the Calcutta High Court and friend of Satyendranath, had come to England in connection with his son Loken's admission into London University. Taraknath thoroughly disapproved of Robi leading a sheltered life under the care of a fond sister-in-law and wasting his breath in a country town. It was at his insistence that Robi had to join the London University and, as was the custom, live as a paying guest in an English family.

At the University he became friends with Palit junior. Loken later joined the I.C.S. and remained one of his ardent admirers all his life.

At the University College, Henry Morley used to take classes in English literature. His way of teaching made a deep impression on Rabindranath. Even in his old age whenever he talked of methods of teaching or of his English days he always spoke feelingly of Morley though he did not read with him for perhaps more than three months.

The Scotts, with whom he was staying, soon came to treat him as one of the family. Two young: sisters felt greatly drawn towards him. There is a plain hint in one of his poems, *Dudin* (Two days) in *Sandhya Sangit.* He later confessed that the girls were in love with him. But he did not, at the time, have the "moral courage" to face the fact. After twelve long years when he re-visited London he did make an effort to look up the Scotts. The house was empty and no one could tell him where they had gone.

Rabindranath was writing a series of letters for *Bharati* on his trip to Europe and his experiences in England. In England what usually struck the Indians most was the freedom of its womenfolk. That at his age Rabindranath would fall for it is no wonder. This was revealed in his open support of free mixing. His guardians at home felt alarmed and his eldest brother Dwijendranath, who happened to be the editor of *Bharati*, was obliged to add more staid and conservative footnotes to Robi's advanced views. Finally, Maharshi asked him to-return home with Satyendranath.

A year and a half he had passed in England; he went back to India without any University degree. He had qualified neither for the Bar nor for any other profession. He was then nineteen. His letters on the European tour were published as a book eighteen months after his return. In the preface the young author had pointed out that the work would show how the mind of a Bengali reacted to England and was influenced by it. That modestaim the book certainly did achieve. And more. For the book has a special merit of its own. This was perhaps his first book to be written in colloquial (*chalti*) Bengali, and an irrefutable proof of the richness and range of that idiom. In 1878 no one wrote in such a racy style.

Robi returned home after an absence of about two years, six months in West India and the rest in England. It was a shy boy that had gone out, but the young man that returned home was fairly assertive. His health had improved by the stay abroad and so had his looks. Now he did not hesitate to speak out his mind before elders or even to treat them to English songs.

The warmest welcome came from his sister-in-law, Kadambari Devi. In her childless, barren life all her affection and love had centred round Robi. He had been her playmate and companion ever since her marriage. She was most happy to have him back. On Rabindranath she was the one single abiding influence throughout his long life—his ideal of love, beauty and grace. Till the last, her memory spreads a glow over his life and works a miracle of a constancy.

Rabindranath found the house in the throes of a new excitement; preparations were under way for staging Jyotirindranath's play, *Manmoyee*. Rabindranath readily joined the rehearsals and even wrote out a song for the play. There was enough hilarity and burlesque in the drama.

In spite of these excitements he had little peace of mind. That he had failed to achieve anything tangible or worthwhile during his stay in England weighed heavily upon his sensitive mind. In a letter we find him writing : "I have come back. The same old roof, moonlight, south wind, are all there as before. The dreams of a lonely heart, a thousand bonds branching out on all sides, the long unending leisure, idle fancy, the same old pursuit of the mirage of beauty, hopes without issue, the deep heartache, the agony of vain sentimentality—the days pass in dreary listlessness."

While abroad, he had written but a few poems. A longer poem *Bhagna Hridaya* (The Broken Heart) was begun in England, continued on board ship and completed after his return to India. The book was entirely his own and nothing but an expression of a romantic poet's state of mind, its joys and even more of its sorrows.

In the meantime he had been commissioned to write a few religious songs for the annual Brahmo festival. The composer was not yet out of his teens, when he wrote his first seven *Brahma Sangit*. And for six decades he composed several hundred religious and spiritual songs. It may be recalled here that it was the Brahmo Samaj that introduced a new type of spiritual song, without reference to any sectarian creed or deity but with a universal appeal. And in this the Tagore family—and Rabindranath in particular—played a significant role. He was musical to the fingertips.

The Tagore family were really crazy over art and music. But there was a method in their madness. For instance, it is the normal practice to fit tune or melody to the words of a song. With the Tagores it was the other way about. In this connection the poet says : "All day long Jyotirindranath Tagore used to pound classical songs on the piano. And now and then the *raga-raginis* revealed strange forms and evocations. Akshoy Chaudhury and I would try to match words for what was being played on the piano." Sometimes his eldest sister, Swarnakumari would join in the game.

A very select group of the intellectual elite of Calcutta used to meet regularly at a club in the Jorasanko Mansion. Some months after Robi's return from England it was decided to stage a new play at the annual meeting of the club. Rabindranath, the highbrow of those days, was commissioned to write a play. The result was *Valmiki Pratibha,* (the Genius of Valmiki).

Biharilal's influence on this drama is quite clear. He was then looked upon as the last word in poetic imagination. The subject-matter of the play was taken from Biharilal and the music from Jyotirindranath. The play was staged in the Jorasanko Mansion; Rabindranath appeared in the role of Valmiki, Hemendranath's daughter, Pratibha, was the little Saraswati. The staging of the play revealed Robi's histrionic talents. Amongst those present on the occasion were Bankimchandra (43), Gurudas Banerjee (37) and Haraprasad Sastri (28). Gurudas was so delighted with the poet and the play that, though not a poet by nature, he composed an impromptu verse. To reveal a new world once more, a new genius Valmiki, a new sun has arisen.

Valmiki Pratibha is really not poetry to be read. It is a new experiment and you cannot enjoy it, unless you see it acted and you also hear the songs. In fact, it is a musical play which is highly seasoned with Western tunes. This also was a bold venture.

It wouldn't have been bad if the days had passed like this—singing, acting, composing. The stern elders took a somewhat different view. They wanted Robi to go back to England and resume his studies for the Bar. This time a nephew, Satyaprasad, made the party and the two left for Madras by sea. But as fate would have it, both changed their minds on reaching Madras. Satya was a newly-wed and had reasons of the heart to recommend retreat. Rabindranath came back because of Satya, at least it proved a convenient excuse. Feeling guilty, the young offenders went up to Mussoorie in order to report to the Maharshi. Luckily for them the Maharshi took a lenient view.

Two of his books, *Bhagna Hridaya* and *Rudra Chanda*, had been published prior to the second trip to England. *Bhagna Hridaya* was dedicated to Kadambari Devi (under a pseudonym known only to the family circle). The second book was dedicated to Jyotirindranath. The pangs of separation came out in the dedicatory verse. We have already suggested our view of this immature drama, an adaptation of his earlier poetic play *Prithiviraj Parajaya* (Defeat of Prithiviraj) written at Santiniketan in 1873 when he was hardly twelve years old. About this loosely constructed lyrical drama of *Bhagna Hridaya* in thirty-four cantos Tagore had lost all interest in later years when once it was going to be reprinted by his publisher, and proofs of the first canto came to him, he simply wrote 'Rubbish' and stopped further print.

Today *Bhagna Hridaya* is almost unread. The author was destined to write more memorable poems in the future. And yet how wonderful the poem had seemed in its own days. Many young poetry-lovers could rattle off long passages from the lyric.

The work received unexpected commendation at the hands of the high and the mighty. One day the Private Secretary of Maharaja Birchandra Manikya came to see the young poet all the way from Agartala. The Maharaja, the emissary said, was delighted with the book and had sent him to convey that piece of information to the poet. For a young man unknown to fame and fortune this was welcome news indeed. His last public recognition, the title *Bharat-Bhaskar* (Sun of India), also came from the court of Tripura when the poet was eighty. The young poet's life seemed to pass in a round of aimless activities. The grandeur of Jorasanko Mansion had in the meantime dimmed, the hum of busy activity had ceased. Dwijendranath, buried under a heap of books on poetry, philosophy and mathematics, was lost to all worldly interests and seemed careless even in the matter of bringing up his children. Satyendranath, now judge in Bombay, was almost an exile. Hemendranath was living in the ancestral house, but his wife was taken up with the problems of a large and growing family. Jyotirindranath and Kadambari Devi did not have any issue and Rabindranath was their favourite. They became his companion spirits, friendly to his poetic effusions and indulgent to his musings. Once when they had gone away on a holiday, young Robi had been left a solitary. It was in loneliness of spirit that poetry came to him as a relief.

The crust of old conventions was gone, and the poetry of *Sandhya Sangit* (Evening Melodies) strained forth in new and fresh forms and striking rhythms. In his Poetical Works (1903) this group of poems bears the title *The Heart-Wilderness:*

> There is a vast wilderness, it is called the Heart;
> whose interlacing forest branches dandle and
> rock the darkness like an infant, I have lost
> my way in its depths.

So long in the dialogues of *Banaphul, Kavi-Kahini* and *Bhagna Hridaya* the poet had employed a dramatic mask to express his feelings of joy and sorrow. In *Evening Songs* the mask was set aside and he spoke in the first person. The idiom was unmistakable, the 'inscape' wholly his. Its freer movement and variety follow from its greater subjectivity. The poet seemed to have discovered himself in a flash. Most of these poems are the works of a poet just out of his teens and literary judgement is bound to describe them as immature. In his *Poetical Works*, which the poet himself brought out, all his writings before *Sandhya Sangity* except *Bhanu Singher Padavali* had been rejected. In later life he wanted to exclude even *Sandhya Sangit*. The reading public prevented him from such a drastic measure. In his Selected Poems or *Sanchayita* Tagore suffered only a few lines from one poem to be included.

From Mussoorie he came to Chandernagore to join Jyotirindranath and his wife. "It was here that I felt for the first time," he writes, "that soul of Bengal flows through her rivers." We shall point out later the influence of Padma and her environs on the work of his middle years. *Nadir palita ei jeeban amar* (This life of mine fostered by rivers), are his own grateful words in a poem written at the end of his life.

He wrote a good deal of miscellaneous prose at Chandernagore. These were scribbled without any plan, and as with the themes of *Sandhya Sangit* there is an air of just-as-you-please about them. He was leading a free and untrammelled life, there was no let or bar to airy fancies and the winds of doctrine. The style was the man.

But in his fiction, *Bouthakuranir Haat* (The Young Queen's Market) he struck out on a new line altogether. The Bengali novel was still young. Bankim's first novel had come over 15 years earlier, for a maiden attempt it had qualities enough though written in the orthodox manner of the days. The story he had taken from a biography of Pratapaditya as found in Pratapchandra Ghose's voluminous 1869 work, *Bangadhip-Parajaya* (the Defeat of the King of Bengal) which he had not only read for himself but read out to his mother and womenfolk of the family, when he was a little boy. Apart from this he had also collected many stories and anecdotes about Pratap from different sources. Pratap was a feudal lord of Bengal during the Mughal rule and wanted to carve out an independent State for himself.

Commenting on the work much later, Rabindranath wrote: "Here the pent-up mind found its release and set out on a journey across the devious ways of the world." His genius was seeking for new images and experiences. *Bouthakuranir Haat* was an early proof of this desire for release. Of course, its characters are little more than puppets and do not seem to develop under the stress of any inherent necessity. There is also something of a window display about them. Bankim, however, commended it soon after its publication. It may be noted that he had congratulated the young writer on the publication of *Sandhya Sangit* as well.

The play, *Prayaschitta* (Atonement), written thirty years later, was based on the plot of this novel. Again, after twenty years, he recast this in *Paritran* (Deliverance) as a drama for the public stage. *Muktadhara* (The Waterfall) came in between the two and is a distant echo of *Prayaschitta*.

Along with this novel, book reviews and essays on a wide variety of subjects were also appearing regularly. In one of these essays we find the old bitterness over *Meghnadabadh Kavya* of Madhusudan still rankling. He held the view that every epic has an ideal or view of life growing round the hero or a noble protagonist and that *Meghnadabadh* was totally lacking in this respect. The killing of Indrajit by Laksman who had stolen into the palace of Lanka like a thief could not, by any stretch of the imagination, be looked upon as a great or edifying event. As regards its description of Hell, that was a mere copy of similar descriptions in the Western classics, and it formed no part of the poem's real theme. The criticism, openly hostile, however, had its points.

In another review on Baul songs, he drew attention—one of the first to do so—to the need for collecting folk songs. "We would then be able," he said rightly "to know our people more closely, and their joys and sorrows, hopes and aspirations would not be such a sealed book to us." Years after, when the Bangiya Sahitya Parishad (The Bengali Literary Academy, 1894) was founded, he appealed once more to the public about its importance and himself volunteered to undertake the task. The editing and publishing of folk songs, folk tales and nursery rhymes and other similar works in Bengal date from this period. (*Bharati* and its young author had shown the way).

Bharati had been running for five years now, and it was felt that without a literary group to back it one could not be sure of a regular supply of printable material. The need for scientific essays was also keenly felt; but the lack of technical terms in Bengali presented a difficulty. To meet these demands it was decided to start some kind of an academy in Calcutta (Kalikata Saraswat Sammelan). The young enthusiasts met the venerable Vidyasagar and he said, "My advice to you is to leave us out; you will not accomplish anything with bigwigs; they can never be made to agree with one another." Later, a meeting was held, the constitution drawn up and office-bearers elected. Dr. Rajendralal Mitra was elected President of the Society. Rabindranath became the Joint-Secretary with Krishna Behari Sen, brother of Keshab Chandra.

Once in the swim they realised to the full the truth of Vidyasagar's warning. Moving in vain from door to door for co-operation and sympathy, Rabindranath acquired a rich harvest of bitter experience. And he wrote, *de profundis:* "The-wise who laugh at ideals are inferior to the simple souls who, even if they do not succeed, are willing to work and suffer for the sake of ideals." The Society died in infancy. But when a few years later the Bangiya Sahitya Parishad was founded, Rabindranath came forward to prepare a list of scientific and technical terms.

4

The Flower Blossoms

THE YOUNG POET had started writing his first novel, *Bauthakuranir Haat,* at Chander-nagore; the last chapters were written after he had moved into a rented house in the Sudder Street of Calcutta. While living there, he had a strange experience, about which he has spoken at some length in his *Reminiscences.*

"One morning the sun was just rising through the leafy top of the trees—all of a sudden a covering seemed to fall away from my eyes and I found the world bathed in a wonderful radiance, with waves of beauty and joy swelling on every side. The radiance pierced in a moment through the folds of sadness and despondency which had accumulated in my heart, and flooded it with this Universal Light."

That very day, in the white heat of inspiration, he wrote *Nirjharer Swapnabhanga* (The Awakening of the Waterfall), which flowed gaily, freely, indeed roared down like a stream released from a cave. *Prabhat Utsava* (The Morning Festival) which came a little later was born of the same ecstasy.

Some years later the poet, looking back remarked: "*Prabhat Sangit* was the first expression of my 'inscape', no wonder it lacks discrimination. Even now I love the world—but the love is not so wild as before." On another occasion he described this group of poems as *Nishkraman* (Going Forth). It was going forth from the darkness, an emergence from the heart's wilderness of *Sandhya Sangit* into a world of light. This meant a great release and detachment from the clouded passions of an imprisoned ego.

That autumn he went to Darjeeling with his brother Jyotirindranath and his sister-in-law. Amidst the majestic Himalayan landscape he had hoped to get back the Sudder Street experience. In vain. The spirit of delight had fled to never more return. He had to be content with an echo and wrote *Pratidhvani* (Reverberation).

Returning to Calcutta he put up in a house on the Lower Circular Road. The Society of Wise Ones was still going strong, and at its annual meeting a play was called for. Naturally Robi had to foot the bill. The musical play *Kalmrigaya* (The Fatal Hunt) was staged in the Jorasanko Mansion on December 23, 1882. The young poet appeared in the role of the blind sage. Some of the songs in the play were set, as before, to foreign tunes. Subsequently, a few songs and scenes were incorporated in the revised version of *Valmiki Pratibha* and the play remained long out of print, *Kalmrigaya* has how been printed with musical notations and proved popular on the children's stage.

Rabindranath was twenty-two, but still a bachelor an unusual thing in those days. Naturally, he had to live with his brothers. Once, with Jyotirindranath and Kadambari Devi, he visited Karwar in the Bombay Presidency (now Karnataka State) where his civilian brother had been transferred.

Situated on the mouth of the Kali river, Karwar, capital of ancient fame, was truly a beauty spot. The Karwar days did not go in vain: poetry, songs and plays on the one hand and miscellaneous essays on the other flowed out in this period of his life. But there was a bitterness in the prose writings. The most outstanding work of this period was no doubt *Prakritir Pratishodh* (Nature's Revenge). This was his first play not cast in the mould of a musical drama. In the English version it is known as *Sanyasi* or the ascetic.

In his own words, "The book is a mixture of poetry and drama. The poems tell of the ascetic's inner story. Round this self-absorbed person moves the everyday world with its many discords. What characterises these discords is their triviality. This contrast may even be described as dramatic. When love bridged the gulf between the two, and the hermit and the householder met, the seeming emptiness of the infinite disappeared." The problem of untouchability, hinted in this drama, has hardly been noted.

Towards the beginning of his series of essays called *Alochana* (Discussion), there seems to be an attempt to explain the play's inner meaning. He writes, "We have argued that the finite is not really limited, but that it concentrates in the minutest point on unfathomable profundity. Today (22) I am able to see that till now it is this idea that has, in different guises, been the 'dominant and range' of all my writings so far."

This idea has, as it were, two aspects. One is confined to the inner world and its guiding formula is *Seemar majhe aseem tumi bajao apart sur,* (the Infinite plays its tune within the limits of the finite); the other is extroverted and forms a part of the way of works. Its leading thought is *Vairagyasadh-ane mukti se amar nay* (my salvation lies not in renunciation). In this play, for the first time, these two ideas, central to the poet's theme, have become explicit and self-conscious.

The party of Jyotirindranath came back from Karwar, and stayed in a garden house in the Circular Road, now Chowringhee, Towards the south of the house was a long stretch of shanties. From his room Rabindranath looked out on to the slum. To him it was all a picture. It is the impact of this scene that he records in *Chhabi O Gan* (Songs and Pictures). The poems, though written in a serious mood, lack depth. A series of essays appearing in the *Bharati* serially and published subsequently as *Alochana* look to be light works. In reality they wield the scourge of satire. Only by combining the two can we have a complete picture of Rabindranath the poet-essayist. But one poem of *Chhabi O Gan* is an exception to the general tenor. This is *Rahur Prem* (the Love of Rahu).

During these days there was a good deal of display and extravagance about his dress and demeanour. His calculated refinement became the butt of much chaffing and open criticism. Many took him to be a *poseur* and pretender to poetry. The impression persisted in some quarters, even when the reasons for it no longer existed.

5

Adulthood

Birth, death and marriage, there's a divinity that shapes them, says the Bengali proverb. Rabindranath's marriage on December 9, 1883, was sudden and unexpected. His wife, a girl of eleven, came from the family of one of the junior officers of the Tagore estate and belonged to the Peerali caste of Brahmins. The marriage took place, in the Jorasanko Mansion, instead of at the bride's place, the usual practice. The girl-bride had an old-fashioned name which would hardly pass in the Tagore circle; so the bride became Mrinalini, a synonym of Rabindranath's favourite 'Nalini'. The wise Maharshi arranged for her education in the Loretto School.

Within six months of the marriage a regular tornado blew over the Tagore family. Jyotirindranath's wife, Kadambari Devi, suddenly committed suicide. The reasons are shrouded in mystery. But that there was some family misunderstanding it cannot be doubted. This was a great shock to Rabindra-nath. One has only to read some of his writings to feel the intensity of her affection for Robi and how much she meant to him. Her image and memory recur throughout the poet's work, the alchemy of imagination turning the facts into a "greater truth". In brief, she became an idealised symbol of deathless love.

And yet deep down in the poet's mind there is a core of strange detachment. "The ability to forget is an integral part of one's life," he has said. In a poem we find him bidding the past adieu, "A new-game is about to begin."

This ability to forget and this detachment are perhaps virtues. Otherwise in a mind weighed down with the past there would be little scope for any creation. It is because of this innate detachment that the poet can create continuously, he is a voyager who can always fare forward. Maitreyi Devi, who heard from the poet, in his old age, many stories about Kadambari Devi, has written with a woman's subtlety and understanding on the subject. We quote a few lines: "I am amazed to think how the memory of an affection which lasted for a few years could have taken such deep roots in his life, could continually sweeten his imagination. With what a glow it must have originally shone! Or maybe the mind of a poet creates its own world, what was she really like, 'the poet in the heart of a poet' ?"

Eighteen-eighty-four was a remarkable year. Towards the beginning died Keshabchandra Sen, the great leader of the Brahmo Samaj. It was from Keshab that a section of the Calcutta gentry had! come to know of the extraordinary spiritual genius of Ramakrishna Paramhansa. Many educated Indians, were drawn towards him. The career of his disciple, the great Swami Vivekananda, and the Ramakrishna Order are now a matter of history.

Perhaps taking advantage of this change of mood, orthodox pandits like Sashadhar Tarkachuramani were trying to spread their fantastic interpretation as Hinduism "scientifically explained". The contention was that all Hindu rituals and conventions were scientifically grounded. Even a thinker like Bankim had suggested the Comtian religion of humanity to be a Hindu ideal. Another powerful intellect of the age was Chandranath Basu. All these men were hostile to the Brahmo group and eager in their defence of Hinduism. Two monthlies *Nava Jiban* and *Prachar,* were mouthpieces of this new movement. Literary men like Bankim and others patronised both papers.

But, as the newly appointed Secretary of the Brahmo Samaj, Rabindranath had to criticise some of the articles of Bankim, who had become a protagonist of neo-Hinduism; there was a fairly prolonged wordy controversy between Bankim and Rabindranath. Most readers have forgotten the details nor is it necessary to rake them up again. In his *Reminiscences* we find Rabindranath writing, "When the controversy was over, Bankim sent me a letter, which I have unfortunately lost. Had I kept it, readers could have seen for themselves how completely he had forgiven me for my part in the controversy."

Keshab's passing away had greatly weakened the Brahmo Samaj. To bring new life into the Adi Brahmo Samaj the Maharshi appointed Rabindranath as its Secretary, while Dwijendranath was put in charge of the *Tattvobodhini Patrika.* As Secretary, Rabindranath had to attend to its various businesses. This was good training but whether it was in keeping with his temperament may be doubted.

But the energies of the young poet could not be taken up with purely socio-religious controversies. His literary life was blooming, he was seeking new friends and moving into newer circles—Priyanath Sen, Probodh Chandra Ghose, Kaliprasanna Kavyabisharad, Ashutosh Choudhury, Jogendranarayan Mitra, Srishchandra Mazumdar and others became his friends and admirers. Mitra undertook to publish Rabindranath's first collection of songs, *Rabichhaya.* In collaboration with Srishchandra he himself published *Padaratnavali,* a Vaishnava anthology while Ashutosh arranged the sequence of *Kadi O Komal* for the Press.

Ashutosh was a brilliant product of the Calcutta University, had been to England to qualify for the Bar. His mind was stored with continental literature. It was from him that Rabindranath used to hear about the latest trends in poetry and the changing climate of opinion in Europe.

Priyanath Sen was a lawyer's clerk in the High Court; but his heart was in literature. He had free access to the highways and byways of literature, local and continental, both classical and modern. Thanks to him a "wider vista of ideas" was opened to the poet. In a quiet corner of the ancestral house, the young poet's days passed in delightful conversation, in the company of a few friends that he had chosen or gathered round himself.

Satyendranath's wife, Jnandanandini, had come to Calcutta in connection with the children's education. The Tagore mansion was crowded with children of all ages. Jnandanandini, though she lived away from Jorasanko, thought of bringing out a new monthly magazine for the children. It was to be called, appropriately, *Balak* (The Boy). She knew quite well that though she might be its nominal editor, and financier, the monthly literary ration would have to be provided by her obliging brother-in-law, Robi.

Here at last was some work for a poet without occupation. And he started to write poems, novels, playlets, essays, travelogues, humorous sketches—a never-ending supply. Some of the poems were later included in the anthology *Sishu* (The Child). In the English version it is *The Crescent Moon*.

For the juvenile readers he wrote the novel *Rajarshi* (The Royal Sage) based on events relating to the royal household of Tripura. The short story *Mukut* (The Crown) also drew upon the same background. Later *Rajarshi* was adapted into a successful play, *Visarjan* (Sacrifice). *Mukut* too was dramatised and turned out to be a favourite with young actors.

The other work *Hasyakautuk* (Charade and Little Comedies) was quite a new thing in Bengali. The idea he got from Western charades. There is hardly any school in Bengal whose students do not know these amusing playlets and in which they have not, at some time or the other, taken part.

The contributions to *Balak* did not interfere with those in *Bharati*. But what a queer contrast there is between *Pushpanjali* (Flower Offerings) and *Rasikatar Phalaphal* (Consequences of a Practical Joke). The first was a sentimental tribute to the memory of his sister-in-law, and the second an amusing skit. Yet the same hand wrote both.

6

The Humanitarian Takes His Stand

THE IMPACT OF Brahmo Samaj was changing Hindu society in many directions. Just as the young progressives were eager to get rid of old, outworn beliefs and habits, so too the orthodox were fondly hoping to preserve the past with as little change as possible, with some tinkering and whitewashing here and there. The spirit of controversy has been preserved in some letters written by Rabindranath and collected in his book *Samaj* (Society). Under the guise of an exchange of letters between a grandfather and his grandson is revealed, in gentle hints, the recurring clash of opinions, the conflict of generations. Products of a forgotten age, the letters are still good reading.

In those times disputes centred round the marriage of girls and their education. As a result of the spread of education among the Brahmos, the age of marriage was going up; one could not 'offer one's fair daughter' at eight or ten as well as educate her. Today, nearly every Indian home contains fairly grown-up unmarried daughters, whether happily so or not, it is not easy to say. Things were quite different ninety years ago, and the literary men worried no end over the issue. Among them as well as among social workers there were, as there are even today, people with minds that looked back and sighed over the vanished glory of ancient days. Tagore wrote a long and challenging essay on 'Hindu Marriage'. This was read in the Science Association Hall. He sharply criticised those who defended early marriage. His essays on this and other matters may not be counted among literary masterpieces, but the false beliefs and practices, which they tried to do away with continue to haunt and harry the Bengali mind and society even today.

Take, for instance, the advent of Kalki avatar. One Krishnaprasanna Sen began a new kind of *tantric sadhana* and changed his name to Krishna-nanda. It was soon rumoured that he was none other than Kalki, the promised Messiah. In every land an incarnation has never been in want of disciples or camp followers. The way the foolish and the faithful are exploited in the name of religion, *guru* and *avatar,* surpasses the worst atrocities of the cruellest institutions of antiquity.

It was impossible for Tagore to put up with such patent nonsense and he lashed out against them in his prose, poetry and plays. Here are a few lines from a verse letter :

> Like grass they sprout everywhere, the Aryans;
> How sharp their tongue against one's feet.
> And they say I, Kalki am I—may be a Kalki of hemp.
> The lanes and alleys are jammed with avatars, avatars, everywhere.

Happily the poet did not waste much time and energy over this kind of futile social reform. Now and then, hoping to do some good, he has joined some controversy and articles flash forth; but the excitement over, he has gone back to his vocation, the life of a poet. The rhythm has often repeated itself in his life time. He has thrown himself into a movement or an idea and then withdrawn. His unfettered spirit has need of provisional bondages. "But I escape over."

"Life was aimless, in those early days," the youthful poet had written. But in some ways it had also been an irresponsible existence. As yet the young Tagore did not, it is true, have to bother about earning a livelihood, and life was for the living. Rabindranath was then the very image of Calcutta aristocracy, its grace and fashion, the observed of all observers, the young man's envy and despair. The poet wrote just as the moods dictated, his studies were purely personal. There was nothing utilitarian about it either.

There were musical soirees, many and frequent. Behind the facade, however, there persisted a strain of unsuspected seriousness, a deep and abiding awareness of the national life. And when the organisers of the Calcutta session of the Indian National Congress (1886) requested him for a song, they were richly rewarded. The poet wrote, *Amra milechhi aj mayer dake* (We have gathered today at the Mother's call). This he himself rendered in opening session. For those present it was an experience.

But immediately after he had his moods, almost an anti-climax. A sudden impulse to visit—of all places—Ghazipur in Uttar Pradesh came over the poet. He had often played with the idea of a leisurely trek of northern India, on a bullock cart along the Grand Trunk Road. This fortunately did not materialise. But why of all places, he should have chosen Ghazipur, let his own words explain: "From my very boyhood the western parts of India have been objects of romantic musings. I had often played with the idea of staying in some place there and feeling the touch of vanished days, of the glory that was India. . .1 had often heard about the rosy acres of Ghazipur and this had greatly attracted me."

The poet travelled with his family, a fifteen-year old wife and a newly born daughter, Bela. But the charm of Ghazipur soon vanished. The rosy acres belonged, alas, to traders who were more interested in selling bottled rose-water than in poetic musings. "Neither nightingale nor poet was welcome there," he wrote rather ruefully. But what the outer eye failed to find, the inner eye did—an ample recompense. A large number of *Manasi* poems, twenty-eight in all, were written here. It is true that *Manasi* includes poems written during three years, but whenever the topic came up, the poet invariably spoke of his sojourn at Ghazipur.

An incident is worth mentioning here. The English Civil Surgeon lived near the house where the poet was staying. On being introduced, the doctor had shown an interest in his works and the poet had felt encouraged to read out to him a free translation of his poem *Nishphal Kamana* (Futile Passion). We do not know if the Sahib understood anything or was just being polite. But this was his first attempt at translating his own poems and here it is :

> All fruitless is the cry,
> All vain this burning fire of desire.
> I clasp both thine hands in mine,
> And keep thine eye prisoner with my hungry eyes;
> Seeking and crying, where art thou ?
> Where, O Where !

Speechless I gaze upon it,
And I plunge with all my heart
With the deep of a fathomless longing :
I love myself. . . .—(*Poems,* pp. 7-8)

With the coming of the rains Rabindranath returned to Calcutta. He would stay sometimes at Jorasanko, at others with Jnandanandini Devi in Wood Street or in some other place. *Balak* closed down after a year's circulation. It was merged into *Bharati* and came to be called *Bharati O Balak.* At this time he was requested by the members of the *Sakhi-Samiti,* a Ladies' Club of Calcutta, to write a play for women characters only. The result of the request, *Mayar Khela* (Play of Illusion) was quite different from the earlier *Valmiki Pratibha* and *Kalamrigaya.* Here the drama was less important than the songs. Incidents were few, sentiment was everywhere but mercifully he loaded it with music still delightful to hear. It was staged for women only in the Bethune College Hall, and turned out to be quite a success. They had never seen or heard anything like it before. Some of its songs are very popular and continue to be heard in musical soirees and on the radio. We quote a few lines from an oft-sung song: *Bhalo bese yadi sukha nahi.* "If there is nothing but pain in loving then why is this love ? What folly is this to claim her heart because you have offered her your own ! With the desire burning in your blood and madness glowing in your eyes why this circling of a desert ?"

Summer 1889. The school had broken up and Jnandanandini was returning with the children to her husband at Sholapur in Bombay Presidency. Rabindranath accompanied her along with eldest daughter now two and half years old; the little boy, only four months old, and his wife were left at Jora-sanko with other members of the family. Rabindranath stayed at Sholapur for about a month. The play *Raja O Rani* (The King and the Queen) was written there. Once a success on the Bengali stage the play is "drowned in lyrics," he himself complained. When he came to rewrite it,the play was not changed. Instead a new prose play was written. This was *Tapat'u*

From Sholapur the faimly came to Poona, where they used to stay in the suburbs of Khirkhi. Rabindranath had a new experience while living there. He had once been to listen to Ramabai, the well-known Maharashtrian social worker. Listening to a lady holding forth on women's valour and rights proved too much for the more daughty male members of the audience and they soon started to parade their superiority in a blatant fashion till the poor lady had to admit defeat. The men must have returned home jubilant. But Tagore was left athinking and he wrote a long essay on the emancipation of women and the movement to further that cause. On the whole he supported it, but with some provisos.

From Sholapur he returned to Calcutta in the middle of the rainy season. His first five-act drama, *Raja O Rani,* was published soon after in August 1889. It was dedicated to his eldest brother Dwijendranath. Rabindranath might have felt now that the even tenor of his days would never cease. But that, alas, was not to be. His venerable father, the Maharshi was getting on in years. Someone had to look after the far-flung *zamindari* which he had patiently built up. Dwijendranath was out and out a philosopher and hardly the right person for the job. When, if ever, he looked into *zamindari* work, out of a sense of duty, he usually gave away money in charity and excused rents on the least pretext. Official work kept Satyendranath away. He visited Calcutta on leave only for a few days in the year; it was hardly possible for him to supervise the family's landed property. Jyotirindranath, without wife and child, had but few attachments. Hemendranath had died before. The brothers Birendranath and Somendranath were of unsound mind. Indeed there was none, except Rabindranath, who could look after the *zamindari.* Maharshi also felt that it would not do to allow his youngest son complete freedom; it was time to break him in.

Rabindranath was at first attached to the Calcutta office of the Tagore Estate. Later he had to go to Shelaidaha on the Padma where he used to live in a houseboat. The experience was new and exhilarating, and he liked it. "Living in Calcutta one almost forgets how very beautiful the world really is," he wrote from his rural retreat. Always senstive to change of scene, in the lonely *zamindari* bungalow at Sahjadpur he once more felt the creative urge and within a few days he wrote a magnificient drama *Visarjan* (Sacrifice) which he dedicated to his nephew, Surendranath. While in Calcutta last, Surendranath had presented him with a self-bound exercise book with an earnest request to write a play in it. In the dedicatory page the poet wrote:

The note book bound by your own hands,

its hundred and odd pages
I have covered with words.

The material of the drama was taken mainly from the novel *Rajarshi.* But some of the characters were newly introduced. It was indeed a new creation. This was his second and last five-act verse drama. The English version, *Sacrifice,* was dedicated "to those heroes who bravely stood for peace where human sacrifice was claimed for the Goddess of War."

Back from Shelaidah, when he was feeling uneasy over the play's publication, a political whirlwind upset everything else for the time being and the play lay forgotten. The year was 1890 and the trouble began over the Viceroy's Executive Council. This was a small body with nearly all-British membership. The problem before the Government was about the number and type of Indian members in the Council and the method of recruiting them by nomination or election. Also, the question of employing Indians to high posts in the administration was being discussed in English official circles.

Rabindranath openly criticised the Government's niggardly attitude. At the Emerald Theatre, Calcutta, he read a paper on 'Appointment of Ministers'. It was more desirable, he said, to have ministers by election rather than by government nomination; in other words, it was a strong defence of democracy in practice. This was Rabindranath's first political essay read out in public. Fifty years after, the poet commented on this yearly effort: "Times have changed since then . . . Then our demands were few and restricted. Like parrots on a perch, we would flutter our wings and scream, for shackles to be spread by a few inches more. Today we say, we accept neither perch nor shackles; we want to spread our wings in the free air. Those days even the demand for a concession made the blood of the British officers boil with rage. I had given them hot rejoinder. But you should know that my defence was on behalf of beggars that had hoped only for crumbs."

The excitement of the city life over, the poet left for Bolpur. Two years before on October 19, 1888, round the two-storeyed building known as Santiniketan, beginnings had been made towards starting an ashrama there. In March, 1888 the Maharshi's trust deed concerning Santiniketan had been completed. The Mandir (prayer hall) had not been built yet. It was constructed a decade later.

It is not easy to visualise what Santiniketan looked like eighty years ago. Except the two-storeyed building there was no other structure in the wide area; on the road from Bolpur were just a few scattered huts. This time while living alone at Santiniketan the muses were kinder and he wrote a few poems, the most memorable being *Meghdut,* a long poem on the rains written in recollection of Kalidasa's famous *Cloud-Messenger.*

From Bolpur he had again to go on *zamindari* work. But his mind was not in it. Most of the time he was a silent listener to the maulvi's sermons, the explanations of the officers, the complaints of the tenants. During leisure he tried to read Goethe's *Faust* in the original. He thought out a play but it wasn't making much progress. Feeling restless (a recurring mood) after a time Tagore went to Satyendranath who was then at Sholapur. There he came to know that his friend Loken and his brother, both in the Indian Civil Service, were going to England on furlough. This excited him and he joined their company. A poem written at the time reveals his restlessness and sense of alienation:

> The whole world is ridden with rules;
> I am the only lawless one.
> They have built their houses close together.
> They work so much and so noisily.
> Day follows day . . .
> Down the ages
> I alone seem to be unable to control myself
> And am left wandering day and night.

This is not just poetry, but the truth of his inner life. Whenever and in whatever way he might say, "I am athirst for the beyond," for him every word is true, perhaps too true.

This time the English tour lasted but three and a half months (August 2 to November 3, 1890). Of these forty-two days were spent on board ship. In London he spent barely a month. Mental restlessness was the reason for the sudden trip; the reason for the early return was no less mysterious. But Bengali literature gained a new book, *Europeja-trir Diary,* a delightful document.

7

A Controversial .Harvest

RABINDRANATH WAS NOW thirty. Three years before (1888) he had written in anticipation that at this stage of life one hardly expects a new harvest. But the thirtieth year, when it came, brought with it unexpected abundance.

There were infrequent visits to the *zamindari* in North Bengal. But all the same, he would often visit the city. During one of these visits he heard from friends about the project to bring out a new weekly magazine. He joined the group and enthusiastically wrote to a friend, "We are bringing out a weekly paper *Hitavadi* and have started a huge company to start work on it." Different sections were entrusted to different persons. Rabindranath was placed in charge of the literary section.

The magazine released a stream of new writings. In the past he had attempted to write short stories but really these had been just sketches. Now we have full-fledged short stories. Journeying through the country in the houseboat, Tagore had acquired much new experience. He had met and known the common man, the rustic, and profited by the contact. The short stories were written out of direct experience and a refined sympathy. The characters were based on the men and women he had come across during his tours of North Bengal villages. This was probably the first time that in Bengali literature stories based on the life of common folk, their joys and sorrows, came to be written. Those who look upon the poet as a dweller in the ivory tower overlook this aspect of his creative expression.

Hitavadi published six stories in succession : birth of short stories in Bengali might be counted from this time. Among his prose writings such as *Akal Bibaha* (Untimely Marriage) kept the literary world agog for some time. This was part of the controversy between him and the Hindu apologist, Chan-dranath Basu. The poet suggested that untimely marriages did not merely mean marrying tender girls but also the equally guilty act of marrying without means of earning a livelihood.

Chandranath retorted by saying that there was 'a Western tinge' in Rabindranath's way of thinking. It is not easy, say what you will, to deny this charge. Rabindranath himself however felt that there was really "no conflict between the Hindu and the European mind; it is only the lifeless conventionalism and grotesque, perverted Hindu chauvinism that is really un-Hindu."

The poet's association with *Hitavadi* lasted for barely six weeks. He must have found it impossible to write serious and edifying literature to order. After breaking away from the group, he wrote a few satirical essays which were published in a new monthly, *Sahitya* (Literature), edited by Suresh-chandra Samajpati, a talented youth. The essays were full of digs at the new-fangled idea of realism in literature. For him realism could not be reality.

His stay in Calcutta was always brief and broken. He had often to visit North Bengal to supervise the family's land interests.

When he came back to Calcutta in autumn, after his

tour of Orissa and North Bengal, he found his nephews excited over the publication of another new journal, *Sadhana.* The leader of the group was Sudhindranath, Dwijendranath's youngest son, a fresh graduate of the prestigious Calcutta University and lover of literature; he became its editor. But they all knew that 'Uncle Robi' would have to provide the life-line. Uncle himself was no less eager and willing. He had often dreamt of an ideal monthly magazine. Here was a chance. Many things needed to be said; the old masters had either retired or gone into hiding, or worse, were peddling rehash. Variety, truth and beauty had disappeared from the literary scene. Home truths had to be uttered once more.

Most of the journal's contents were by Rabindranath, poems, stories, diaries, essays, reviews, etc. In the course of a year (1891-92) he wrote no less than eleven short stories, most of which were tragic. The first was *Khokababur Pratyabartan* (The Return of the Young Master). It began with the furies of the river Padma in spate and ended on a note of the futility of human existence. *Sampatti Samarpan, Kankal, Jeebita O Mrita, Swarnamriga, Jai Parajaya, all* were sad. *Dalia* had a slender historical thread, melodrama alone could save it from a fatal ending. An English playlet, *The Maharani of Arakan,* based on *Dalia* was staged in London in 1912. In *Tyaga* (Renunciation) the hero showed a surprisingly bold spirit when he told his guardian that he would not give up his young wife, and that he did not accept the caste system. It showed some moral courage; for the Adi Brahmo Samaj itself was not wholly free from that incubus.

Two of the stories, *Muktir Upaya* (The Way to Salvation)

and *Ekti Asharey Galpa* (Grandmother's Tale) were later adapted as plays; *Ekti Asharey Galpa* became *Taser Desh* (the Kingdom of Cards), the other retained the original title. But in the revised version both were new creations different from the original.

Sadhana first came out in November 1891. On 22 December the Mandir at Santiniketan was founded. As yet Rabindranath had not been involved in prayers and sermons; he was just a singer at the ceremony.

After the function at Santiniketan was over, he had, as usual, to proceed to the Estates. For sometime the muse had been chary of her gifts. This time at Shelaidah on a spring morning, though there was no touch or trace of rains anywhere, he suddenly wrote a magical line : *Gagane garaje megh ghanabarasa* (the rain clouds clap in the sky). A poet can always imagine. A golden barge, loaded with freshly harvested paddy, steered by a singing boatman, while the reaper is left alone on the bank on the plea that there is no room for him.

In what an unhappy hour he must have written that poem *Sonar Tari* (The Golden Boat) ! The controversy over this slender piece is almost without parallel in Bengal's literary history. There is hardly anyone who has not thrilled to its evocation and none perhaps that has understood it. The poet's own exposition fails to satisfy, is at best second order reality. The poem lives, magical, mysterious, irresistible, pointing at epiphanies that no words can capture.

Many of the poems in the *Sonar Tari* volume belong to this period. Along with this he was doing more pedestrian work also, such as writing short stories and essays and *belles lettres.* But nothing of course gave the same satisfaction as a poem did. "A thousand pages of prose cannot give the same joy as the writing of a single poem," he said frankly and truthfully.

Rabindranath was now regularly supervising the *zamindari;* it was on the whole not such a disagreeable occupation. Travelling from place to place he reached Rajshahi where Loken Palit, his boyhood friend happened to be the District Judge. The letters exchanged on the pages of *Sadhana* between the friends have not lost their freshness yet.

At Rajshahi also lived Akshoykumar Maitra, by profession a lawyer, but by choice a historian and art critic. There were others as well. At their request Rabindranath read, at the Rajshahi Association, a paper on *Sikshar Herpher* (The Vicissitudes of Education). There hardly exists a more cogent discussion on the problems of education through the medium of the mother tongue. When the whole country was almost hypnotised by English and busy singing its praises, it was a bold thing to advocate-openly the mother tongue as the medium of instruction. With the help of a metaphor Rabindranath pointed out that the education that we receive in the schools and colleges remains in the outer court of our mind; the barrier between what one has learnt from books and one's life is impassable, it does not change or modify our lives to any great extent. The medium of instruction, he advocated, should be the mother tongue at every stage of education.

The *Vicissitudes of Education* is important as his first

major essay on the subject and for its emphasis on the study of the mother tongue. The suggestion was revolutionary and thinkers and public men sent him congratulatory letters. But from the Education Department of the Government there was naturally no response.

From Rajshahi, Tagore went to Natore, where he accepted the Maharaja's hospitality. While there, he had a severe attack of toothache. Sickness is no respecter of persons and it did not spare the poet. Even then he was writing humorous letters to his niece, Indira Tagore. Anyhow, when he returned to Shelaidaha the heart was without songs, and he pining for them. In a letter he writes : "The Muse, like all ladies, is a jealous mistress. Hence I am in some mental distress, poetry is indeed my first love —I cannot bear long separation." A little after this he wrote *Manas Sundari* (Intellectual Beauty), one of his finest poems.

But the thrills of intellectual beauty were far removed from the cares and anxieties of everyday life. To harmonise the inward dream with the reality outside was quite a job. His wife wrote from Sholapur that she was returning to Calcutta with the children. The over-long stay at the sister-in-law's place must have made her uneasy. The nonplussed poet wrote back: "I know for certain that the longer you stay at Sholapur the better it well be for all of you. I earnestly believed that the children would profit by their stay. However, in this life not everything is within one's own control."

Mrinalini Devi returned with the children to Calcutta and set up home at Jorasanko. Her third daughter, the fourth child, was born in January 1893. Owing perhaps to these family problems-Rabindranath was for the first time unable to attend the annual fuction at Santiniketan. But as usual he composed some religious songs, Brahma Sangit, for the Magh Festival.*

He had to go to Orissa once again. This time his young nephew, Balendranath (22) joined him. He was serving his literary apprenticeship under Rabindranath and was also being trained to look after family affairs. At Cuttack they put up with Biharilal Gupta. Along with Surendranath Banerji and Rameshchandra Dutta, Biharilal was a member of the second batch of Indian Civil Service men. Between his family and Rabindranath there was a good deal of intimacy. In a letter to his wife the poet wrote : "Biharibabu, I noticed, suffers from the same fastidiousness as I do. He is easily put out. But, unlike me, he does not growse and grumble, which must be a godsend for his wife."

During his stay at Cuttack, Gupta had invited the English Principal of the local Ravenshaw College to dinner. A perfect John Bull, his offensive against the Indian people and civilisation must have hurt the poet to the quick. At that time there was a controversy over the extension of the jury system in India. The Principal thought that the moral standard of Indians was pretty low. They were indifferrent to the sacredness of life; hence it was better to keep down

* The Magh Festival : Rammohan Roy established Brahma Sabha in 1828, and the opening ceremony of the Brahma Mandir (church) took place two years later on the 11th of Magh (10th month of the Bengali year). This date coincided with the 23rd January in 1830. Now it generally coincides with the 25th January.

the number of such people on the jury. Referring to this incident out of the bitterness of his heart, Tagore wrote : "Those who do not hesitate to speak in this vein, sitting in an Indian family where they are invited guests, one may well imagine with what eyes such people look upon us." His essay *Apamaner Pratikar* (Redress of Insult), written a little after, was perhaps based on this memory.

From Cuttack they went together in a horse-carriage to Puri. There were no railways then. From there they visited Bhuvaneswar and Konark. Looking at the temple he wrote, "It is like reading a new book."

But there was no time for day-dreaming. They had to go round the estates by boat or palanquin. Some of the best poems in *Sonar Tari* were written in this peripatetic fashion. No wonder he has written so freely and feelingly about the wayfarer. Has he not been one, all his long life ?

8

The Nationalist Takes Shape

AFTER A SHORT stay in Calcutta he had again to move to North Bengal. There he wrote the dramatic poem *Bidaya-Abhishap* (Farewell Curss), the story of

Kacha and Devajani, one of the first poems of its kind in Bengali. One feels a trace of Browning's dramatic lyrics in this. He was a keen student of Browning even in his later years. The day on which the lyrical drama was written, in a letter he had said, "I have for long thought that men are rather incongruous, while women have a certain consistency." It is a fact that most of the poet's writings of the period reveal a keen awareness of the basic problems of existence. His *Panchabhuter Dayari* (Diary of the Five Elements), for instance, is an intellectual monument. A neglected classic, it consists of dialogues and arguments on life and literature among the five elements in a humorous vein.

Returning to Calcutta he found the educated bourgeoisie in a state of agitation. Rabindranath could not keep himself aloof, and wrote several essays on the questions of the day. What were these questions ?

The time of which we are speaking is 1893. In 1861, little after the Sepoy Mutiny, the first Indian Councils Act had been passed; nearly thirty years after, in 1892, the Act was revised. The Indian politicians now demanded some form of representative government. Not only were those demands not acceded to, but some seats were reserved for special groups and communities. In other words, communalism was forced into the body politic. Also, Indians were cleverly kept out of many high Government positions. Also, the exchange ratio between shilling and rupee was so manipulated that in foreign exchange deals the Indians would lose heavily. Because of this and other discriminatory measures the educated Indians felt extremely bitter. Even a Government pensioner like

Bankimchandra (a Rai Bahadur) wrote, "So long as this attitude of conqueror and conquered persists, we shall continue to remind ourselves of our past glory. Till we are on a footing of equality with the English, let us pray, heart and soul, that feelings of racial animosity (*jati-bairi)* may remain with us as strong as they are now." Feelings ran high and Rabindranath could not but join. He wrote an essay, *Ingrej O Bharatvasi* (The English and the Indians) for a public meeting. Bankimchandra had been proposed as the president of the meeting. The wise President wanted to have a look at the paper; perhaps he feared that the young poet's language might stray into areas forbidden by the Indian Penal Code. Rabindranath went to Bankim's house and read out the essay to him and had his approval. The meeting was held in the Chaitanya Library, on Beadon Street with Bankim in the Chair. This was their last meeting, for Bankim died shortly thereafter.

Apart from this paper, Rabindranath also wrote a number of other articles, *Ingrejer Atanka* (Fear of the English), *Subicharer Adhikar* (The Right to Justice), *Raja O Praja* (The Ruler and the Ruled), *Rajnitir Dwidha* (The Hesitations of Politics), etc His love of the country is writ large in every one of these warm-hearted articles. At one place out of bitterness he had written, "Europe's ethics is for Europe only. The Indians are so different a people that a civilised code is not suited to them."

It was from this period that the canker of communalism entered the Indian body politic. This had an evil effect on the social life of the Hindus and Muslims alike. Hindu nationalism was born in Maharashtra under the leadership of that astute hero, Lokamanya

Balgangadhar Tilak. Homage to Shivaji and Ganapati Puja became national festivals. As a result of militant Hindu nationalism a society for the protection of cows was founded in Poona. That became the symbol of Hindu religiosity. Appropriately, very soon the slaughtering of cows became a must for the Mussalmans. For the Hindus it became equally necessary, for maintaining the purity of the religion, to protect the cow. Bloody fights ensued and many died on either side. The English, had they wanted it, could have put an end to the unseemly and unnecessary conflict. Many Hindus believed that it was not the Government's real intention to end the troubles; on the contrary it was interested in keeping alive the spirit of religious hatred between the two communities, and with Muslim help to bring down the pride of the Hindus, who were becoming 'national'.

Rabindranath had fondly believed that, faced with the danger, Hindus of all classes would be gradually drawn towards each other. But it was hoping against hope, national integration is still a far cry.

The two literary figures, Bankimchandra and Biharilal, whom young Rabindranath looked upon as his ideals, died within two months of each other in 1894.

A memorial meeting for Bankim was arranged and Rabindranath requested the poet Nabinchandra Sen to preside over the meeting. Nabinchandra wrote back that he was against the idea of holding a memorial meeting; as a Hindu he failed to understand what a memorial meeting meant, the thing was purely European. Rabindranath, as the Chief Guest, read out his essay on Bankim. Anyway, the memorial meeting was held (April 28,1894) under the chairmanship of Gurudas Banerji. He pointed out that in our country the father's funerary ceremonies are held in the open; likewise the expression of our sorrow at the passing away of a great and philanthropic soul was in the nature of a social duty. The poet's profound regard for Bankim was beautifully conveyed in his address. Even after this on several occasions he spoke enthusiastically about Bankim.

Biharilal, the 'Lord of Lyricism' in Bengali poetry died; but no public meeting was held. In a long article Rabindranath paid his tribute to Biharilal who had inspired his early lyrics. The Bangiya Sahitya Parishad (Bengali Literary Academy) was founded in 1894. Rabindranath had been associated with it from the very start. During the first year of the Academy he acted as one of its Vice-Presidents. He was also a member of its Subcommittee on Technical Terms.

Once, on his away to the *zamindari,* at the invitation of Nabinchandra Sen, then sub-divisional magistrate of Ranaghat, Rabindranath had halted there for a day. This is how Nabinchandra describes the young poet of thirty :

"I saw before me the adolescent of 1876 in the full orb of youth. How beautiful and serene a stature, glowing with genius. The long face shining and fair like the lotus bud about to bloom; and the curly hair parted and dressed in the middle; the brow, like a golden mirror, set in the midst of curly hair; the face, set off by the beard and moustache dark as a bee; a pair of polished golden spectacles on his shapely nose. The gold frame and the complexion vied with each other. Looking at him you are reminded of the portraits of Christ. He was wearing a white dhoti, and a chadar or tunic. On his feet were soft sandals, suggestive of the intolerable hardness of Western footwear."

Almost from the founding of the Sahitya Parishad the poet had turned his attention to collecting the ballads of rural Bengal, especially the 'feminine ballads'. He wrote a long and perceptive article on the subject, and opened before the literati a new world. When Dakshinaranjan Mitra put together his collection of folk tales, *Thakurmar Jhuli* (Grandma's Bag), it was Rabindranath who wrote the preface.

His days were divided between North Bengal and Calcutta. It was a tiring life. Staying in Calcutta "one gradually loses the power to think or feel or imagine. One ceases to have the leisure and enthusiasm for expressing what one feels—within one's mind there is a continuous dissatisfaction." So he came to Bolpur. Except the two-storeyed Guest House of Santiniketan and the prayer hall, there was nothing but the bare plains of Birbhum. In this solitary world he was all alone. Analysing his own temperament he wrote in a letter :

"I am ashamed to confess that, as a rule, the company of men distracts me. There is round my personality, a certain sense of limit which nothing will permit me to violate. And yet I do not find it natural to remain totally aloof from human contact. From time to time I feel an urge to participate in the life of the many. I feel the need of the warmth of companionship. This conflict can be harmonised in living with intimate spirits, who do not tire the mind with tension, indeed, who offer you that easy happiness which gives a natural and delightful direction to the faculties of the mind."

The self-examination is reflected throughout his life. In his poem *Aikatan* (Orchestra), he said the same thing, in a different key.

A new chapter was opening in Rabindranath's life. Two of his nephews, Surendranath and Balendranath had, with no experience and little backing, started a business at Kusthia. The Tagore family traced its wealth to the business acumen of 'Prince' Dwarakanath. These two cousins perhaps hoped to see history repeated; in this they were soon joined by Uncle Robi. Though a poet, Rabindranath was a man like any other man and like them he knew, that in order to live and live well one should earn money. But the business was quite an adventure.

In a letter we find him writing : "I had known only from books that work was an excellent thing. Now I can feel that the true worth of a person is in the work he does. . . . The more varied the activities that I am turning my hands to, the greater grows my respect for the thing called 'work'. . . . Men from distant places meet there. Today I have joined that wide throng." In *Chitra* there is a poem called *Nagarsangit* (City Music). It is a hallelujah to 'the work is worship' cult.

Kusthia, Calcutta and villages of the *zamindari*— he was all the time on the move from one place to another. On top of it all there was the editorial work of *Sadhana.* This he did with great conscientiousness. He regularly wrote stories, essays, and topical comments. But the new feature was book reviews. This kind of work had been begun by Bankimchandra in *Bangadarshan.* Rabindranath's work in this genre raised Bengali to the standards of Western criticism.

But *Sadhana* was not a paying proposition. In those days monthly magazines could not depend on the income from advertisements. The uncle and nephew had invested all their extra money in business at Kusthia; they began manufacturing sugar, crushing cane in competition against a British firm which had so far the monopoly in this. So it became quite difficult to meet losses on account of the magazine. After running for four years *Sadhana* stopped publication. The poet wrote to his friend Srishchandra almost with a sigh of relief, "After a long time I am once more face to face with my old friend, idleness." That is his creative norm.

To supply the whole year round the miscellaneous demands of a monthly magazine, was growing quite intolerable. But the real trouble was that it was against his nature to be absorbed in one form of activity or one set of thoughts for any length of time. So he felt relieved to be free of the responsibility of the monthly magazine. 'Old friend, idleness' did not mean that he was passing the long days in relaxation or a state of suspended animation. Some of the best poems of *Chitra* were written at about this time—*Purnima* (Full Moon), *UrvaSee Bijayini* (The Victorious Lady), *Swarga Hoite Bidaya* (Farewell from Heaven), *Sindhupare* (On the Seashore), etc.

Sadhana had ceased publication after four years. Tagore was staying at the *zamindari* at Patisar. The river, Nagar, was indeed rural, narrow and meandering, slow and sluggish, about to dry up. In the insufferable heat of April he was staying in his houseboat—hardly the proper background for any genuine work or serious studies. The windows of the houseboat were closed; only through the half-open shutters appeared a small portion of the world outside (it was like looking at the world through the wrong end of a telescope). It was like looking through the windows of the Chowringhee House during 'Chhabi O Gan' of his earlier days. It was the vision of a world extremely limited in range. The painting was bare—both as regards ideas and images. A poet of nature, he had described her beauties in many of his poems, where man was secondary. Man was given only as much place as was necessary to make nature meaningful. It was in the verses of *Chaitali* that man and nature make a harmony. That is, the first notes of welcome to man were heard in this tiny volume of verse, mostly sonnets. In the course of *zamindari* work he had come across the common man of his country. In *Galpaguchha* (Short Stories) he had written about them; it is of them that *Chaitali* also speaks.

The poet had to go to Orissa again. It was the same *zamindari* work. Family problems were getting complicated; there were talks of breaking up the Tagore Estate. So far the entire property had been one unit. Now that the grandsons of Debendranath's younger brother—Gaganendra, Samarendra and Abanindra—had come of age, it was the Maharshi's wish that the property should be divided during his lifetime so that there might be no trouble later. Sajadpur fell to the share of Gaganendranath and his brothers and the Orissa property to Hemendranath's descendants. Rabindranath had to do a lot of travelling in this con-nection, since he alone knew the details of the transactions, some of the bitterness, usual in these matters, had spilled over. *Chaitali* contains traces of this. The poet prays again and again for quiet and peace.

It was during these peregrinations in Orissa that he wrote the dramatic poem *Malini.* Unless he had a supreme sense of freedom somewhere, in some corner of the mind, he could hardly have written such a lovely piece in the midst of endless travel and what was little better than pettifogging.

Malini and *Chaitali* were not printed in separate book form; but a few months after, they were included in a collection of poems which was published by his nephew Satyaprasad Ganguly in October, 1896.

The responsibility of contributing miscellaneous writings to *Sadhana* was over. The active pen lay idle. The business at Kusthia was in full swing. But occasional release did come. His friends in Calcutta requested him for a new play. He wrote *Vaikunther Khata* (The Manuscript of Vaikuntha), just as four years before he had written *Goray Golad.* It was a delightful piece and the amusing goings-on of Kedar and Tinkari make it impossible to be angry even with their villainy.

Within a month of *Vaikunther Khata* was published *Panchabhuter Dayari* (Diary of the Five Elements). In Bengali there has been no book like this before or after.

The Bengal Provincial Conference was being held at Natore (in Rajsahi). The *zamindar* of Natore, Maharaja

Jagadindranath, was its convener. Rabindranath, one of his close friends, was present with many of the young men of the Tagore family.

Towards the end of the nineteenth century, Indian politics was confined to the upper and middle class educated Indians. Meetings and conference addresses, resolutions, debates, etc. used to be in English. Whatever was said or done, was really meant for the ears of the British rulers. The Indian leaders had not yet felt the need for speaking to the masses in their language. The President of the Natore Conference, Satyendranath Tagore, retired civilian, delivered, as usual, the Presidential Address in English.

Rabindranath and other young men were totally opposed to the use of English for conducting the business of the meeting. He wrote : "When, with the help of Jagadindranath, I first tried to introduce the use of Bengali in this meeting, W.C. Bonnerjee (the first President of the Congress) and other leaders spoke sarcastically about me and my efforts." Rabindranath had planned to have his own back at the time of thanking the volunteers. But fate willed otherwise. In the afternoon (June 1897), a terrible earthquake left the conference in mere shambles. They just managed to save themselves and return to Calcutta in safety. In one of his books Abanindranath has left delightful descriptions of the Natore conference.

This political event was, however, only a sideshow. It was really the period of lyrics. But a change came soon. We have seen that invariably, after a period of intense lyricism, Tagore has taken to writing stories—the form of expression varied from time to time. This time it was lyrical drama or narrative poem : *Gandharir Abedan* (Mother's Prayer), *Sati, Narakbas* (A Season in Hell), *Lakshmir Pariksha* (Trial of Lakshmi). Among the narrative poems, *Bhasa O Chhanda* about the historicity of Ramchandra legend, 'What is truth' was the root question for the bard :

> Narad said smiling, '!What you write shall be the truth,
> That which happens is not entirely true,
> The land of your imagination, poet,
> Is Rama's birthplace, truer than Ayodhya....

In some of these lyrical dramas, the poet has raised the eternal questions of truth and religion. The second he would answer at length, the first would elude till the end.

The task of editing *Bharati* soon devolved upon Rabindranath. It was practically a family affair, and for the last two years the periodical had been edited by his two nieces. Ten years prior to that, his eldest sister Swarnakumari Devi had looked after it, and before that Dwijendranath, the eldest brother. The journal had been started twenty years before, when Rabindranath was sixteen. Now he was thirty-five.

A journal was always a stimulus to the poet. Once again came a spate of stories, essays, book reviews and miscellaneous articles.

'1he nineteenth century was drawing to a close. During the last few years political awareness in the country had taken a new shape among the masses. The events inspired by Tilak's Hindu nationalism we have already hinted at.

In 1896 during the plague epidemic the Bombay administration enacted measures which were hardly to be distinguished from tyranny. The cure was worse than the disease. A little before this a secret society had been established at Poona to fight the British. Two of the members, the brothers Chapekar, shot the Plague Officer and a Magistrate on the day fixed for the celebration of Shivaji's birthday. The Government saw the hand of Bal Gangadhar Tilak in all this, and he was sentenced to a year's imprisonment. For some time past Bengal and Bombay newspapers and periodicals had been relentless critics of the Government. Their language was frequently irresponsible;, nor were the facts reported always objective. In order to put a stop of these 'irresponsible' writings, the Government introduced a Sedition Bill. Calcutta was then the capital of India. The day before the bill was passed into an Act there was a huge rally at the Town Hall. Rabindranath read a paper *Kantharodh* (Gagging the Voice).

When disaffection grows among people it is as well to allow it to be expressed, such was the view expressed by Tagore in his speech. He said, the more open the criticism in the papers, the more could one know people's real minds. To have to live in a gagged world would be a terrible state indeed. "Rigid laws and intimidation, *zubberr-dusti,* were bound to lead to contrary results. If political agitation could be dubbed treason against the State, why should not the tyranny of administration be a treason against the citizens. *Prajadroha* as opposed to *Rajadroha* ?" He added, playing on words. "An administration that works against the wishes and interests of the people-should be accused of treason."

A few days later, at Dacca was held the Provincial Conference. The Rev. Kalicharan Banerji,. an advocate of the Calcutta High Court, a devout Christian and ardent patriot, was the President. In keeping with the existing convention he-read out his speech in English; but Rabindranath himself provided a summary in Bengali. The opening song had also been sung by Rabindranath. Of course it was in Bengali.

9

The Poet as Father

WE HAVE TALKED of his public and creative activities. What about the man Rabindranath and his personal problems ?

The children were growing up. He held definite-views about education, and did not send the children to any of the Calcutta schools, though other children of the Tagore house used to attend school and college. The Jorasanko Mansion was a hive of families, and the children were being brought up according to miscellaneous ideals. The Maharshi, now an old man, was living in another part of the city, in a rented house. Rabindranath also did not like to live at Jorasanko with his wife and children. Returning to Shelaidah from Dacca he wrote to his wife: "I am anxious to take you away from Calcutta." Accordingly, he brought over his family to Shelaidah, and arrange privately for the children's education. Three years after, in 1901, a boarding school, Brahmacharya Ashram was established at Santiniketan. Of this we shall speak later.

The business at Kusthia was on its last legs. Balendranath was ill, Surendranath appeared to be indifferent; Rabindranath was busy editing *Bharati.* The joy of literary creation and the anxiety over family problems, his days alternated between the two. When at last he had time to look into the business enterprise, it was too late—the thing had rotted from within. Balendranath's "most faithful" Manager had decamped, leaving a loan of seventy thousand rupees to be paid. The entire responsibility came upon Rabindranath, for neither Balendranath, nor Surendranath were yet legal partners in the *zamindari.*

The loan might have been paid up in the usual course, had Rabindranath not been so eager to close the show. This has happened often in the poet's life, he would rigorously wipe out all memory of failure, so that no trace of the past might remain. In correcting his scripts, for instance, he was so thorough that it was quite impossible to make out the original draft. Of course, in his private correspondence there is ample material for reconstructing its history.

Rathindranath, the eldest son of the poet, in his

Memoirs writes : "At Shelaidah we lived an entirely different life, away from all contact with society and completely confined to ourselves. My father had become greatly concerned about our education* He was determined that we should not go through the grind of stereotyped school teaching prevalent in our country." So at the Shelaidah *Kuthibari* (Manor House), a private school for children had been opened. The English teacher was one Mr. Lawrence, an odd but lovable gentleman. Jagadananda Ray looked after mathematics, and one pandit taught Sanskrit. Rabindranath himself spent much time over the lessons.

All the while poetry came in short, sudden trickles. *Kanika* contained brief poems from two *to* ten lines. His experience in business had brought him in touch with many kinds of men. He had seen that most men carried a mask to cover the hypocrisy within. The poems have a sting unusual in the works of the poet. At this period he also started writing a number of verse narratives which were published first in *Katha* and later collected in *Katha O Kahini.* In all he wrote about twenty ballad-like poems, all great favourites with children.

In spite of staying with his family at Shelaidah, he had frequently to come to Calcutta. The Calcutta young men could hardly do without "Rabibabu". Once he had to settle a dispute in the Bangiya Sahitya Parishad. For the last six years the Parishad had been housed in a well-known aristocratic family mansion of Calcutta. The younger group was opposed to the idea of holding the meetings of the society in a plutocrat's palace; they called for a change of venue. Rabindranath joined hands with the younger group and a house was rented for the purpose. Later, there was a gift of land, on the Circular Road, by Maharaja Manindrachandra Nandy of Cossimbazar (Mur-shidabad). Among the recipients, on behalf of the Parishad, was Rabindranath (1900).

The poetic vision soon changed and a sudden rebellious mood came upon the poet. He no longer cared for legends of far-off times. Enough of dream excursions into the past ! Now he sought for the poignant moment—here and now the actual experience of everyday life asked for attention and embodiment.

So, when the management of *Bharati* called for a contribution, the story that he sent was a comedy called *The Bachelors' Club.* And a new series of poems known as *Kshanika* bore the same strain of hilarity. The poems were written mostly during 1900, some at Shelaidah, a few in Calcutta and a few even at Darjeeling, where he had gone on a short visit with the Maharaja of Tripura, Radha-kishore Manikya. The book was dedicated to his friend, Loken Palit. *Kshanika* is surely among his greatest works. Its apparently tripping verse hints at deeper values, while *The Bachelors' Club (Chirakumar Sabha),* fiction in the form of a comedy, is not entirely a comic piece. Whether bachelor-hood is socially desirable is the problem dealt with in a rather comic vein. At that time Swami Vivekananda was busy organising a new band of ascetics. Was the comedy a criticism or a fling at that ? In one of the poems in *Kshanika* he has said :

> Never, never shall I an ascetic be:
> Let them say what they feel.

What was said so gaily took on a deeper tinge a short time after, and in *Naivedya* we hear : "Not in renunciation my deliverence lies."

As it is, he had a family to look after. A dutiful husband and affectionate father, sympathy and sense of duty were not confined within the family circle. He always did his best to help his friends and disciples whenever he came to know that they were engaged in serious research. He supplied plots of stories to writers, meticulously revised the scripts of many and wrote introductions, by way of encouragement.

The help was not confined to literary men, as will be seen in case of Jagadishchandra Bose, then a promising lecturer in Physics in Presidency College, Calcutta. Jagadish was then on leave in England, engaged in research. Rabindranath was anxious that his researches should continue without let or hindrance. An Indian engaged in scientific research work was something the British authorities could neither understand nor imagine. Rabindranath wrote to his friend in England, "The way of knowledge is India's way, she has no other way. The way of austerity and spiritual striving is our way. In the past we had given many things to the world, but none remembers that. We have once more to acquire the teacher's role, that is how we can hold our head high."

Substantial assistance was needed in order that Jagdish could carry on his work in England. The Government was unwilling to grant him leave, not to speak of financial help. In this predicament Rabindranath appealed to the Maharaja of Tripura, Radhakishore Manikya. The Maharaja was an admirer of the poet and he sent him ten thousand rupees.

Thanks to this, Jagadishchandra's work in England went on uninterrupted.

Rabindranath wished the Maharaja to be an exemplar of Hindu royalty and help liberally in noble causes. In the matter of modern knowledge Tripura was pretty backward; the Maharaja who lived in the provincial town, was not familiar with the leaders of Calcutta society. Rabindranath wanted the Maharaja to come out of his rural shell of Agartala into the urban society of Calcutta where he arranged a reception. The play *Visarjan* was staged in December 1900, on the occasion and the noble ideal of his ancestor, Govinda Manikya, presented before him for emulation. Rabindranath himself appeared in the role of Raghupati.

In this way Radhakishore Manikya was gradually drawn to the poet and he soon came to depend upon him for advice and guidance in many matters such as the education of the princes, administration of the State, appointment of ministers, etc. But it is easier for a camel to pass through a needle's eye than for a rich man to go to heaven. In a letter Rabindranath wrote: "Men of property might be large-hearted but they are often surrounded by small-minded folk, and in spite of their sincere desire to do good, the attempt fails, it is impossible to engage them in any useful activity."

In 1901 *Bangadarshan* came out in a new series, with Rabindranath as editor. He was now forty. The management was in the hands of Saileshchandra Majumdar, the brother of his old friend Srishchandra. He had opened Majumdar Agency, a publishing firm in Calcutta. They were the first publishers of many of Tagore's books. Round this shop and publishing house there gradually grew up a literary club.

In the new *Bangadarshan* Rabindranath contributed not only poems and essays but serialised a new novel, *Chokher Bali* (Eyesore). Some time before he had written the draft of a story *Binodini.* The demand of the new magazine made him elaborate that in the form of fiction. So long he had been writing short stories: his last work *Nastaneer* (Broken Nest), was at first described as a novel. But it is better to call it a novelette. It might be said that this was his first psychological story. This was followed by a full-fledged novel. It was in many ways a departure from the romantic novels, of the day. The psychological novel in Bengali really began with *Eyesore* as *Binodini* is known in English translations.

Apart from the novel, and in spite of the fact that times have changed, his nationalistic essays are still read and are worth reading. The Indian situation was getting more difficult, and people seemed to suffer more. The intellectuals felt the need for arousing the Indian masses. The problem was, how to unite and utilise this vast but weak society, the enormous dormant power. Many of the intellectuals believed that the Indian problem would be solved by the power of the idea of the Hindu-ness (Hindutva) of the Hindu: in other words, Hindu nationalism.

It was to this end that apologists like Ramendra-sunder Trivedi, Brahmobandhab Upadhyaya and others bent their energies. It is necessary to point out that the attitude of these thinkers was different from the earlier exponents of Hinduism like Bankimchandra, Chandranath and Sashadhar Tarkachudamani. Rabindranath too joined hands with them and engaged himself in the neo-Hindu movement but with a difference. Earlier, in the poems of *Naivedya* (Offering), he had been putting his ideas of God and nation into shape. Now in the pages of *Bangadarshan* he expressed the same ideas in a series of prose essays. In a sense these essays are a commentry on some of the poems of *Naivedya* and the two should be read together.

Varnashram was the basis of the unity of the Hindu, Rabindranath declared. And yet he added, "Those who think that the Indian ideal is a breeding ground for ascetics and nothing else, turns them all into Brahmins, are false prophets. Such pride is indeed a slur on that noble ideal. India in her glorious day was great in diverse ways of human activities, in strength, wealth, knowledge and spirituality; counting beads was not her only duty all day through." But Rabindranath's Brahmin is really cast in the image of an idealised superman. It may be doubted if such a person ever existed. That he is rare in our present century we all know.

The hundred poems of *Naivedya* give a perfect conspectus of Rabindranath's mind. His social, political and spiritual tenor is well revealed in these poems:

> Let honour come to me from Thee through a call
> to some desperate task,
> In the pride of poignant suffering.
> Lull me not into languid dreams;
> Shake me out of this cringing in the dust,
> Out of the fetters that shackle our mind.
> Make futile our destiny;
> Out of the unreason that bends our dignity
> Down under the indiscriminate feet of dictators;

Shatter this age-long shame of ours,
And raise our head
Into the boundless sky,
Into the generous light,
Into the air of freedom—(*Poem 24*)

It was now nearly three years that, away from noisy Calcutta, Rabindranath had been living at Shelaidah with his children. For his wife, the lonesome Shelaidah life turned out to be no better than an 'exile'. In this rural retreat, without company she was far from happy. This worried the poet and he had written, perhaps in self-defence:

No dealings shall I have in the city's market places,
In human society I shall prove to be of no use.
I shall get nothing, nor shall I borrow from anyone,
An idle life shall I pass in the heart of the village.

For many reasons it became difficult to continue this idealised, idle life in a village. The girls were coming of age and had to be married. The eldest son, Rathindranath, must prepare himself for the University Entrance Examination. It was necessary to secure the services of an experienced teacher to coach him. The poet had to admit that none of these things could be done without getting away from Shelaidah. But he was totally opposed to staying in the family house in Calcutta. He preferred to settle at Santiniketan. The idea of starting a boarding school came to him at that time. Rathindranath would be a student there.

First he came to Calcutta, where his eldest daughter Bela (Madhurilata) was married to Saratchandra Chakravarty, a son of the poet Biharilal Chakravarty. An M.A.,B.L., Saratchandra had his legal practice at Muzaffarpur in North Bihar. Compared to the bride, the groom was perhaps a little elderly. But the Tagores were a family of Peeralis and Brahmo too. Few dared to marry into such a family and 'lose caste'. A son-in law like Sarat-chandra was not easy to come by. On the other hand Sarat's family did not belong to the upper stratum of Brahmanical society, the orthodox higher castes would not marry into their group; so a marriage with the Tagores meant social prestige. In a sense both parties gained. According to family conventions Saratchandra had to be initiated into the Brahmo faith, after which the Maharshi sanctioned a sumptuous dowry.

Within a month of the eldest daughter's marriage, the next daughter Renuka, or Rani, was also married. The groom was a doctor, Satyendranath Bhatta-charyya, L.M.S. Shortly after the marriage he left for the United States to secure a "homeopathic feather on his allopathic cap."

At the time of her marriage Bela was fourteen and Renuka only twelve. In a sense both were early marriages, though in the Tagore family some of the girls were married after graduation. Rabindranath had not sent any of his daughters to school nor did he coach them for any University Examinations. The arguments about the right age of marriage which he had so vehemently set forth in some of his early writings did not apply in the case of the two marriages in his own family. One reason for this might have been the economic dependence on his father. Nor was his wife as spirited as her sisters-in-law. Mrinalini Devi's attitude was the normal motherly attitude, the quicker the girls were married the better.

After her marriage, Bela left for her new home in Muzaffarpur. Rani's husband was abroad. Rabindranath finally left Shelaidah and settled with his family at Bolpur i.e. Santiniketan; at first they put up at the Santiniketan Guest House, as there was no other house to live in. On the eastern side of the ashrama land there was a plot by the roadside. This he purchased and here he built a small thatched house for the family residence. In the Santiniketan buiding only vegetarian food was served; also it had been meant to be a Guest House, one could not stay there permanently.

As we have seen, Tagore had been thinking of starting a boarding school at Santiniketan. Some years earlier his cousin Balendranath had a house built with the idea of opening a Brahmavidyalaya; Rabindranath's boarding school started with that building as a nucleus. That house was part of the (old) Visva Bharti Central Library for many decades. Maharshi Devendranath had already established an ashrama and built a prayer hall at Santiniketan; and made a liberal endowment for their maintenace.

It was the auspicious seventh of Paus, the day of Devendranath's initiation into Brahmo dharma in 1843, that Rabindranath chose for inaugurating his Brahmacharya Yidyalaya, as he called his boarding school.

Brahmabandhab Upadhyaya (or Bhavani Charan Banerjee as he used to be known), that curious amalgam of a Roman Catholic and Vedantist, and an uncompromising nationalist soon joined Tagore's school. It was he who turned or tried to turn Rabindranath's boarding school into a genuine Brahmacharyashram. It is true that in his letters and essays Rabindranath had written at length on the ideals of *gurugriha vasa* (living with the Master as of old), but to be tied to Santiniketan, to run a school and develop an ashrama was, for him, hardly a feasible proposition. He would be a truant even from his own school.

The school started with only five pupils on the rolls. These were all recruited from Brahmabandhab's own school in Calcutta. But Brahmabandhab stayed at Santiniketan only for four months. Politics drew him away. The experience of the last few months had dimmed the poet's dream of an ashrama according to ancient Indian ideals. For instance, at the start he had hoped to run the school without charging any tuition fees from the students. He had hoped that his countrymen, enamoured of his idealism, would contribute liberally for his Brahmacharya-shram; for everywhere people were talking about the glories of ancient India Hinduism. After the summer vacation in June 1902, came a Headmaster, a young graduate, Manoranjan Banerjee, a relation of Brahmabandhab. It was decided to charge fees from the students. It was, of course, easier to turn, outwardly, the young students into little ascetics, wrapped in holy ochre garments. But the teachers were not ascetics; they had families of their own and worldly needs and ambitions. Money was needed at every step. The economic nexus had asserted itself. The poet's dream of an ashrama was almost nipped in the bud. The word 'ashrama', however, continued to be used for years after; now one hears *little* of it. That is another story.

10

The Intrusions of Reality

THE POET HAD hoped to live a quiet family life at Santiniketan. But this was not to be. Soon his wife fell seriously ill and had to be removed to Calcutta. After a protracted illnes she passed away on November 23, 1902. This happened just eleven months after the formal opening of the school. At the time of her death, Mrinalini Devi was hardly thirty and Rabindranath forty-one. The eldest son Rathindranath who was fourteen was preparing for the Entrance examination. Mira, the youngest daughter, was eight. The little boy, Shamindra, was six. Bela and Rani were already married.

In a series of poems *Smaran* (Remembrance) Rabindranath paid tribute to the memory of his wife. Even in some of the pieces of *Utsarga* (Offering) one hears the same sad undertone:

> O thou terrible, silent and bare, I salute thee
> Come thou to my broken abode. . . .

In another poem of the period he writes:

> You have turned me into a wayfarer—
> Oh it is as well, as well,
> I shall walk the solitary way.

For Rabindranath sorrow has been, at all times, a personal affair. He has not been a stranger to suffering, but he has never allowed himself to be shaken or broken-hearted on account of these mishaps. He knew that the world's demands have to be met, and his greatest immediate problem was over his second daughter who had been ailing for some time. At first it seemed to be sore throat, but it turned out to be tuberculosis. He brought her down to Santiniketan and put her up in the new cottage. But Rani showed no signs of improvement. The doctors recommended a change of place, and he took her to Hazaribagh.

In those days (1902-3) to reach Hazaribagh one had to take the 'push-push', a sort of palanquin-cart drawn and pushed by porters from Giridih, the nearest railway station. Rabindranath had been to this part many years before on a pleasure trip with his nephews and niece. But this time, with a sick daughter by his side, the saddened poet was trudging his way to Hazaribagh in search of health and happiness. They stayed there for some months. But Rani's health did not improve. It was decided to take her to Almora.

In spite of the death of his wife and his daughter's illness, he continued to fulfil his commitments for *Bangadarshan* as usual. While at Hazaribagh, he started writing a new work of fiction, *Naukadubi* (The Wreck). A trickle of verses flowed alongside, some of it touched with tears, but few noticed this.

Before leaving for Almora, he had sent his youngest daughter and son, Mira and Shamindra to be looked after by his sister-in-law, Jnandanandini, in Calcutta. Rathindranath was staying in the school boarding house. Bela was with her husband, at Muzaffarpur. Thus the compact family life had broken.

The hardships of carrying a sick daughter from

Giridih to Almora are better imagined than described. The reserved coach was attached to a passenger train at Madhupur; and it took about two days to reach the last railhead. Arriving at the hills of Almora he wrote to his friend, Priyanath Sen "My boat sails through tempests—I have no idea if some day I shall reach port and be at anchor. The children are scattered; the school is at one end and I, with a load of sicknesses, at another. I long to bring together the scattered family and once more wish to live in peace."

Misery and sickness apart, his creative mind was not wholly dampened by family worries. The novels and essays for *Bangadarshan* went on without pause. But the greater part of his time and energy were being spent on the editing of his *Poetical Works.* These had been first published in 1896. But this time, 1903, the plans were a little different : the poems were classified more or less according to theme, to show the growth of the poet's mind. In this task he received much help from Mohitchandra Sen, a young professor of Calcutta. It was under his editorship that the volumes were published by the Mazumdar Library. Rabindranath wrote an introductory poem to each of the parts, these were collected some ten years after in 1914 as *Utsarga,* which he dedicated to C.F. Andrews.

During the Almora days, while collecting the children's poems from his earlier writings for the eighth volume of the series he had felt a certain incompleteness in the series. So he wrote a new lot, of about thirty poems. Thus *Sishu* (The Crescent Moon) was a collection of both old and new poems. On reading these poems Mrs. Sen, wife of Professor Sen sent a query : "All the poems seem to be written on behalf of a boy, why was it that there-were no poems on behalf of a girl ?" Mrs. Sen was-the mother of two young daughters. In reply the poet wrote back : "I had my little boy (Khoka) in mind and the joyous relationship between the boy and his mother are the last pleasant memory of my family life. So, whenever I try to write something, it is these emotions that colour my mind like the clouds after sunset."

Even after three months of stay at Almora, Rani's health showed no signs of improvement and she insisted on being taken back to Calcutta. Perhaps she had felt the coming end. Within a few days of returning to Calcutta, Rani passed away in September, 1903. In the course of a year he had lost his wife and a daughter. He was particularly fond of Rani, though the family considered her a problem child.

The school at Santiniketan had not crossed the second year of its existence and the absence of the chief sometimes led to petty bickerings among the teachers. But the optimist poet wrote : "Every day I am amazed to feel that through all vicissitudes the institution is gaining a newer vitality and a stronger foothold." The faith was led by the presence of a young and sensitive teacher of sterling character, Satischandra Roy who had lately joined the school. All his life Rabindranath has called to mind this young idealist, in whom he saw the image of his ideal or may be it was an idealised version of his imagination. But within a year his faith and the growing life of the institution met with a rude shock in the sudden death in February, 1904, of Satischandra Roy who was hardly twenty-one at that time.

The school re-opened after the Magh festival, but it was temporarily removed to Shelaidah. Professor Mohitchandra Sen now joined as the head of staff. A philosopher and litterateur, he had edited Tagore's *Poetical Works.* Now he felt like giving form to the poet's ideal, a task which soon proved too much for him.

The experiment failed. The philosopher was burdened with undue responsibility and took upon himself impossible tasks. His health deteriorated and in the end he had to go away. Now Bhupend-ranath Sanyal was put in charge. No two men could have been more different, Mohitchandra a Brahmo of the Nababidhan Samaj, well versed in Western philosophy and humanities, and Bhupend-ranath an orthodox Hindu, punctilious about rituals. Naturally, there was a good deal of change in the working of the school under the new set-up.

It is 1904, the time of agitation over the proposed Bengal partition. Long before 1947 Bengal had been partitioned once in 1905. Then it was a province that had been cut into two. At that time the crack had set, though some traces of it were perceptible ever after.

Lord Curzon was the Viceroy (1899-1905); Calcutta was the capital of India as well as of Bengal, and Simla was the summer capital of the Indian Government. It was absolutely essential for the prestige of British imperialism, to curb the new nationalism in Bengal. With that aim in view, the Government had put forward the proposal of having a separate province for the Muslim majority areas in North and East Bengal. Curzon had suggested at Dacca, where he held a Durbar, that the new province would mean more power to the Muslims. He applied the masterstroke of divide and rule, and Bengal was to be partitioned.

There was countrywide protest. But it had not yet taken the form of a boycott. People believed that British policy might be changed by a liberal display of mere verbal, wordy protests, resolutions and lawful demonstrations. What an illusion ! At this time Rabindranath read an address on 'Swadeshi Samaj' (July 22, 1904). Before Tagore no one had analysed the problems of the country so fearlessly and suggested solutions so clearly. Sending petitions to the royal masters, or memorials with assorted signatures, rhetorical display on public platforms and abusing the British in the newspapers —these were the usual methods of expressing our disapproval. Rabindranath pointed out the real remedy, and he asked people to turn once more to the villages. The country folk living in villages must be saved, and a new mass consciousness aroused. How this was to be done, he discussed in detail. The song "Let us go back and hearken to the call of the earth" was written twenty years after. But it is the same voice.

The redoubtable professional politicians laughed away these suggestions as a poet's ideas. They said that to work on the lines of Rabibabu would be the end of politics. Half a century later we see that what the poet had said about village reconstruction and rural uplift is the mainstay of our national planning. Along with the scheme of partition the government launched a scheme, under the pretext of spread of literacy among the masses, for breaking up the provincial speech. To all this Tagore gave a ringing rejoinder. But since the partition was scotched, the scheme of introducing dialects was also dropped.

In spite of the later colourful presentation of the poet as a staunch internationalist there is no denying that at this period of his life he did add fuel to the fire of nationalist upsurge with his exciting poems and songs. The Maharashtrians had made of Shivaji the national hero. The wave of the Shivaji cult touched the shores of Bengal, and Rabindranath responded with a glowing tribute to Shivaji in August, 1904. From that day, the vogue of hero worship in Bengal has never ceased.

The time for the partition drew near. In spite of all protests the British administration was adamant while the Bengalis declared that until partition was rescinded they would boycott British goods. In a song Rabindranath wrote "I shall not buy a noose, thinking it to be an ornament." The people boycotted British-manufactured cloth; but the poet was unable to accept this purely negative approach to the problem. Negation and agitation were not enough. Within a few days of the announcement about the boycott he read an article *Abastha O Byabastha* (The Situation and the Remedy) in the Town Hall of Calcutta, "The nation's working potential has to be focused in a special committee of action. A Hindu and a Mussalman shall be the chiefs of this committee. We shall be entirely obedient to them, pay our taxes to them, shall obey them, do their orders, accept their ruling in all matters, honouring them we shall honour the country." He further added;

"The administration of the villages we shall have to take into our own hands. We shall protect the peasantry, educate their children, improve agriculture and save both landlords and peasants from suicidal litigation. Let not the idea of seeking help from an alien administration cross even our imagination. It is not enough to confine boycott to a refusal to buy foreign cloth, salt or luxury goods; we have to non-cooperate with its administration and establish self or home-rule in the remote rural areas, the nation's heart." A parallel government, in fact.

To the boycott enthusiasts he said that he had no faith in tempering our demands or lowering our standards for the sake of some temporary advantage; it was quite easy to be excited, but such a facile reaction was not the safest or the best. Because the English were not going to accede to our request, we shall not go to them, there was no logic in that argument.

Though, intellectually, he was criticising the state of the country, on the emotional side, as we have seen, he was nourishing the movement with his stirring national songs. On the eve of the partition he wrote quite a few songs in the typically *baul* style and these caught on marvellously. The partition became a *fait accompli* on October 16, 1905. The poet's answer was his famous song :

Let the earth and the water, the air and the fruits of my
country be sweet, my God.
Let the homes and marts, the forests and fields of my
country be full, my God.
Let the promises, and hopes, the deeds and words of my
country be true, my God.

Let the lives and hearts of the sons and daughters of my
country be one, my God.*

He also suggested that there should be no cooking on that day, and all men should have a dip in the holy Ganga and tie bands *(rakhi)* on the forearm as a symbol of friendship. Rabindranath himself took part in the processions that went round the city, and tied these *rakhi* bands on all alike, irrespective of status, caste or religion.

Within a week of the partition the Chief Secretary to the Bengal Government sent a circular to the Heads of educational institutions warning the students against taking part in the political movement. Two days after the publication of the circular on October 22, 1905, the leaders in a meeting decided that the only remedy lay in opening National Universities and making our education independent of foreign control and interference. In his school he tried to lay the foundation of the *swaraj* (self-rule); visits to the surrounding villages were encouraged; everyone's mind was turned to the one idea of rural service; a Poor Fund was opened and an evening school in the village started. In school administration, collective responsibility of the teachers took the place of rule by a Headmaster; the students had their own autonomy and they looked after their own affairs, including discipline. Teachers and students joined hands in building up one composite unit, the school or the ashrama. Now, in the school and the community, 'a

* Another of his songs, *Sonar Bangla* has become the national song of Bangladesh.

poem without words', came to occupy an important place in the mind of the poet.

The diehards of the Government were not worried over the educational experiment of the nationalists; what they were determined to check was the boycott movement because that directly hit the Manchester millowners and British shippers. Severe measures were adopted to curb it. Indian leaders were either clapped into prison or placed under orders of detention; a punitive police force was. stationed in towns and villages, and no effort, legal or otherwise, was spared to put an end to the boycott of British goods. The heads of educational institutions were reminded that they should be more vigilant and see that no student joined politics or anti-British demonstrations. The Government's wrath was specially directed against the Hindus of East Bengal. Thanks to the Government officers and their henchmen these efforts met with a fair measure of success. The maul vis, the conscience-keepers of the Muslim community, declared that it was a sin to join the independence movement of the Hindus. It must not, however, be forgotten that there were, at all times, a few Mussalmans who belonged to the Indian National Congress. But they were looked down upon as stooges and renegades by the faithful.

It was during this nationwide agitation that the Prince of Wales (afterwards George V, grandfather of Queen Elizabeth II) visited Bengal in December 1905. The red carpet was duly spread and he was taken through the scheduled routes; he attended sumptuous parties, visited places of interest and could hardly have known or felt what the people of the province were clamouring for and why.

Yet all was not well in the State of Bengal and the Prince must have guessed it, as his letters home make clear.

Rabindranath's days were passed alternately in Shelaidah and Bolpur, also sometimes in Calcutta where he had to go in response to calls of duty or to keep engagements. The poems of *Kheya* (Crossing) belong to this period. The book was dedicated to his scientist friend, Jagadishchandra Basu.

In the meantime he had taken a decision to send his eldest son, Rathindranath and his friend, Srish's son, Santosh to the United States for training in agriculture and animal husbandry. They had already by 1904 passed their Entrance examinations. Instead of sending them to the Calcutta colleges, he had arranged for their private coaching at Santiniketan. He wanted them to be well grounded in the Indian lore before going abroad. Satish Roy, Mohit Sen, Bhupen Sanyal, Vidhusekhar Shastri and others, a formidable band of teachers, was commissioned to take classes for the two young scholars who remembered the rigorous schooling long after. In those days Indian prodigies and prodigals went, rather were sent to England; the brilliant ones competed for the heaven-born Civil Service, others joined the Bar. Boys from middle class homes with slender means were sent to Japan, to learn such utilitarian trades of the manufacture of biscuits, soap and shoe polish. Rabindranath was sending these two boys to America to learn new techniques in agriculture. India's basic problem is and has always been food, sufficient and nutritious food. Later, according to his wishes, his youngest son-in-law also joined them there.

After seeing off Rathindranath and Santoshchandra

at the Calcutta port, the poet went to Barisal, in East Bengal, where the Provincial Conference of the Congress was holding its sessions in April, 1906. Barisal was also the venue for the first Bengali Literary Conference, with Rabindranath as the President-elect.

Barisal now forms part of Bangladesh. But half a century ago it used to be the storm centre of the boycott agitation. Thanks to the inspired leadership of Aswinikumar Dutta, Liverpool salt had disappeared from the local market and the sale of imported textile had become a thing of the past. Dutta was the convener of the political conference.

The idea of a literary conference had been first mooted by Rabindranath in his essay *Abastha O Byabastha.* That was perhaps why he had been elected the First President. But as we shall see the conference did not meet. The over-zealous representative of His Majesty's Government, the District Magistrate, saw to it. The repressive measures and the hooliganism of British police did the rest. The 'mild' lathi charge by the police drew blood in April 1906, on the Bengali New Year Day, a bad beginning. Thirteen years after, on that fateful day history was to repeat itself at Jallianwala Bagh where hundreds of unarmed and innocent men lost their lives due to indiscriminate firing. From Barisal the leaders returned to Calcutta. The poet went back to Bolpur.

From the beginning of the Swadeshi movement, there had been a difference of opinion among the leaders, as to the method of political work to be adopted. This gradually developed into bickerings. This Tagore had never liked. He had hoped for a few quiet days at Santiniketan. That was hot to be; and he had to come down to Calcutta to read his paper on *Deshnayak* (The National Leader). To quarrel, he said, only reveals the excitement of weak minds, it is a form of self-indulgence. He said frankly that in our national struggle against the British, one-man rule in the party was essential, and he appealed to the people to elect Surendranath Bannerji, the 'uncrowned king of Bengal' as the supreme leader.

A few days later, in a meeting of the Dawn Society, speaking on the Swadeshi Movement, Rabindranath observed : "One cannot hope for much result in this state of wild excitement. I too have not escaped its infection." It is clear from this statement that he was slowly outgrowing the movement and its mood. In another public meeting wefiud him saying : "It is now time for us to build smaller organisation." To this end he proposed Village Societies. "These shall be our first training ground in self-administration." He worked out a detailed programme and gave it a trial in his own estate. It was not, as may be imagined, much of a success. The nation or the people were not ready, nor perhaps was the poet an ideal revolutionary.

Within a year of the partition, the National Council of Education got busy on August 15, 1906. There were unending arguments over the aims of education, syllabuses and methods of instruction. As we have already said, Rabindranath took a leading part in all this, and his articles, *Siksha Samasya* (Problems of Education), *Siksha Samskar* (Educational Reform), *Jatiya Vidyalaya* (National School), *Tatah Kim* (What Then ?), were read before large, appreciative audiences. When regular sessions started he delivered a series of lectures on Comparative Literature which were later collected in *Sahitya.* He was connected with the National College of Education in other ways too. For two years, 1906-7, he was its Convener and Examiner in Bengali language and literature. In spite of his intimate relation with the Council he did not however permit his own institution to be involved in the experiment. The Ashrama was an institution outside the sphere*of politics, above the battle and open to all. But at times, in spite of him, the dust of politics darkened the serene atmosphere of Santiniketan.

The poet was now a permanent resident of Santiniketan, and busy editing and publishing his *Prose Works.* The *Poetical Works* had been published three years before in 1903-4, under the editorship of Mohitchandra Sen. Now the first volume of prose works, *Vichitra Prabandha* (Miscellaneous Essays), came out in 1907. They bore the significant inscription : "The copyright of these works rests with the Bolpur Brahmacharyashram."

Devendranath Tagore passed away in January 1905. This altered the family situation considerably. Dwijendranath shifted to Santiniketan. His son, Dwipendranath, one of the trustees of Santiniketan also moved in and stayed in the Guest House, the 'Santiniketan' building. Rabindranath had built for his own use a small two-storeyed house on the eastern side, later called 'Dehali', where he lived for many years. Among his children, Mira and Shamindra were with him, living in thatched cottages under the care of a distant female relation.

Mira, fourteen, was married in 1907 to Nagendranath Ganguly, a handsome, brilliant young person and a member of the progressive Brahmo Samaj i.e. the Sadharan

Brahmo Samaj. The poet was attracted by this energetic intellectual. The marriage took place according to the rites of the Adi Brahmo Samaj and was held in the prayer hall at Santiniketan. But in many matters Nagendranath maintained his individuality. He threw away the holy thread which the family priest wanted to pass over his head. After the marriage, Nagendra was sent to Illinois University to study agriculture. The poet had to bear the expenses of a son and a son-in-law abroad. He had a hard time of it. His wife's ornaments had been sold to meet the expenses of his school. Now his Puri house was disposed of to liquidate the debts and meet the new items of expenditure. His own life at the time was bare and simple—a 'combined hand' was cook and odd-job man. His eating habits were plain and did not differ from those of an average Bengali house holder. For his bed he had a simple cot, a simple desk and some writing material nearby. It is necessary to speak of these facts, to cure the public mind of the cherished image that Rabindranath was a sybarite. He doubtless loved beauty, but was never afraid of austerity.

11

Politics and the Literary Conference

THE POLITICAL SITUATION in the country was changing fast; the difference between the dissentient groups known as 'moderates' and the 'extremists' had become almost unbridgeable. A clash seemed inevitable. The daily English paper, the *Bengali* (editor : Surendranath Bannerji) and the Bengali weekly *Hitavadi* (editor : Kaliprasanna Kavyavisharad) spoke for the moderates; while Sisir Kumar Ghose's English daily, *Amrita Bazar Patrika* and Krishnakumar Mitra's Bengali weekly *Sanjibani* put forward the extremist point of view. Even more strident was the newly started weekly *Nabashakti* (New Power) edited by a Barisal man, now residing at Giridih as a mica-mine owner. Another more violent weekly paper was *Jugantar* which favoured armed insurrection. Brahmabandhab Upadyaya had come out with a new daily, *Sandhya. Jugantar's* language was virile and addressed to the intelligentsia, *Sandhya,* more racy and full of colloqualisms also advocated revolution but not of the *Jugantar* brand. A new English paper appearing on this confused scene was *Bande Mataram.* It had, as its chief editor, Bipinchandra Pal, one of the leaders of the extremist group. The paper's motto was : 'Autonomy absolutely free from British control'.

Bipinchandra was one of the first to put forward the idea of complete sovereignty of the people. Among its contributors was Aurobindo Ghose who had given up a lucrative position at Baroda to take up, at an exiguous salary, the post of the Principal of the National Council of Education, which was then located in a rented house on the Bowbazar Street. Aurobindo's one and only aim was to spread the revolutionary doctrine among the Bengali youth. One of his unsigned articles in *Bande Mataram* was accused of being seditious. Bipinchandra who was on the editorial board of the paper, was summoned to the court as a witness; but he refused to answer the questions put to him and thus became one of the first non-violent non-cooperators. In the eyes of the law this amounted to contempt of court. He was sentenced to imprisonment for six months. Aurobindo was acquitted for the time being.

On coming to know that Aurobindo had been accused of sedition, Rabindranath wrote a long poem and himself took it to Aurobindo at his residence. Is was published in the *Bangadarshan,* when the case was *sub judice,* a bold thing to do. The poem was prophetic in its recognition of Aurobindo's greatness, his idealism and sacrifice.

But there were other activities too. The most important was the Literary Conference at Berham-pore, of which he was the President. The convener and the host was Maharaja Manindrachandra Nandy, a patron of learning known for his charities.

Back in Calcutta from Berhampore he received a telegram from Monghyr that his youngest son Shamindra had an attack of cholera and that his condition was causing anxiety. The boy had gone with a friend to spend the autumn holidays there. The poet left for Monghyr at once. Shamindra breathed his last on the lap of his father.

Rabindranath was particularly fond of the boy and he must have felt the loss keenly, but outsiders saw little of it. He came back to Santiniketan, left detailed instructions about the school, and took away the daughters, Bela and Mira, to Shelaidah. Rathindra-nath was still in the United States. The poet stayed there for five months and for the first time did not attend the Paus celebrations. He came to Calcutta for a couple of days in connection with the Magh festival, where he conducted the service. The theme of his address was 'Sorrow'.

During his stay at Shelaidah his mind turned once again to the idea of rural uplift. In a letter he writes : "At the moment I am taken up with our village commune. I have thought of setting an example of village uplift in our *zamindari.* A few East Bengal lads have joined me in this." These were mostly young revolutionaries affiliated to the Anushilan Samiti of Dacca, a terrorist organisation. One of these was Kalimohan Ghose. Young Kalimohan had given up his college studies when, his head full of revolutionary ideas, he met the poet. The poet saw his mettle and broke him into the ways of more constructive work. He remained till his death one of Tagore's lieutenants in the rural reconstruction work at Sriniketan.

At Shelaidah he read in the papers that owing to violent partnership the Surat Congress (December 1907) had ended in a fiasco. The difference between the Moderates and the Extremists did not remain confined to a frank exchange of views and wordy battles, but a liberal showering of chapp als (sandals) had brought the Congress to an ignominious end. The Barisal Provincial Congress could not be held because of the governmental repression. In Surat no third party was needed. Internal division was enough to achieve the end.

To his friend Jagadishchandra, then in England, Rabindranath wrote: "You must have heard of the Congress going to pieces—the parties have little else to do than to pick holes in each other's armoury. The Government is breathing a sigh of relief—now is no time for sedition—the heat that we had generated is being used solely in setting fire to our own house. We shall not need any outside agency to beat and destroy—neither Morley nor Kitchner (Commander-in-Chief of the British Army)—as we ourselves will be able to do that."

About two months after the Surat Congress the Bengal Provincial Conference held its session at Pabnain February 1908. Rabindranath was elected President. Anonymous letters started pouring in. He was warned that if he agreed to preside over the Conference, Pabna would see Surat repeated. The extremists took him to be a moderate; they wanted someone as president of the Conference who could attack the British violently, and indecorously. The police thought otherwise; to them Rabindranath was no less suspect and unpredictable. They kept strict watch over him, censored his letters and made him feel uncomfortable. In fact, however, Rabindranath did not belong to any group or faction. He took a detached and rather idealised view of things, but he never favoured political chicanery or weak compromise. Behind all that he wrote or said was implied philosophy of Man, of human ideals and possibilites. It was a politics of a poet and a seer.

The Pabna Conference went off without disturbance. He reiterated, with even greater emphasis, what he had already suggested in *Swadeshi Samaj,* the introduction of village co-operatives, small-scale industries, labour-saving appliances, extension of communal development schemes, etc. He held that all these would add up to our national unity and strength and without these we could not hope to succeed in politics or anything else. Let us hear the poet speak : "We shall be swept away into oblivion if we cannot achieve harmony between our sociol conditions and the demands of the modern age. The watchword of the day is unification, consolidation, organisation. An aggregate of individual as may have many fine qualities but it can never stand up to a people that is organised. We must therefore organise our villages for survival.

"Our national consciousness is not spread uniformly throughout the community .... National unity is not becoming real because of the separation between the educated classes and the masses. The unity of national consciousness that we need cannot be brought about by argument or advice alone. A sense of kinship will pervade that entire community only when the educated classes are united with the masses in a common programme of work."

As expected, the presidential address was delivered in Bengali. This was the fulfilment of an old dream of the poet. From 1895-1907 all the Presidential addresses had been given in English. Rabindranath was the first to break this unhealthy convention. It may be mentioned in passing that thirty years after he gave the Calcutta University Con-vocation address in

Bengali. This was an innovation and still remains so. But his own University has—so far—failed to honour the lead.

Barely two months had passed, when the sensational news was flashed in all the papers that in Muzaffarpur, a small town in north Bihar, one Mrs. Kennedy and her daughter had been killed by a bomb explosion. Two young boys, Kshudiram and Prafulla Chaki had been involved. Kshudiram was arrested but Chaki committed suicide to avoid arrest. On inquiry it was found that the bombs were really meant for Calcutta's Presidency Magistrate, Mr. Kingsford; but unfortunately two innocent English ladies had been killed by mistake. The boys, it was discovered, were members of the Bengal Revolutionary Party. Most of the members were arrested soon after, in a dilapidated garden-house at Manicktollah, Calcutta, where evidence of conspiracy was unearthed.

The country was shocked and left wondering. It was obvious that politics in Bengal was moving down a dangerous incline, very different from earlier gentlemanly appeals for gradual constitutional reform. While the sedate party leaders were busy in mutual fault-finding, while Rabindranath was wrapt in his dream of rural India, the firebrand young had been playing for high stakes. They knew that essays and addresses would avail nothing and had taken to violent means. And— strange compliment—Rabindranath's verse was on their lips. They recited :

> Life and death we hold as slaves,
> Fearless is our heart.
> Time has come
> To cut the old mooring.

The revolutionaries—Aurobindo, Barin, Hem Kanungo, Upendranath Bannerji, Ullaskar and others, thirty-eight in all—were under-trial prisoners at the Presidency Jail.

On hearing, in the court room, the death sentence, young Ullaskar burst out :

"Blessed am I to have been born in this land, and that I had the luck to love her. . . ." One of Tagore's most beautiful songs, which gained rather than lost by this change of context.

For writing an article on the bomb outrage, Lokmanya Tilak, against whom the administration had an ancient grudge, was sentenced to six years' imprisonment. The people were taken aback. Rabindranath left Santiniketan and came down to Calcutta, where he addressed a public meeting. He never supported the cult of the bomb, but neither could he lecture the young revolutionaries. Their patriotism he openly admired. As a people the Bengalis, he said, had carried long enough the stigma of being cowards. The present incident, whatever it merits, could not but wipe away that age-old ignominy. The mood was easy to understand. And yet, personally, he was profoundly opposed to murder, secret societies, and killing.

There was in fact a hint in his address of the message on non-violence, which Mahatma Gandhi was to put before the nation a few years later in more unequivocal terms. Rabindranath said openly —and then it needed some courage to say this— that no great aim in life could be achieved by hatred and violence. Truth is born of austerity and self-control. In fits of passion, men are apt to forget that excitement is not strength.

On the other hand, he had been all the time insisting

that national service meant upliftment of the rural people and the villages. As we have seen in his own way he had tried some kind of an experiment in his own estate. But, thanks largely to the over-zealous Indian police, the work could make little headway. The young men whom he had collected, were thwarted by prying policemen. The villagers thought discretion the better part of valour. In their daily round the police would often inquire if any young men had come to the village and what was it that they had said. The poor rustics were naturally cowed down by these inquiries and the poet's ideal of rural service remained a disembodied ideal till, some years later, he turned to Sriniketan and had apparently, less interference to put up with.

The face of Bengal was fast changing. By the end of 1906 the Muslim League had been formed in Dacca, and the Muslims were more and more moving away from the national movement. In the beginning they had been lukewarm, now they were frankly inimical to the Congress workers. This and similar incidents led the poet to heart-searching.

In one of his addresses before the Sadharan Brahmo Samaj in Calcutta the poet raised a pertinent question : "To whom did the history of India belong ?" In the early days of *Bangadarshan* he too had talked of the Hindu-nation theory. But the bitter and complex experience of the few previous years had revealed to him its inadequacy. The fullness of the Indian theme could not be found in this simple formula. The history of India, he said, was not the separate history of a sect, caste, race or religion, and the Aryans who had conquered the land from the non-Aryans were not its only makers. The country's culture was born of their combined efforts. The Turks and Moguls, who entered India, as conquerors, lived and died on Indian soil and merged into the Indian body, they too had a place of their own in the history of India. The coming of the British too was in the inevitable chain of sequence and perhaps not exactly an accident. Today the East and the West have come closer together and they must evolve some kind of unity and harmony. This will be a test of India's power of absorption or cultural synthesis, a word and an attitude not much known in those days. The speech must have appeared odd to his audience which shared neither his faith nor his vision.

The play, *Prayaschitta* (Expiation), was written partly from this holistic point of view. This comes out in his portrayal of Dhananjoy Vairagi, the apostle of non-voilent non-cooperation. Dhananjoy said (what must have been the poet's own thought) that the State does not belong to the king alone, it belongs to the people as well. The followers of the arch-rebel Dhananjoy sing, "Oh, in this land of ours, we are all kings." This was the poet's version of the democratic creed, the soverign right of the people. On its inner side the play was the vehicle of a far-reaching social revolution. It, however, failed to be popular; and no wonder, for he had presented Pratapaditya, a newly discovered and idealised hero, as a tyrant. For some years the Bengalis had been digging up national heroes, Maharashtra could boast of a Shivaji. What had Bengal to show ? Pratapaditya, Udayaditya, Sitaram, Kedar Roy, Sirajuddaulah, Mir Kasim were all dressed up for the role. But Rabindranath did not feel it in his bones to glorify Pratap and deck him with a set of fancied virtues. The play was never put on the professional stage. The public preferred Kshirodprasad's unreal Pratap.

In some of the songs of *Prayaschitta* one can feel the first hints of the *Gitanjali* period. The poet was soon to enter a realm of deeper, subtler experiences. These songs were the first faint cry of the rapture yet to be. Dhananjoy Vairagi is a strange, almost mythic creation. Some have seen in him an image of Gandhi, then leading satyagraha in far away South Africa. Is this another proof that art imitates life ? Or was there reflection of Tilak, who was leading a movement which he termed 'passive resistance'?

The school at Santiniketan had now well over a hundred students on its roils. Thanks to Professor Vidhushekhar Shastri and the newly arrived Sanskritist Kshitimohan Sen, *Varshamangal* (the Festival of Rains), was held in the school premises for the first time in 1908. This time Rabindranath wrote a delicate play for children, *Saradotsava* (Festival of Autumn). He had already composed some autumn songs, which easily went into the play. Afterwards he was to write songs and plays round nearly all the seasons. As may be expected, there was a unity of theme behind all these plays. As he put it, "from *Saradotsava* to *Phalguni,* I can see that the refrain is the same". In autumn the King stirs out in search of adventure. In spring also he does the same. In *Phalguni* (Cycle of Spring), the youths are wanderers for ever. In search of what ? In the rains Panchak yearns to stir out of the rigid walls of the *Achalayatan* (Immobile Citadel). Even in *Dakghar* (Post Office), not a seasonal play, Amal longs to go out into the wide world without, that beckons him. In all these can be heard the ageless cry, *Charaiveti* (fare forward), breaks through the crust, the crust of habit and convention, and comes out into the open where freedom spreads her joyous wings. But this was not, as some imagine, an invitation to nowhere, an aimless cruising in the void. It was really a romantic search after a balance between the rival claims of the past and the present, a creative unity between the individual and the universe, a deep and serene poise.

It is necessary to add that the plays had been written with the school children in view. Hence they have no women characters. Later, when coeducation came into force the change was reflected in the cast of his plays as well.

The poet was spending the autumn holidays at Shelaidah in 1908, when news reached him of the death of some dear relations and friends—his youngest son had died just a year before. He himself was far from well. All the while a great inner change was taking place within him. Along with a desire to serve the people, whom he loved, a yearning for the Absolute, the beloved was in his inmost heart. The mood had grown after the death of his youngest son. The eternal quest had returned. When he returned to the ashrama his mind was full of musings and a longing for the spiritual life. He put up at the Santiniketan building, his own abode Dehali was being used as a girls' dormitory. Every day in the morning, while it was still dark, he would go to the prayer hall, where a few teachers and students joined him in silent meditation. At their request he would sometimes say a few words. These he would later write down on returning home. These were 'the Santiniketan sermons'. As a fresh commentary on India's ageless wisdom and a help towards understanding the poet's inner life these remain indispensable. A few of these meditations found their way into *Thought Relics.*

This was also the period of *Gitanjali.* The songs came in a thin trickle. But what precious drops ! The tunes would hum in his mind; music, mood and meditation wafted the poet to a world of the ineffable. He was like one possessed. But it was hardly possible to live, uninterrupted, in a world of pure inner intensities. Songs and meditation apart, regular instalments of a new novel, *Gora,* had to be sent in time to *Pravasi,* where it was serialised. Besides, the estate needed looking after.

He stayed at Santiniketan for full five months- without a break. Nearly every day at the early hours he spoke in the chapel. But, as always, ***to*** be tied to one idea or place for long was irksome to the poet. He feared that sermonising might easily turn into a habit and defeat its very purpose. After a time he wished to escape from his tasks and his environment, and eagerly grasped at an invitation to visit Kalka in the Simla Hills. The occasion was to escort his daughter, Mira, to Kalka where the elder brother of his son-in-law, then in America, was an officer in the Kellner Company. But the poet did not stay there long. Kalka was hardly the right place for a poet musing on the Infinite,

When the rains came, he hurried back to the bank of the Padma, his old love. But again he had soon to come away. After three years in the States, his son,

Rathindranath, was coming back in 1909 September after completing a course in Agriculture at Illinois University. Let Rathindra speak for himself : "Towards the end of 1909 I returned home. The house at Shelaidah was being got ready for me, I was to look after the estates. I could at the same time have a farm of my own and carry agricultural experiments as I pleased.

"Hardly had I got home when Father took me out on a tour round the estates. It was novel experience for me to travel with father—just two of us in a houseboat. Successive bereavements and particularly the loss of Shamindranath Tagore had left him very lonely and he naturally tried to pour all his affection on me as soon as I returned , home."

As the boat meandered through rivers and canals there was deep content in the poet's soul. Everything was bathed in a mellow vision. On the anniversary of the partition of Bengal he had written in a letter that the time had come when its significance could be no longer confined to Bengal alone. "We must cross this narrow boundary and turn it into a good morrow for the whole of India. Only then will it have earned its rights to be counted among our 'holy' days—the day on which Buddha, Christ and Muhammed will become one." The problem was not of Bengal alone, nor of Hindustan alone. His mind was now taken up with the idea of unity of all religions and nations.

From his river trip he came to Calcutta to read a paper on *Tapovan* on December 2, 1909. A few days later in his address on Paus festival and on the Magh festival he spoke on *Visvabodh* (Realisation of the Infinite). All this pointed to a growing awareness. Mere intellectual discipline and thetraining of the senses were not enough to rouse our manhood. The soul's union with the universe, a Yoga or 'yoking together', was the essence of true education. The passions, lacking self-control, are time-honoured enemies of this higher consciousness. India has always urged men to give up all hatred. Rabindranath emphasised the main tenets of the Indian ideal of education with clarity, conviction and feeling.

At the time he was a strict vegetarian; even during illness it was not easy to persuade him to a non-vegetarian diet. Once his youngest daughter, Mira, had brought a little soup for him. This he had quietly turned away, out of respect for the terms of the Santiniketan deed, which forbade non-vegetarian food in the ashrama precincts.

12

Santiniketan and Brahmo Samaj

THREE DAYS AFTER the Brahmo festival in Calcutta, Rathindranath was married with pomp and splendour. The bride, Pratima, was a young widow, the daughter of Binayini Devi, Gaganendranath's sister. In the context of the Tagore family, and the Adi Brahmo Samaj, this was indeed a daring act. On the occasion of his son's marriage Rabindranath dedicated the novel, *Gora,* to him. It had been commissioned, three years earlier, by his friend Ramananda Chatterjee, the editor of *Prabasi,* in which journal it had been serialised from August 1907 to March 1910. But we learn from the editor that never, not even once, was there the slightest delay in the receipt of a manuscript.

These were years of much unhappiness and many bereavements. It is hardly possible for the Bengali reader today, who has supped full of 'progressive' writing, to realise the controversy touched off by *Gora.* Many of its problems have today only historical significance. But apart from the problems of a period, *Gora* raised some perennial problems too on which the last word is yet to be said.

Since 1908 Rabindranath came in close contact with Ramananda Chatterjee, editor of *Prabasi* and *Modern Review.* They soon became close friends and were of great help to each other. At this time *Prabasi* started a section called 'Sankalan' (Collectanea) and Rabindranath put some of the teachers at Santiniketan to select suitable passages from different journals and translate them into Bengali. Tagore himself was a close reader of foreign magazines, the back issues of *Bharati, Sadhana* and *Bangadarshan* are full of his clippings. But before the script was sent to *Prabasi* the poet would carefully go through the writings; sometimes he would re-write, partially or *in toto.* The troubles taken by him in licking an author into shape, in encouraging others to authorship, were truly amazing. One example will suffice. At the time of joining Santiniketan, Vidhu-sekhar was but a traditional Sanskrit pundit. It was the poet who persuaded him to study Buddhism and Pali. Under his fostering care many of the teachers became reputed scholars. The poet had a high regard for research and never accepted the idea of a teacher who just went through a set of prepared lessons. Only the lamp that burns can spread the light, such was his view, a view every educationist shares.

A little before the summer break-up, Rabindranath's 50th birthday was observed in the school. It was a homely affair though in later years this became something of a national festival. The school closed for summer vacation; and the poet moved to Tindharia, a small township in the Himalayas. This was the period of the *Gitanjali* songs, songs that were destined to change the tenor of his own life and the lives of many others as well. Sometime before he had been induced by friends and admirers to write his autobiography. By constant changes and chiselling it finally became *Reminiscences,* but he never brought it up to date.

When the school closed for the autumn holidays he went away to Shelaidah. This time he did not put up in the houseboat, his old favourite, but in the manor house. He had with him his son and daughter-in-law, also his daughter and son-in-law, Nagendranath, who had come back from America. After long years the lonely poet breathed the atmosphere of family life. He almost seemed to have started the life of a housholder over again. He was hoping that his U.S. trained son and son-in-law would join hands in trying to solve the problems of the peasantry. For their use a laboratory for agricultural research was being put up; the house itself was undergoing a face-lift. Santosh, who had also come back was put in charge of a dairy at Santiniketan.

During his stay at Shelaidah he wrote the symbolic drama *Raja* (The King of the Dark Chamber), the first of its kind in Bengali.

Back in Santiniketan, he looked into the details of school administration. One fact is worth mentioning : his address on Christ on Christmas, 1910 during the Paus celebrations. Such a thing had never happened before. In fact at one time the Maharshi had been rather put out by Keshabchandra Sen's 'Christomania' and quasi-Christian rituals, and expressed his fears openly. His son now accepted Christ as a symbol of Divine love. Since then Santiniketan's prayer hall has had a special Christmas service every year.

The same year, on the occasion of the birth of Mahaprabhu Sri Chaitanya, he gave an address in the Mandir in March, 1911. It was understood, if not decided, that Santiniketan should observe all-Saints' days without any dogmatism, religious or nationalistic.

These few facts help us to understand to some extent, how the poet's religious attitude was changing. The 'Hindu Only' attitude, which he had championed earlier, was now moving out. There was now a greater eagerness to know more about other faiths and the lives of saints. Even in Indian culture there were other, heterodox, non-Brahmin tendencies; for instance, the mediaeval saints. Kshitimohan Sen, an expert in the mediaeval religious lore helped him in the new orientation. This was in keeping with his own deeper tendencies and those of the age.

From now on his religious thoughts and experience looked forward. Hoping to interest a wider public, he gave an address on 'The Fulfilment of the Brahmo Samaj' in which he pleaded eloquently for the spiritual ideals of the Brahmo Samaj and Rammohun Roy. For a while he even interested himself in the reform of the Adi Brahmo Samaj, and took charge of the *Tattvabodhini Patrika,* turning it into a sort of mouthpiece of the Brahmacharya Ashram at Santiniketan.

Several religio-philosophical essays were written and some read out in public meetings. He argued that the distinct character of a religion need not work against its universality. There could be no real difference between the highest ideals of Hinduism and other religions. Every religion is the product of a land and its people, a country and a culture, and expresses itself through a particular idiom and language; yet it may indeed be universal as well. The seeds of this universality, he held, were to be found in the Brahmo faith.

The co-operation of some Brahmo youths had led him to believe that it might be still possible to salvage the Adi Brahmo Samaj. But it did not take him long to realise that to infuse new life into that moribund society would be no easy task. It may be pointed out that the Maharshi had kept the management of the Adi Brahmo Samaj strictly restricted to friends and relatives. It was a public trust, but in a sense he never really trusted the public. For all its universality the Adi Samaj continued to be centred largely in a single family and in course of time it ceased to exist.

The poet was fifty-one on May 8, 1911. This time the birthday celebrations at Santiniketan were on a bigger scale. In fact, it was almost like a festival.

Soon after, he left for Shelaidah, where he wrote a new kind of play, *Achalayatan,* a satire on irrational habits and customs, the blind superstition of a decadent and tyrannical culture. It was widely misunderstood, especially by the conservative Hindu; but at no time did he criticise the ideals of the Hindu religion. What he had never been able to accept or condone was the loathsome burden of popular rituals which, in the guise of religion, weighed on a dehumanised convention-ridden society. A little earlier in his essay on *Tapovana* he had written : "The more impure we have become due to our lack of true spiritual culture, the more has this meaningless externalism battened upon us. I can never accept the inertia of this literalism of a decadent period as the external message of India.".

No wonder a section of the public, suffering from 'the inertia of literalism', felt deeply hurt. They thought that the author was making fun of their faith, at least trying to strike a superior pose. In a letter to a well-known critic, the poet wrote : "If my play fails to stir the waters of somnolence I shall consider it a failure. When we strike at this massed immobility and it is neither hurt nor stirred, such an attack I would call useless. The more a man loves the ideals of his country, the more hurt he feels at their degradation. To swaddle oneself, indiscriminately, with the good and evil in one's land, I cannot call that love of one's country." ''Everything is true', such an argument is a sign of mental sloth, since if that is so, truth has no meaning.

"I am athirst for the Beyond." For Rabindranath, a

born wanderer, this is indeed something more than a poetic fancy. "I have come to the conclusion", he said even two decades after, on his seventieth birthday "that I was meant to be a companion of the Ever-Changing." How true ! Ever curious to visit a new country and meet new folk, till the end, his travels took him to every part of the world. The Song of the Open Road appealed to him. And so when he heard that Rathindranath was planning to go to Singapore in the Far East by ship with his wife he at once threw himself into the scheme. That plan, however, fizzled out and they drew up a more ambitious itinerary; they decided to go to Europe.

But for reasons of its own that trip too did not materialise. The disappointed poet went away to Shelaidah and wanted to be left alone. The letters he wrote at that time reveal a strange despondency and restlessness. Later he returned to Santiniketan before the autursn holidays. But the nostalgia persisted, thoughts of death haunted him. The mood spread its shadows over the beautiful symbolical play, *Post Office,* which he wrote at this time. Writing it must have brought some relief.

Two of his plays which found a place in world literature are *King of the Dark Chamber* and *Post Office.* Their cast is castless, and they belong to all times. Hence perhaps the perplexity among literary pundits whose preconceived notions they set at naught.

By the end of 1911, Tagore was in Calcutta. He was to read a paper at the ensuing Theistic Conference. While in Calcutta he was approached by a very important person of the Bar with a request for composing a hallelujah for the

King-Emperor, George V, who was coming to the city in the Christmas week, more or less when the Indian National Congress would be in session. On 12 December, 1911, at the Delhi Durbar, the King-Emperor had annulled the partition of Bengal, and as a show of gratitude the elite of Calcutta wanted to felicitate him; and the poet had been asked to compose a suitable song for the occasion. He was amazed at the effrontary. Provoked, he wrote out a hallelujah not for the King-Emperor, but for the supreme Dispenser of People's Commune—*Janaganamana.* The high official, who had commissioned the poet to compose the royal panegyric was intelligent enough to see through the motif of the poem and he felt that it could not be applied to the King-Emperor. The song was sung as a national song at the Congress; and a month later at the Maghotsava* on 25 January, 1912 as Brahma-sangit or a song in praise of God the almighty. Later it was to become India's national anthem.

The Calcutta stay was highlighted by a public reception, a birthday celebration in the Town Hall on January 28, 1912. It was the Bengali Literary Academy (Bangiya Sahitya Parishad) which had taken the initiative. This was the first public recognition of a literary genius in Bengal. Before Tagore no literary figure had been thus honoured.

In February 1912, he came back to Santiniketan after two months' absence. The school was passing through hard times. The East Bengal Government had sent a secret

* The Maghotsava (i.e., Magh Festival) now generally coincides with the date, the 25th January; in 1830 it coincided with the 23rd January.

circular that Santiniketan was not a fit and proper place for the education of the sons of Government officers. This had the desired effect, and many guardians quickly withdrew their wards. The poet was hurt to the quick to see his schoolboys leaving Santiniketan one by one with tears in their eyes. Also the Bengal Police had taken grave objection to the apointment of a teacher who had been convicted for writing a book of verse which had been proscribed as seditious. Pressure was put upon the poet to get that teacher removed. He paid no heed to it. But it was an unequal fight and in the end, to save the school, he had to yield. But he gave him a job in his *zamindari.* Kalimohan Ghose was another of these marked men. He also was sent away to England for studying pedagogy and thus absolved of all past odium.

Tagore was leaving for England in March; before that he read out an essay on the main currents of Indian history in which he tried ***to*** explain the inner drive and meaning of India's spiritual quest and culture. The meaning of history, he suggested, pointed towards unity in diversity and not an insistence on separatism. This was a rather different note from the elitist view strongly popular among the orthodox.

At last he was leaving for England on 19 March, 1912 from the Calcutta port. Many friends and relations had come to the jetty to see him off. But where was the poet ? At the last moment news came that he had suddenly fallen ill the previous night; and the voyage had to be cancelled. Under doctor's orders he enjoyed a month's absolute rest.

Feeling a little better, the poet came away to Shelaidah. There, amid its unhurried, untroubled air, songs came back, shyly, one by one. Most of the *Gitimalya* songs were written thus. Also to fill his leisure hours, he translated some of his poems into English, a somewhat unexpected venture with even more unexpected results.

On the last day of the Bengali year he returned to Santiniketan, unannounced, almost incognito. But once there, he conducted the evening as well as the New Year morning services. In the meantime arrangements for the postponed trip to England had been finalised. But his mind was not free from worry. Why was he going to England ? He had been there twice before, but now at fifty-two ? The open letter that he addressed to the inmates of Santiniketan on the eve of his departure deserves to be read in this connection. In self-defence he argued that a foreign tour was necessary to relate his educational experiment with the wide world outside. "A visit to Europe can be the most fruitful pilgrimage for an Indian, if his mind is unhindered by ancient bias and his eyes seek truth." There was also the quite practical reason of medical treatment. So to England he went.

13

England, New Friends and a Changed India

RABINDRANATH, HIS SON and daughter-in-law, left for England on May 24, 1912 from Bombay. He was all the time composing songs, translating some into English and writing his travel diary in the form of letters for the *Tattvabodhini Patrika,* of which he was then the editor. These were later put together as *Father Sanchaya* (The Earnings of the Road), 1939.

The party reached London on June 16 and put up at first in a hotel; but soon shifted to rooms of their own. Among the people he knew in London was William Rothenstein who had visited India in 1910. Himself an artist, Rothenstein had soon discovered Abanindranath and Gaganendra-nath and visited their house at Jorasanko. He writes : "I was attracted, each time I went to Jorasanko, by the uncle, a strikingly handsome figure, dressed in white dhoti and chadar, who sat silently listening as we talked. I felt an immediate attraction, and asked whether I might draw him, for I discovered an inner charm as well as great physical beauty, which I tried to set down with my pencil. That this uncle was one of the remarkable men of his time no one gave me a hint."

The first person whom the poet went to see was Rothenstein, with whom he had a fitful correspondence. He had shown interest in Tagore's short stories as well as in his poems which appeared in translation in the *Modern Review.* Rabindranath gave him an exercise book containing some of his translations.

"That evening," writes Rothenstein, "I read the poems. Here was poetry of a new order which seemed to me on a level with that of the great mystics. Andrew Bradley, to whom I showed them, agreed. It looks as though we have at last a great poet among us again. I sent word to Yeats, who failed to reply; but when I wrote again he asked me to send him the poems, and when he had read them his enthusiasm equalled mine. He came to London and went carefully through the poems, making here and there, a suggestion, but leaving the original little changed.

"Tagore's dignity and handsome presence, the ease of his manners and his quiet wisdom made a marked impression on all who met him. One of the first persons whom Tagore wanted to know was Stopford Brooke; for Tagore, being a prominent member of the Brahmo Samaj, which was closely allied to Unitarianism, had heard much of him and of Estlin Carpenter."

Within a few days Rabindranath was introduced to the leading writers and thinkers of the day. The young poets came to sit at Tagore's feet; Ezra Pound was for a time most enthusiastic. Among others whom Tagore met were Bernard Shaw, H.G. Wells, Galsworthy, Andrews Bradley, Masefield, J.L.Hammond, Ernest Rhys, FoxStrangways, Sturge-Moore, and Robert Bridges. Tagore was struck by the breath of view and the rapidity of thought that he found among his new friends. "Those who know the English only in India do not know Englishmen," he said, which is true enough.

At the dinner held in his honour on July 10 at Trocadero Restaurant, Yeats presided and paid handsome tribute to the Indian poet. He said, "To take part in honouring Mr. Rabindranath Tagore is one of the great events of my artistic life. I have been carrying about with me a book of translations into English prose of a hundred of his Bengali lyrics written within the last ten years. I know of no one in my time who had done anything in the English language to equal these lyrics."

Rabindranath replied in the following terms : "I have not the power adequately to express my gratitude for the great honour you have done me. This is one of the proudest moments of my life. I have learned that, though our tongues are different and our habits dissimilar, at the bottom our hearts are one. The monsoon clouds, generated on the banks of the Nile, fertilise the far distant shores of the Ganga; ideas many have to cross from the East to Western shores to find welcome in men's hearts and fulfil their promise. East is East and West is West. God forbid that it should be otherwise—but the twain must meet in amity, peace, and understanding, their meeting will be all the more fruitful because of their differences; it must lead both to holy wedlock before the common altar of humanity."

It was here that Rabindranath met C.F. Andrews for the first time. Andrews, a missionary attached to the Cambridge Brotherhood, was then a Professor in St. Stephen's College, Delhi. He writes in *What I Owe to Christ:* "I walked back along the side of Hampstead Heath with H.W, Nevinson but spoke very little. I wanted to be-alone and think in silence of the wonder and glory of it all. , . .There all alone I could think of the-wonder of it: The infinite sky is motionless overhead and the restless water is boisterous." Andrews became the lifelong friend and associate to Rabindranath.

It was decided that *Gitanjali* should be published on behalf of the India Society. Yeats agreed to write an Introduction, some of the background material for which he collected from the poet's friend, Dr. D.N. Maitra.

The poet spent some time in the English countryside. The contrast with Indian villages could not but make him sad. He also visited some schools and in a series of essays and letters gave his own impressions. While in England, he met Colonel Narendra Prasanna Sinha, brother of S.P. Sinha (later Lord Sinha), who had a large house which he wanted to sell with adjoining land at Surul, a village within a mile of Santiniketan. Tagore bought the estate for Rs. 8,003. He wanted his son, Rathindranath to continue his agricultural experiments there. Rathindranath was beginning to tire a little of Shelaidah. His father too wanted to have him near, and Surul was close to Santiniketan.

After four months in England the party left for America on November 28, 1912. For the poet the land was *terra incognita,* and the two-hour detention at New York customs was not the best of introductions.

From New York they went straight to Urbana in Illinois, where his son had been a student once and where one of his Santiniketan teachers was then studying. Tagore knew some of the faculty through correspondence.

A small, quiet town, Urbana's population did not at that time exceed ten thousand. Its open sky, fresh air and unbounded leisure made the poet almost forget that he had come to America. He decided to spend some time at Urbana. Rathindranath eagerly took to biological research at the University, while his wife Pratima's time and energy were mostly taken up with house-keeping. In America maids and servants were a rarity, though labour-saving devices no doubt came to the aid of the harassed housewife.

As a nation, the Americans are wonderfully fond of lectures. They love to talk and they love to hear people talk. Mr. Vail, the Minister of Urbana's Unitarian Church, requested the poet to address the Unity Club. Every Sunday the Club held discourses on the saints and sages of different faiths. The Unitarians, who resemble the Brahmos in some ways, had got wind of the fact that Rabindranath was a member of the Brahmo brotherhood.

The poet was in a fix. Fortunately, he had with him the translation of a few of his sermons and religious essays. He hurriedly put them into shape and read one of these before the Club. This was his first experience of public speaking in the West. He was naturally apprehensive. But the address went down very well. By the end of the year 1912, invitations from academic and other circles began to pour in. Harriet Monroe who had founded and edited *Poetry, Magazine of Verse* (1912) published six poems of Tagore in the December issue. It was the first journal to publish his poems in the New World. This was a Chicago journal; and soon after Tagore was invited by the Chicago University for a lecture. At the end of January, 1913, he came to Chicago, where he lectured on the Ideals of the Ancient Civilisation of India, and the Problem of Evil. But the stay had to be cut short.

He was called away to Rochester, a small township near New York, where a religious conference of liberal-minded people of all faiths was sitting. Well-known philosophers and theologians, including Rudolph Eucken from Germany, were attending. Eucken had been in correspondence with Ajitkumar Chakravarty, a brilliant and sensitive member of the poet's school, from whom he had come to know much about Rabindranath. So when they met at the Rochester Conference they did not meet as strangers.

Rabindranath's theme at the conference was 'Race Conflict', a problem not unknown to America. According to *The Christian Register,* Rabindranath's speech lilted the proceedings of the Conference to the height of sheer sublimity and poetic passion. It was generally felt that no one else had shown such insight or the same literary stature as the speaker from India.

From Rochester he proceeded to Boston. Harvard was not far off, and the authorities of that University immediately extended an invitation for a course of lectures. The lectures over, he returned to Urbana, passing through New York. By then he had already spent six months in the States and longed to return to England. His son had to discontinue his researches and join his father on the move.

America had given him new points about his school at Bolpur. He felt that a technical section ought to be opened; a laboratory was needed; so was a hospital and a research centre. He even liked to think that one day the little place might grow into a university. Had the old dream of an ashrama gone the way of all dreams ? Or was this the shape of the modern ashrama to come ? The poet's mind was gradually freeing itself from the nostalgia of an idealised poet and its exaggcrated glories. This was partly a result of his Western experience, the impact of insistent, cosmopolition ideas.

As usual he wrote many letters from America, sent books on methods and problems of education also a large number of books on science and scientific subjects. He had always a strong bias for scientific training for the young. Hence the idea of a laboratory. In fact Santiniketan school had a laboratory when more expensive institutions in other parts of the country were doing without one.

While in America he came to know that the India society had published *Gitanjali* and that the book had been received well. When he reached England the papers were full of it. It was almost embarrassing. "These waves of praise do not please me," he writes modestly to his niece at home, "I begin to feel a conflict within me." This is an old trouble with him—honour weighs upon him, at the same time he cannot bear indifference and criticism. Indeed, two souls dwell in a poet's breast.

By now he had got over his initial shyness in facing an alien audience and he spoke at the Caxton Hall, London, on a number of occasions. These were later put together in *Sadhana,* a collection of religio-philosophical essays. In fact most of these were either adaptations or elaborations of his earlier Bengali work *Dharma* and the Santiniketan Sermons. Though for the most part annotations of India's ageless wisdom they also revealed the poet's unmistakable temperament and here and there some novel interpretations. Really, they formed a kind of quasi-philosophic confession of his religious life. The fact of an Anglo-American audience may have however modified the matter of presentation.

Two of his plays, *Raja* and *Dakghar,* were now translated as the *King of the Dark Chamber* and the *Post Office.* Both were staged with great success, and have continued to be acted in European capitals ever since.

In June, he underwent an operation and had to be hospitalised for about a month. It gave him a forced rest cure. After his discharge from the hospital he stayed for some time in a house on Cheyne Walk. And here the Muse came back once again after a lapse of several months.

On September 4, 1913, the poet boarded the ship, *City of Lahore,* at Liverpool. Kalimohan Ghose was also travelling with him. Pratima Devi and Rathindranath had gone on a Continental tour and would join him at Naples. He reached Bombay on October 4. He had spent more than sixteen months outside India, covered with glory and rich in experience. There was more to follow.

India had seen many changes in the meantime : the Partition of Bengal had been withdrawn in April, 1912; East and West Bengal had been united; Bihar and Orissa had become separate provinces, no longer tied to the old Bengal Presidency; Assam had again become a province;

but the most significant change that had taken place was the shifting of the capital of India from Calcutta to Delhi. And last but not least, the terrorists were as active as ever, as the attempt on the life of the Viceroy, Lord Hardinge, would show.

The English experience brought him a new friend, Rev. C.F. Andrews. Andrews, then attached to St. Stephen's College, Delhi, had already visited Santiniketan during the poet's absense. The poet's ideal and his personality had cast a spell on him. He had liked the place and thought of coming over permanently along with his friend, William Pearson, a sometime ordained missionary in Calcutta, later unattached to any church or group.

But life at home was not a bed of roses. During his absence critics had once more trumped up the old unavailing charge that Rabindranath's writings lacked a basis in reality and were, in fact, subjective fantasies with no reference to the life of the people. On top of it a popular dramatist tried to make fun of the poet in a farce specially written for the purpose. This the audience did not allow to pass without protest, and shrieks and shouts drowned the play. Some of it the poet had anticipated. While abroad he had written almost prophetically: "When I go back what littleness, what abuse and bitterness, conflict and hatred, I shall have to face ! But one cannot always pass by these unpleasantnesses, one has to face them. We cannot always avoid what we do not like."

His Calcutta experience showed how right these fears had been. The Tagore family at Jorasanko itself was the scene of much pettifogging. He was tired with these bickerings and two days later left the city and came away to Santiniketan. "I cannot tell you what a relief that was," he wrote to one of his pupils abroad.

The school was in full swing after the autumn holidays and the poet was turning out fresh songs every day. Then something happened. On November 13, the evening paper, *Empire,* flashed the following news : "It is the first recognition of the indigenous literature of this (British) Empire as world force; it is the first time that an Asiatic has attained distinction at the hands of the Swedish Academy, and this is the first occasion upon which the £8,000 prize has been awarded to a poet who writes in a language so entirely foreign to the awarding country." The same evening Tagore got the telegram of the award from Calcutta. His only comment was : "Henceforth I shall have no peace," which was true enough.

Thompson, the British biographer of the poet writes : "Rabindranath told me the award was not altogether a surprise. When in England, he had been asked to send copies of his books and press cuttings to the Nobel Prize Committee." Of course this he did at the instance of his British friends.

The whole country went wild with excitement. Criticism and controversies were silenced for a while. Citizens of Calcutta came to Santiniketan by special train on November 23 to congratulate the poet. The news of the Nobel Prize was however not the only reason for this gesture. Arrangement had already been made for a public reception at the Town Hall, Calcutta. But when the news came, the organisers decided to come over to Santiniketan and offer their greetings to the poet in his abode of peace.

The reception was held in Mango Grove. Speeches and

messages were presented in an unending series. All was going on well. But the whole thing took an unexpected turn when the poet rose to offer his thanks-giving speech. Usually gentle and always polite, he seemed to strike a very different chord. The re were grievances buried in his mind and they came out. It was a sad and strange thing to happen. it is said that the same morning he had received a most rude letter; in the meeting itself among the front benchers he had seen a few who had consistently opposed him. To the poet the reception must have looked like a got-up show. His unusual and strongly worded address hurt almost everyone present, his admirers no less than others. The speech— perhaps the poet's one *faux pas* occupied the Calcutta papers for quite some time.

Another explanation of the poet's reaction to the reception might be that the day was the death anniversary of his wife while his youngest son had also died in the same month. A poet is also a man.

Here a little incident is worth recording. The period of which we are speaking (1912-13) saw the culmination of the satyagraha movement in faraway South Africa. It was a protest against the inhumanity with which the Indian settlers were being treated by colonist settlers of South Africa. The leader of the movement was a Gujarati barrister, Mohandas Karamchand Gandhi. Rev. C.F. Andrews and W.W. Pearson were going there to make an on-the spot inquiry. They were not yet among Santiniketan's permanent residents; but they were frequent visitors and it was clear that they would soon be its inmates. Before they sailed for Africa they came to Santiniketan for the poet's blessings. A farewell meeting was organised in their honour and the poet wrote in a message to Andrews: "Along with Mr. Gandhi and others, you are fighting for our cause" This was probably his first reference to Gandhiji.

The Paus festival address this year (1913) was keyed to a new international pitch. "Ours in an ashrama where there are no groups," declared the poet. The partisan views which he had sometimes championed on behalf of the Adi Brahmo Samaj had changed in the meanwhile. Now he would claim that men of all nations could accept the ashrama as their own. He had special reasons for saying this. Santiniketan had a fair sprinkling of people belonging to foreign faiths. Captain Petavel and his wife, Andrews and Pearson, were all British and Christians.

From Santiniketan he went to Calcutta, where the University honoured him with the degree of Doctor of Literature. Lord Hardings was the Chancellor and Ashutosh Mukherji the Vice-Chancellor. The decision of award had been taken before the Nobel Prize. In conferring the Degree the Chancellor, Lord Hardings, the Viceroy of India, said, "Upon the modest brow. . . . the Nobel Prize has lately set the laurels of a world-wide recognition, and I can only hope that the retiring disposition of our Bengali poet will forgive us for thus dragging him into publicity once more and recognise with due recognition that he must endure the penalties of greatness."

The official award of the Nobel Prize took place a month after this. The reception was held in Government House, presided over by the Governor of Bengal, Lord Carmichael, who represented the Swedish Academy.

In 1914, Pramatha Choudhury came out with an *avant-garde* monthly magazine *Sabuj Patra* (The Green Leaf). As usual, the poet was at once drawn to the new venture. The songs of *Gitimalya* and *Gitali* left behind, he longed for clear, powerful prose, and a more vigorous verse. The new magazine offered him that opportunity. The essay *Bibechana O Abibechana* (Consideration and its Absence) acted as a safety valve. The country had once been led to move forward, but now, he said, the Bengali mind was once more busy erecting walls of platitudes. There was obstruction at every step and progress was impeded. To breathe fresh air one must break through. To some, all this smacked of heresy. In his first poem of the Balaka group, *Sabujer Abhijan* (The Green Adventure), he said, with gusto:

> Leave behind the highway,
> Become a homeless wanderer,
> And blaze a trail into the Unknown.
> Danger lies ahead,
> Let Sorrow be thy companion.
> Knowing this my heart dances !
> Stop seeking precepts in age-old manuscripts.
> Come ! O Liberated, the Evergreen !
>
> Casting off
> All that is weak, infirm and worn,
> Scatter life in an endless stream.
> With the intoxication of the Green
> Thou hast made the earth brim,
> And thy light flashes in the crumbling cloud !
> Throw round the neck of Spring thy own garland,
> Come ! O Deathless, the Evergreen !

This was a call to youth, the eternally green. A new era

was opening, the articles and the poem were its passionate prelude.

Another incident, not literary, may be mentioned here: the house-warming ceremony at the Surul Kuthi. While in England the poet had purchased the house and the adjacent land. At great expense the house had been renovated and remodelled; the jungle cleared even an engine and dynamo had been set up for the supply of electricity. The Shelaidah experiment was wound up and some of the equipment, library and laboratory, were brought over and fitted for Rathindranath's work. Money was no longer much of a problem. Were not the Macmillans sending regular cheques against the sale of translations ?

14

The Ebb and Flow of a Poet's Mood

RATHINDRANATH HAD PURCHASED a house near Nainital, sixteenth mile from Kathgodam, in Kumaon hills. Tagore, with the whole family, went there to spend the summer months. In the new surroundings, the poet appeared to be quite cheerful. But there is no accounting for moods; as from nowhere, dark, premonitory thoughts crowded back upon him. He felt the wings of an unnamed evil spread over a crouching, groaning world.

In some of the *Balaka* poems there is an 154 open hint of coming doom. Was it an intimation of the European War, or an expression of inner sorrow and struggle ?

The clouds dispersed as suddenly as they had gathered. From his letters to Andrews one can see the ebb and flow of a poet's mood, by turns rapt and restless. Essays, poems and stories for *Sabuj Patra* continued as before. So did the songs of *Gitaliy* which had become almost a daily service. His greatest happiness and relief lay in the music of his songs.

One of the stories, *Strir Patra* (Wife's Letter) touched off a prolonged controversy, perhaps more among the reactionary social thinkers than among the literary men. The story plainly points to the cracking of the walls of outmoded convention: it stresses the individual rights of women, rights neglected almost throughout our history.

The question of emancipation of women now enters a new phase in Bengali literature. Just as the European bourgeoisie had been shocked by Ibsen's *Doll's House* in the nineties of the last century, so was Bengali society by stories like *Strir Patra, Haimanti, Bostomi*. The novelette, *Chaturanga,* and the novel *Ghare Baire* (Home and the World) added fuel to the fire. The literary pundits and keepers of the social conscience did not spare Rabindranath. It was an unintended compliment that he had succeeded in exposing real evils.

July 1914 was the beginning of World War I, in a ledge of the European mainland. The fire soon spread over the whole of the Continent and sparks fell across West Asia. India also felt the heat of the flames because it was the part of the British Empire. Deeply wounded, in his weekly sermon Rabindranath spoke from the depth of his heart: "The world's evil has burst in a bloodtide. Oh, Lord, take away this evil and spare us from annihilation." So far as the rival powers were concerned, the prayer of course went unheeded. The poet looked within and saw that "the sins of a few have to be paid for by all."

With high hopes and a big project Rathindranath had came to Surul : but the plan of rural reconstruction had to be soon abandoned. Rathindranath and others were down with malaria and had to go away elsewhere. His son-in-law, Nagendranath, stayed there for time, but in the end he too left.

For some time they all settled in Calcutta, a somewhat battered disillusioned co'Tjmunity. The dream of rural reconstruction, of scientific agriculture, first at Shelaidah and then at Surul, had faded. The Santiniketan dairy, under Santosh's supervision, was in a similar plight; paid men were looking after the dairy, while Santosh Chandra Mazumdar was busy with school work and miscellaneous jobs.

The poet felt disturbed by the thought that his ideas were not being practised as they should have been in Santiniketan. In its present shape the school was far from what he had intended. Andrews and Pearson had come in search of higher ideals in life, ferrying weak students across the waters of the matriculation examination was surely not their aim. There were obstructions against running the school of new lines—obstructions from guardians, teachers and students. He wished to move out and see things from a distance, with a new perspective. But he did not perhaps know that he himself was probably the greatest obstacle in 156 giving shape to his own ideas. Every time the school was taking shape he thought that it was falling into rut and his restless spirit called for a newer scheme or reorganisation. The straining after the new and sometime absurd has been at once the source of its vitality and a constant stumbling-block. It has always been on the move, in a state of flux. Its most pervasive quality has been its atmosphere, now alas rather rudely shaken.

After the autumn holidays he spent a few days at Buddhagaya with some of his young friends. Years before he had been here once with Sister Nivedita, Jagdish Bose and others. This time his mind was completely taken up with the *Gitali* songs.

From Gaya he moved to Allahabad and put up with Pyarimohan Banerjee, a relation of the Tagore family. He spent three weeks there and the last few songs of *Gitali* were composed here. His singing mood was over; and the old lyrical and even the romantic demure began with a new series of poems. A faded picture of Kadambari Devi in the house recalled the forgotten days and he wrote the immortal poem *Chhabi* (Picture).

Art thou a picture mere, on canvas limn'd ?
That starry cluster, distance-dimm'd
That throngs its nest
Of heaven's breast;
That tireless travellers' band
Journeying through the darkness, lamp in hand,
The sun and moon and stars that speed
Through wheeling year by year:
Art thou not real like those, indeed ?
Art thou, alas, a picture mere ?

The *Sajahan* poem may also be studied in this context,

both meditations on love.

He came back to Santiniketan in time for the Paus festival. But within a month he came to Calcutta to conduct the Magh festival there, after which he once more retired to solitary Shelaidah. The Kuthi house stood empty, the dream of settling his son and son-in-law there had been rudely shaken. He went back to his old houseboat.

Three young artists, students of Abanindranath, visited him while he was there: Nandalal Bose, Surendranath Kar and Mukulchandra De. The poet was very happy with them. Later on all three became closely associated with the poet and his institution.

The poet came back to Calcutta, where Dr. D.N. Maitra was trying to organise the 'Bengal Social Service League'. The poet was asked to inaugurate it and he said: "The moment we put our shoulders to the wheel of work we shall be saved from the bugbear of dialectics and the futility of empty scholasticism. A great force has come to the land. . . .We need not despair." The huge mass movement which was just emerging, few had seen it so early as the poet had done. He welcomed the new spirit.

Returning to Bolpur he preferred to stay at the Surul Kuthi, alone. The ashrama folk had asked him for a Spring drama. The outcome was *Phalguni* (Cycle of Spring). The Viceroy invited him to Barrackpore. But the poet lost in his librettos, politely avoided the invitation. *Phalguni* went ahead.

During his North Indian tour the poet had come to know that Gandhiji was returning to India from South Africa.

After reaching a compromise with General Smuts he had withdrawn the Satya-graha movement on behalf of the Indian settlers and had left for England to meet the Colonial Secretary and acquaint him with the situation in South Africa. But the fate of his Phoenix School, its staff and students was left undecided. Some of the children had never seen India before and were now being sent back *en masse.* But who would give them shelter and look after them ? Mr. Gandhi was then not a well-known figure in India. Thanks to Andrews, the group was accommodated at Santiniketan. Rabindranath sent a letter of welcome to Gandhiji.

From England, Gandhiji and his wife, Kasturibai (Kasturba Gandhi), came to India and to Santiniketan on February 17, 1915. But the news of Gokhale's death made them go to Poona immediately. The poet too happened to be out of station. On March 6 Gandhiji came back from Poona and the two met—the poet and the man of action.

Gandhiji later went round Santiniketan and was not particularly happy over the administration of the school. In his characteristic fashion he recommended more self-help among teachers and students, a rigorous regimen. When enthusiasts reported this to Rabindranath at Surul, he heartily approved of it. An experiment always held an attraction for him, the counsel of self-help sounded simple.

The Phoenix School lads did not believe in employing cooks or servants. They did everything on their own. It was a community with severe, near-ascetic standards. Somehow the fever caught on and the services of cook, servant, water-carrier and sweepers were dispensed with—with interesting results. The community, of nearly two hundred, chose to be self-reliant, self-sufficient. While peeling vegetables, some doing it probably for the first time in their lives, they heard the school bell ring and rushed to the classes, some to teach, others presumably to learn. One can easily imagine what a mess or a merry-go-round it must have been while it lasted and how unlike the even tenor of a poet's school. The experiment was soon given up. But though the austerity drive did not succeed, Santiniketan has kept it apart as a day of remembrance. March 10, when the experiment was first launched, has been marked off as 'Gandhi Day' when, at least for half the day, the daily chores are done by the residents, a pleasant diversion, if not a parody.

Gandhiji left for Rangoon on March 11. On coming back he took away with him the students of the Phoenix School to the Kumbha Mela at the confluence of the Ganga and the Yamuna, where thousands of monks and mendicants from all parts of India gathered, being held at Allahabad. It had been decided to shift the Phoenix School elsewhere, to some other part of India. The boys from South Africa had stayed at Santiniketan only for four months, but Gandhiji never forgot the gesture and the hospitality shown by the ashramites and the founder.

On March 20, 1915, the Governor of Bengal, Lord Carmichael visited Santiniketan. Gone were the days when Government servants had been warned against the impropriety of sending their children to Santiniketan. Now the highest British dignitary in Bengal came to pay his respect. Now that its founder had been feted in Europe, he and his institution had to be patronised.

A reception was held in the mango grove in honour of the distinguished guest. Some changes and repairs, in the prayer hall and outside had to be made for the occasion. Some did not like this. The small semi-circular platform put up on the occasion and named after Carmichael is still there. Just before the school broke up for the summer -recess, *Phalguni* was staged. The poet himself appeared in the role of the blind singer. It was an unforgettable impersonation. But was it only an impersonation?

An event which caused some stir soon after was the Knighthood, conferred upon the poet on June 3, 1915 on George V's birthday.

15

The Poet Itinerant

RABINDRANATH HAD LONG wished to visit Japan. On his way to Tibet, Kawaguchi had passed through India and had met Rabindranath. In the middle of 1915 Kawaguchi sent him an invitation from Japan, but there were too many hurdles which could not be removed then.

In April 1916 the poet was invited for a lecture tour in the United States. Major Pond, the director of an agency, offered him 12,000 dollars. The poet was so eager to go abroad that without weighing the pros and cons of the proposition, he readily accepted the terms. At the time he had little idea what peddling lectures would mean. About Pond and his ilk he knew nothing.

On May 3, 1916, he left for Japan. With him were Andrews, Pearson and a young artist, Mukul De. On May 7 the ship touched Rangoon harbour. It was his birthday and the poet dedicated his book of poems, *Balaka**, to his friend and companion, Willie Pearson. The city of Rangoon gave him a big reception. From Rangoon the ship meandered through the Straits which suited the poet, halting at Penang, Singapore, Hong-Kong, for loading and unloading.

On May 29 the ship reached Kobe. The poet stayed with a Gujarati merchant. Kobe was out-and-out a commercial port and the poet did not feel at his best. From there by way of Osaka he came to Tokyo, At Osaka, the Press Association flooded him with requests for a public address, his first in Japan.

At Tokyo he was the guest of Taikkan, one of the foremost painters of Japan, whom he had known in Calcutta several years before. A series of lectures and receptions followed, beginning with the Tokyo University and the City's Ueno Park. But, living in a large city, one cannot see Japan. At the invitation of Harasan, a wealthy Japanese, Tagore spent some time in a country house at Hakaan. "I am being looked after like a king. I do not think I shall ever set my eyes on a more beautiful spot." Such were the happy poet's reactions.

*Translated by A. Basu as *A Flight of Swans.*

This was the third year of the First World War. Japan was an ally of the Entente and an aggressor on the Chinese mainland. After centuries of bondage and tyranny China had recently become a republic but was still plagued with internal dissensions. On top of it came the unprovoked Japanese attack. To add insult to injury, the militant Japanese made harsh demands which went against the idea of Chinese sovereignty. The poet was a witness to all this and wondered at this other face of his idealised, aesthetic Nippon. Mortally hurt, he openly denounced the spirit of Japanese aggressiveness. Needless to say, the military junta was not pleased with this unsought advice from the poet of a slave nation. Japanese officialdom saw to it that the poet was deprived of a chance of speaking in public. The day on which he left Japan the only person who had come to see him oif was his unhappy host.

Andrews had already gone back to India. With Pearson and Mukul the poet left for America. The ship reached Seattle on September 18, 1916. Mr. Pond's conducted lecture tour started at once. On his way to Japan as well as during his stay there he had written the lectures he was to deliver. These were later collected in two slim volumes, *Personality* and *Nationalism.*

Nearly every day and some times even twice a day and for full two months, often repeating the same set of lectures, he came to New York; from there he was taken to Boston and Yale Universities and a few other places. His patience was sorely tried; and, typical of the poet, at considerable financial loss he cancelled the contract of the lecture programme, and hastened home.

The poet returned to India in March, 1917 after ten months spent abroad. These travels and contacts were slowly changing his point of view. "For me the barriers of nation have ceased to exist," he wrote in a letter, "only when my soul can make all countries into one country will I have my release."

The tour of 1916-17 differed in some ways from that of 1912-13. The first tour had been made in a spirit of pilgrimage. Expressive of his spiritual longing he had taken with him *Gitanjali,* a viaticum, for a sick and hag-ridden Europe. For himself he had brought back its sense of restlessness and questioning, so necessary for the East, and with the advent of *Sabuj Patra,* started new types of stories, novels and poems.

This time too he had carried a noble message for Japan and America and warned, with a poet's sensitiveness and a prophet's fury, against the spirit of aggressive nationalism and its dangers for the world. Not that he was blind in the nobler aspects of nationalism. These he had pointed out in many of his essays written during the Swadeshi days. But he was moving beyond the patriotic phase.

As Brajendranath Seal pointed out in the reception held in the poet's honour: "On his first visit he had carried with him in his *Gitanjali* the word of peace to care the unrest of Western individualism. He had sung of the soul's peace in tune with the play of the Lord. This time, in answer to the social unrest and tension, he revealed the secret of Indian's age-old wisdom of peace and compassion. Then he had spoken of the eternal companion, now he spoke of the glory of the Eternal Individual."

Returning home he found that the Vichitra Club had developed into a flourishing institution. A number of his admirers had become members of the club. But he was not happy. He heard disquieting news about Rathindranath. The automobile business, in which his son was a partner, was on the verge of collapse. Rathindranath was too intelligent to be hoodwinked; he forced Rabindranath to sever all connection with the firm. This timely action saved his son from many complications which cropped up with the liquidation of the firm and one of the partners having absconded.

This was one side of the shield. On the other side, the Indian nationalist papers were now very bitter with Tagore. The nationalism Rabindranath had attacked was an enemy of our common humanity, a violent, greedy spirit that lived upon weaker nations. His *home-made* critics did not always appreciate the poet's standpoint or were perhaps then not in a mood to listen to wise counsel. In some cases there might have been real or imaginary grievances. Besides his political opinions, his writings too had become the storm-centre of criticism. The champions of 'purity' in literature had once again raised their cudgels against the poet; they might have their reasons to be angry with him. Those who found favour with him were also not entirely innocent. In a spirit of bonhomie, and in an effort to ingratiate themselves with the poet, they would often exaggerate the views of the critics. And the poet was rather sensitive, the gossip used to excite and tire him by turns. Moreover he was also beginning to feel the loneliness of age. In a letter from Santiniketan he wrote "I am feeling very lonely. Don't think that just writing can fill the gap. The school is now my only companion."

There were reasons for worry nearer home. His eldest daughter, Bela was on her death-bed. His relationship with the son-in-law also come to be strained.

Indian politics had entered a new phase. As before, the terrorists were busy with their bombs and revolvers. The World War was on. The Government had passed a new Defence Act and held twelve hundred Bengali youths in detention in prisons and forts, or inaccessible detention camps.

Mrs. Annie Besant, the founder of the Home Rule League in Madras, was under orders of detention. In Western India, Lokamanya Tilak, released after six years of jail life, had again launched a movement for liberating India. He was however silenced by the Bombay Government, and obliged to sign an undertaking. Thus all the movements which aimed at independence were ruthlessly crushed.

The poet's mind was agitated over these and other issues. He wrote to the papers protesting against the Government's repressive measures and expressed sympathy for Mrs. Besant. The citizens of Calcutta wished to protest against the detention of Bengali young men. The authorities of the Town Hall refused permission to hold the meeting in their premises. First, at the Rammohan Hall and then at Madan's Alfred Theatre, Rabindranath read a long article, *Kartar Ichchae Karma* (As the Lord Proposes). A new song, *Desk, Desk Nandita Kari* was composed.

Thy call has sped over all countries of the world
And men have gathered around thy seat,
The day is come.
But where is India ?
Does she still remain hidden, lagging behind ?
Let her take up her burden and march with all,
Send her, mighty God, thy message of victory,
O Lord ever awake.

This was, once more, the Rabindranath of the earlier Swadeshi days—heroic, brilliant, the poet of a nation in chains writhing to break away. In his essay he criticised the injustice of an alien administration. Montague had announced in the British Parliament in August, 1917 that responsible Government could be given to India only by successive stages. Referring to this the poet said, "We accept every possible risk of making mistakes in our demand for self-government; we are ready to march on, even though we are likely to stumble now and then, only the freedom to make mistakes confers the freedom to attain truth."

But at the same time he raised the larger question, why such a state of things had come to pass. He explained our intertia in terms of an infatuation with the past, and a compromise with beliefs we do not hold to be true. In other words, our politics was playing second fiddle to British policy, and our society was being ruled by old out moded conventions. We have to emancipate ourselves from both bondages—such was the burden of his simple argument. The poet's social criticism aimed against the country's age-old complacency did not go unchallenged. We agitate for political freedom, but refuse to apply the same liberal attitude towards our odsolescent social rules;

this is the continuing crisis of our country and the root of so many of its problems.

Clouds were gathering on the political horizon. The extremist members of the Bengal Provincial Congress voted for the internee Mrs. Annie Besant as President of the coming National Congress to be held in Calcutta in 1917. The elders did not agree, with the result that the younger members succeeded and elected Rabindranath as the President of a new Reception Committee. For a few days the country, especially the city of Calcutta, was in the grip of a mounting excitement. All kinds of people were coming in and going out of Jorasanko House. The poet was the hub of all this frantic activity. At last the All-India Congress Committee agreed to accept Mrs. Besant as the President for the coming sessions of the Congress and the poet resigned the Presidentship of the reception committee. Rai Bahadur Baikunthanath Sen, the original President, concluded the deliberations of the meeting. Mrs. Besant was released and came to Calcutta on September 5, 1917, where she had a private meeting with the poet.

But how long could politics hold the poet's attention ? The chaos of the Congress over, he at once plunged into his play *Dakghar* in which there is not even the remotest reference to politics. The play was staged twice in Vichitra Club. One evening was for members only, another for distinguished visitors which included Annie Besant, Balgangadhar Tilak, Madanmohan Malaviya, M.K. Gandhi and others. Its new style of acting and the distinctive decor were appreciated by all present.

We might mention here one or two events that took place towards the end of 1917. A commission of enquiry into the affair of the Calcutta University was sitting then. The Chairman was Sir Michael Sadler, Vice-Chancellor of Leeds University. Sadler had written to the poet, asking for his views on education. The poet said, *inter alia,* "Great care should be taken in teaching English as a second language. But in schools, colleges and at universities the medium in all subjects should be the mother tongue." This had always been his view.

Towards the end of 1917 the Secretary of State for India, Mr. Edwin Samuel Montague, paid a sudden visit to India. He had declared in Parliament that India would be given responsible self-rule by stages. He had come to India to feel the pulse of the nation. He heard the views of all parties, himself keeping mum. Montague met Rabindranath in the premises of Bichitra. It is believed that in a letter to Montague the poet had explained the situation in the country as he saw it.

The New Year (1918) found the poet at Santiniketan in the role of a schoolmaster. He was preparing lessons, taking classes, correcting exercises. A few short stories were by-products of the period.

In May he was again in Calcutta, where he came to know that Pearson had been arrested by the British Police at Peking and sent to England as a detenu. The same evening Andrews left for Delhi, to find out the facts about Pearson's arrest. He returned after a week and reported that the Viceroy Chelmsford was extremely annoyed with 'Wille'. While in Japan, Pearson had written and published a pamphlet criticising British rule in India. The book was seized by the police and proscribed.

The death of his eldest daughter, Bela, on 16 May was a bigger blow. She had been ailing for a long time and he was prepared for it. He used to go to see her every day. On the last day on his way to her house he heard that Bela had passed away. He did not go further, but came back. In the evening he was present at the Bichitra Club as usual. There was no change in his social courtesy and the conversation was as natural as always. It is on occasions like these that one realises how deep were the sources of faith in the poet's mind and soul. Was the poem in *Palataka* (Fugitive), one wonders, about Beta's illness and passing away ?

> Always I hear, 'gone away' 'gone away' ....
> Never say 'she is gone'
> It is a lie. I cannot bear it ... .

16

The Training of People's Mind

A NEW CHAPTER begins now in the history of Santin ketan as well as in the life of the poet. Two years earlier in 1916 from America he had written: "The school at Santiniketan must become a bond between India and the world. We must find a centre of humanistic culture for all the races of the world. The era of narrow nationalism is ending and a great worldwide brotherhood is preparing. The fields of Bolpur shall be its first inaugural."

The day after the Pans festival in December 1918 was held the foundation ceremony of Visva Bharati.* The Gujarati guardians had made a liberal donation towards the celebration. The sacred mantras, in letters of gold and silver, lie still buried under the foundation stone. But the promised building did not come up on the selected spot. The donors were not happy over it.

Annie Besant had gone back to Madras after the Congress sessions in Calcutta. There she also planned a National University, which included engineering, commerce, agriculture and other courses with a practical bias. Rabindranath was made the first Chancellor of this University.

A Chancellor should now and then visit his University. Soon a chance presented itself, for there came an invitation from the State of Mysore. At that time Jnansharan Chakravarty was the Dewan (Chief Minister) of Mysore and the invitation from the Bangalore Dramatic Club was largely due to him. In January 1919 with the young artist Surendranath Kar as a campanion the poet went on a tour of the South.

At Mysore and Bangalore the poet gave a large number of addresses on Indian culture and the ideals of the Centre of Culture at the Visva Bharati. Resting for a while at Ootacamund he started a whirlwind tour of Tanjore, Madurai and other places. Lecture

* Not to be contused with the University (1951).

followed lecture till he reached Madanpalle, a centre of Theosophist activity. From there he wished to go to Madras. But at that time in Madras, a powerful Brahmanic group, which controlled public opinion through the Press, had launched a strong anti-Tagore propaganda. The poet's only fault, it seemed, was that he had approved of Vithalbhai Patel's bill on inter-caste marriages. This the Brahmins of Madras could not forgive. A few days later he reached Adyar, near Madras. There, as Chancellor of the National University, he gave three addresses on Culture and Education (March 10-12, 1919). The most important of these was on *The Centre of Indian Culture.* Based on an earlier essay, *Tapovan,* it contained an account of his own experiment, Visva Bharati.

Here are a few lines from the address: "The main river of Indian culture has flowed in four-streams—the Vedic, the Puranic, the Buddhist and the Jain. It had its sources in the heights of the Indian consciousness.

"But a river belonging to a country is not fed by its own waters alone. Contribution have similarly found their way to India's original culture.

"The Muhammadan for example, has repeatedly came into India from outside, laden with his own stores of knowledge and feeling and his wonderful religious democracy. . . . In our music our architecture, our pictorial art, our literature, the Muham-madans have made their permanent and precious contribution.

"And there has descended upon us the later flood of

Western culture. But a river flowing within its banks is truly our own, but our relations with a flood are disastrously the opposite. So, in our centre of Indian learning, we must provide for the coordinated study of all these different cultures— the Vedic, the Puranic, the Buddhist, the Jain, the Islamic, the Sikh and the Zoroastrian. And side by side with them the European and only then shall we be able to assimilate the last."

He added, "We must make room for the study of all our great vernaculars. . . . We must include our literature in order truly to know the psychology of our people and the direction towards which our underground current of life is moving."

The South Indian tour over, in Calcutta at the Empire Theatre he placed before the public his scheme or dream of Visva Bharati. The address, for some reasons, was given in English; another novelty was the sale of tickets. This practice he had learnt in America, it had been followed in the southern tour. Later he spoke on the same subject at the Bose Institute, where admission was by cards.

Lecturing over, he returned to Santiniketan and stayed at Dehali. Here he got busy over a four-page newsletter called *Santiniketan* (1919 April). This was printed at the tiny printing press which had come as a gift from Lincoln city, U.S.A. The machine had to be fed regularly. As expected, the greater part of the journal was supplied by the poet's miscellaneous writings, including new songs. Beside this he was taken up with school work. The Visva Bharati classes began after the summer vacation in July 1919. The poet himself was taking classes in literature, while others were also doing their bit. The students were resident scholars.

In his writings he was making new experiments; small stories and fairy tales; new songs were welling up like acts of daily worship. The stories were later collected in *Lipika,* the first faint cry of prose poems which were to come later.

The Nobel Prize and the foreign contacts had meant a rush of visitors, Indian and foreign, and a rapid increase in correspondence. He used to answer every letter in his own hand; and for long had received no assistance from anyone. The load was growing heavier every day. In a sad moment he wrote: "I sometimes wish I could keep a secretary. But funds will not permit that luxury. For Rathi too has financial troubles, it is the same with the school; so I keep my eyes and try to preserve my peace of mind."

It was unlikely that the routine activities of a school would engage him for long. Relief soon came, thanks to Gandhiji. Rabindranath was invited to preside over the Gujarati Literary Conference at Ahmedabad. That summer was one of the hottest and the school had to be closed early. Towards the end of March 1920 the poet left for Ahmedabad, the city where he had spent happy days in his early youth. With him went Andrews, Santoshchandra and a young student, Pramathanath Bisi. The party was the guest of Ambalal Sarabhai, the famous industrialist. To describe the Sarabhais as merely plutocrats would be unfair; they are a gifted family.

This was Rabindranath's first visit to Gujarat after

he had become a world figure. Gandhiji's ashrama at Sabarmati was on the other side of the river. Rabindranath went there one evening and spent the night at the ashrama. In the morning after the prayer meeting he came back to the Sara-bhai mansion. From there began his tour of Kathiawad. After some days he reached Bombay. At that time, April 13, the first anniversary of the Jaliianwalla Bagh massacre was being observed (April 13). Bombay's leading barrister and Congress worker, Mohammad Ali Jinnah, was its organiser. At his request the poet sent a written address.

He wrote: "A great crime has been done in the name of law in the Punjab. Such terrible eruptions of evil leave their legacy in the wreckage of ideals behind them. What happened in Jaliianwalla Bagh is itself a monstrous progeny of a monstrous war. . . . The disruption of the basis of civilisation will continue to produce a series of moral earthquakes, and men will have to be ready for still further sufferings."

From Bombay to Baroda, as guest of His Highness the Gaekwad Sayaji Rao, a reception was held at the Nyaya Mandir (High Court). While in the city the poet one day attended a meeting of the depressed classes. Pained at what he saw and heard about them he requested Tilak to find a solution for the problem. But Tilak was then on his deathbed and could not possibly take up the work. Long after this Gandhiji began his Harijan Movement.

17

The Travels : Continued

WITHIN A FEW weeks of returning from the Gujarat trip the poet again left for Europe with his son and daughter-in-law. The last time he had been there was in 1912-13. After that had come the World War (1914-18). The end of hostilities had been declared in November 1918. This was followed by the parcelling out of Europe among the powers; but in Eastern Europe a new power—the power of the masses—was arising. Soviet communism had emerged after the collapse of the Romanov despotism.

The ship reached Plymouth (1920 June); Willie Pearson came to receive him at the port. They had parted at Tokyo (1917) and met after three years. As soon as it was known that Tagore was in London friends began to call on him. There were parties and dinners as usual. But this time there was a studied aloofness in the air. The English had not forgotten Tagore's rejection of the Knighthood offered by their King on his birthday.* Robert Bridges was expected to preside over a meeting at Oxford; at the last moment he "could not come." How could the poet-laureate preside over the meeting of one who had turned down royal favours ? Rabindranath stayed in England for about two months.

* The Knighthood had been conferred on Rabindranath Tagore in 1915. But he protested against the Jallianwalia Bagh massacre by renouncing Knighthood in 1919.

Among new acquaintances were the Irish leader, Sir Horace Plunket and the emigre artist, Nicholas Roerich.

Parliament was then holding an enquiry into the Jaliianwalla Bagh massacre. Montague, the Secretary of State, had to submit a report to a Committee. The report happened to be in favour of the Indians and the British public was quite annoyed with Montague. Rabindranath sent him a letter of thanks, its only immediate reaction in India was that he was taken to task by the extremists !

The poet met Montague at India Office and told him that Indians were not clamouring for the punishment of General Dwyer, who had ordered the firing at Jaliianwalla Bagh, or the Governor, O'Dwyer. They would be content if the Government publicly admitted its mistake. But then to admit a mistake British prestige would be at stake. Montague assured him that Government would be careful in the future, so that such events did not recur. From the trend of events Rabindranath could feel that India was not likely to profit from the Parliamentary discussions. In a letter he wrote, bitterly, "The British officers may perpetrate any atrocities they like in India, these will make no difference among the ranks of the British electorate." From France he wrote to Andrews at Santiniketan: "Your Parliament debates about Dwyerism in the Punjab and other symptoms of the arrogant spirit of contempt and callousness about India have deeply aggrieved me and it was with a feeling of relief that I left England." He was in Paris.

Paris was an unknown city to Tagore; so was its language. Fortunately he came across Sudhir Rudra, son of Principal Sushil Rudra, of St. Stephen's College, Delhi. But for young Rudra the poet and his party would have been put to much inconvenience. Soon something turned up. M.Kahn, a millionaire, took him under his wings. A well-furnished house set in the midst of a garden by the Seine, away from the city, was placed at his disposal.

Many French savants came to meet him, the philosopher, Henri Bergson, Le Brim, Sylvain Levi, Comtesse de Noailles, and others. Bergson, it was obvious, was acquainted with the poet's writings. In the meantime a request for lectures came from the Netherlands. The poet readily accepted the invitation and he visited almost all the cities of Holland. A Dutch paper wrote that in Holland the poet was no stranger; his works, either in English or in Dutch, had been read by thousands. In fact, the "spirit of Tagore" was quite a popular phrase.

The greatest honour came at Rotterdam, where he was asked to give an address in the city's main church. So far no non-Christian had been honoured like this. In neighbouring Belgium, the gallery of the High Court was the venue of the poet's address.

Back in Paris, he thought of going once more to America. But Major Pond, the impresario of the earlier tour, wrote back to say that he was unable to arrange for a lecture tour. But the real reasons went deeper. These he came to know only after reaching the States.

From Rotterdam the poet and Pearson left for America. Rathindranath and others stayed back in Europe for some time. In New York, they stayed in a hotel.

But what curt coldness everywhere ! There was no

reception and invitations were scarce. There were no doubt a few lectures at Brooklyn, New York, Harvard, and one or two other places, but people did not seem to be in a mood to listen to the message of internationalism or universalism or the message of non-attachment. A busy nation, they understood the gospel of work and judged by results. Rabindranath wished to meet Mrs. Carnegie, but this was politely declined. After about a month of no work, he was asked to address a junior club of socialites. It was not a great success. The meeting over, Professor Woods asked him about the British Government's attitude towards him and his school at Santiniketan. It was then that the poet understood why Major Pond had avoided him, and the Press was so lukewarm. His renouncing of the Knighthood had crossed the Atlantic and hurt even the democratic American no less. Allies of England, the Americans were not in a mood to be charitable, though for himself the American is a plain "Mister" and proud of it. The poet felt that his chances of getting financial help for the Visva Bharati were very dim. But America's honour was retrieved a little by a small group of literary men and women; the Poetry Society held a reception in New York. From New York he went to Chicago to spend a few days with Mrs. Moody. News reached him at Chicago that Major Pond had at last been able to arrange a course of fifteen lectures in, of all places, Texas.

For full fifteen days Major Pond hauled him from city to city. "It is my tyrant *Karma* which is dragging me from one hotel to another. Between my two hotel incarnations, I usually have my sleep in a Pullman car," wrote the bemused and bedraggled poet. The days went by, crowded with lectures and interviews. Texas was a comparatively backward state; still, after the memories of New York, it was a relief.

The poet had come to America with a million-dollar dream. The dream did not come true. All the while Andrews was regularly reporting from Santiniketan a lack of funds. The poet had left him in charge of the school; in case of need it was Andrews who went about to find money. But there was a silver lining. In the spring of 1921 Sam Higginbottom and Mrs. W.V. Moody told Tagore in New York of a young Englishman Leonard Elmhirst, who was then studying agriculture **at** Cornell University. He had his M.A. in history from Cambridge, but was anxious to go to India and study its village problems at first hand. Elmhirst met the poet and was at once impressed with his idea of rural reconstruction and promised to join him in the experiment. His friend Mrs. Dorothy Straight, a prominent member of the Junior League, provided funds for Visva Bharati. She was later married to Elmhirst and for long years the couple continued to help liberally the work at Sriniketan, Visva Bharati's Institute of Rural Reconstruction.

So, the American tour, apparently without result, did not entirely fail. He did receive some financial assistance, but more than that he had gained a genuine friend and collaborator in Elmhirst.

After three weeks he came to Paris. In Paris he met Romain Roliand. They had corresponded with each other but this was their first meeting. Another remarkable person, at once a thinker and a man of action, he came across was Patrick Geddes. Tagore became a patron of

Geddes' Montpellier Institute.

From Paris he left for Stasbourg at the invitation of Professor Levi and the University. After World War I, Alsace-Lorraine had been returned to the French. It was now undergoing a process of Gallic transformation. Levy's scholarship and courtesy impressed Tagore and he hoped to bring him over to Visva Bharati as a Visiting Professor.

From France to Switzerland; through Lucerne, Basle, Zurich everywhere he met intellectuals and artists. At Lausanne he came to know that on his birthday (6 May 1920) the Germans had presented a large number of their classics to his University. He was deeply touched by this homage, something he had never known or expected. He wrote to his German friends: "The generous greeting and the gift that have come to me from Germany on the occasion of my 61st birthday are overwhelming. I truly feel that I have had my second birth in the heart of the people of that country, who have accepted me as their own."

Via Darmstadt and Hamburg he reached Denmark. In Copenhagen he was greeted with thronging crowds. After an address at the University the students reached him at his hotel in a torchlight procession, and stayed on till late hours singing national songs. At Stockholm the members of the Swedish Academy were waiting for him at the station. A huge crowd had collected outside. The annual Folk Festival was going on and he did not like to miss it.

According to the rules of the award, as a Nobel Prize winner Tagore had to address the Swedish Academy. At the end of his address Archbishop Upsala said : "The

Nobel Prize for literature is intended for the writer who combines in himself the artist and the prophet. None has fulfilled these conditions better than Rabindranath." At the Archbishop's request the poet had to visit Upsala and speak at the Cathedral. This was a singular distinction, since while the Archbishop was present in the city no person belonging to another denomination was allowed to speak from the altar.

From Sweden he came to Germany. At the Berlin University scenes of frenzied hero worship marked a public lecture by Rabindranath. In the rush for seats many girls fainted. The police had to restore order. The lecture had to be repeated next day. He had also to speak before Prussian Academy, a society of learned men and intellectuals. After the speech his voice, in Bengali and English, was recorded. The discs were specially processed to last for years. The Academy presented its valuable journals to Visva Bharati.

From Berlin to Munich and then to Darmstadt, at Count Keyserling's school. The Count, once a prince, was now almost penniless. In 1920 he had started a *Schule der weisheit* (School of Wisdom). As a young man Keyserling had visited India (1911) and met the poet in the Jorasanko Mansion. In those days many foreigners used to visit Abanindranath's art collection. Keyserling was deeply attracted to the poet, though they had been barely introduced to each other. He wrote in his *Travel Diary* ; "Rabindranath the poet impressed me like a guest from a higher, more spiritual world. Never perhaps have I seen so much spiritualised substance of soul condensed in one man."

The week he spent at Darmstadt came to be called

'Tagore Woche' or the Tagore Week. People came from neighbouring places to ask questions, some would send questions by post. The poet answered these in the afternoon meetings with the help of an interpreter.

One day he visited the Workmen's Union at Darmstadt. Beer bottles lay open on the table and the room was filled with cigar smoke. The poet had to find a corner in that uninviting atmosphere. But after he had spoken a few words, a change came over the place. The beer jugs and bottles went under the table, the cigars were allowed to burn out, many turned round in their chairs to catch the poet's voice. Tagore counted this meeting as one of his greatest triumphs, as indeed it was.

He was now anxious to return to India. But he could not turn down an invitation from Vienna. Professor Winterniz and his Czech disciple, Professor Lesny, were admirers of the poet and experts in Indology. At their eager request he had to visit Prague.

Now he was tired of being on the move always; letters from home were also far from reassuring. Soon after he had left, Gandhiji had launched his non-cooperation movement. Santiniketan too was no longer peaceful, the political excitement had touched many of the ashramites. In July 1921 the poet returned to India almost in a hurry.

18

Politics vs. Intellectual Achievement

AFTER A LONG time the poet found release in a new world of creation. The past months had been full of activities. From America had started the whirlwind. Returning home he had been entangled in political debate and argument and in further schemes for Visva Bharati. He sometimes feared lest responsibility outdid the spirit of play. The new urge for writing poems was perhaps to get rid, if only for a while, of all sense of adult responsibility. The poems were later included in *Sishu Bholanath* (Child).

Before the autumn holidays a revised version of *Saradotsava Rinashodh* was staged at Santiniketan, Rabindranath appearing in the role of the Sanyasi. It was diversion from the drabness of everyday life. The revised version of *Saradotsava* was rather weak and it was never republished or staged.

Pearson returned during the autumn of 1921. With him came Leonard Elmhirst, to take charge of the rural reconstruction work at Surul. A little later in November, as the institution was about to re-open, came Professor and Madame Sylvain Levi. With Levi the research department of Visva Bharati started with arrangements for the study of Chinese and Tibetan. The same year during the Paus festival December 23, 1921 the poet made a public trust of his institution. So long the entire responsibility had rested with him. And he had, almost single-handed, to provide the finance. This was no longer possible, 184 the Institute was growing too fast. On this day he also made a gift of all his Bengali works published till then along with as all his movable and immovable properties at Santiniketan to the Trustees of Visva Bharati. He also credited the interest from the Nobel Prize award to the institute.

The poet sincerely believed that without an international atmosphere, education for the future would be incomplete. In a letter he wrote; "At Santiniketan the guest house of the new age has been opened, and the coming truth announced." Further: "We must make room for Man, let not the Nation obstruct his path."

Visva Bharati's activities were of course growing in many directions and called for close supervision. After many a misadventure in business his son, Rathindranath, had changed his residence from Calcutta to Santiniketan. Now he took charge of the office of the University; Professor Prasanta Mahalanobis of Presidency College, an ardent devotee of the poet, came forward to help Rathindranath in his administrative duties. For a few years the two together steered it through stormy waters. In Surul, Elmhirst was going ahead with the work of rural reconstruction in and about Bolpur, Kalimohan Ghose was his lieutenant.

Outside Santiniketan, the country was in a ferment. Gandhiji had decided to launch a no-tax campaign in Bardoli, Gujarat. The news reached the poet in the quiet of Santiniketan and he heard other reports as well. In an open letter to a Gujarati litterateur, the poet once more pointed out the dangerous possibilities of applying nonviolence to politics. "Like every other moral principle *ahimsa* has to spring from the depth of the mind and it must not be forced upon men through some outside appeal." Once the mob had been roused to fury against the British, precepts of pious non-violence might not work. True nonviolence is a stiff, psychological discipline and it is not easy to train a mob into its inner laws. The letter was published on February 3, 1922. The next day an infuriated mob, in the name of the Congress, killed some native constables in a police station at Chauri Chaora, in the United Provinces. Two days after the incident the rural reconstruction work began, under the guidance of an Englishman. The money came from America, the field of work was a Bengal village. The East and the West had met at Sriniketan. Outside raged the storm of politics.

So the days passed—Santiniketan, Calcutta and sometime Shelaidah, where he had still to supervise the work of the estate. He had often to go to Calcutta either for work connected with Visva Bharati or to take part in meetings or conferences. But during the hot summer months he stayed back at Santiniketan all alone. The Levis had left for Nepal, Pearson and Elmhirst had gone to the hills. The rains had come and the poet was busy writing songs. After the opening of the school the *Varsha-mangal* (Rain Festival) was celebrated in Calcutta (1922 August). This was the first time that Santiniketan students and a few girls of high society in Calcutta appeared on the public stage of the city. There was naturally some criticism from the orthodox, but not by the audiences, who saw and heard a lovely pageant the like of which they had never seen before and they wanted more.

Visva Bharati's needs were multiplying and there were

no regular funds: "I am moving from place to place, a beggar's bowl in my hand. It will be better to say, hanging round my neck. I am not an expert in this art, nor am I pleased with it. My days are far from happy. In my tired moments, Visva Bharati seems a mirage. An idea is living, but it cannot be preserved in the iron safe of an institution. It is lucky if it finds a place in the hearts of men." From his tours Tagore returned to Santiniketan a little before the Paus festival. This was Visva Bharati's second year. During this short span of time, the Institute had attracted quite a few foreigners—Winterniz, Lesny, Bogdanov, Collins, Stella Kramrisch, Shlomit Flaum. Besides, Andrews and Pearson, at Sriniketan there were Elmhirst, Miss Green and Arthur Geddes. The list will show how Visva Bharati was branching out in different directions. All these Europeans lived with the simplest of furniture and in the plainest of houses. Their salary too was pretty poor. The poet had to provide all this, hence the frequent lecture tours for raising funds. So far as creative work was concerned, it was rather a fallow period.

The summer vacation he spent at Shillong, the hill station and capital of Assam. There he wrote a play, *Yakshapuri,* which was later revised and published as *Kaktakarabi* (Red Oleanders).

Yakshapuri flourishes on goldmining and forced labour recruited from rural areas. Its king like *The King of the Dark Chamber* never appears before the workers; the land is ruled by an unscrupulous head man with whip and occasional use of religious sermons. In this *El Dorado* appears a young girl, Nandini, who charms everybody from the labourer to the king. The king discovers to his dismay that his own officers have exploited his own people shutting him in his lonely palace. He revolts against the tyranny of his own officers. But in the meantime Nandini's love, Ranjan, had been killed for his refusal to be conscripted. Tagore interprets his drama thus: "In Red Oleanders there are certain underlying principles at work, which we can quite easily recognise in our own daily existence. The habit of greed for things, for power, for fact, with all the ramifications the greed is able to set between man and man—is arranged against the explosive force of human sympathy, of neighbourliness, of fellowship and of love, the force which we may term good. Good is here arranged against the dehumanising force of Mammon, of selfishness, of evil. Until Nandini came they had not realised that the times were out of joint."

When he returned to Calcutta he found a new change in Indian politics. Sri C.R. Das, a leading barrister of the Calcutta High Court, had renounced his practice to join the non-cooperation movement. But the negative Gandhian philosophy did not appeal to him. So, along with Motilal Nehru and a few other stalwarts of the Congress, he had formed the Swaraj Party and decided to enter the Legislative Council (which the Congress had boycotted in the last election) and act as opposition to the Government. His party wanted to defeat the Government by a vote of 'no confidence'. Reporters asked Rabindranath for his views. He welcomed the move. It was a sign of life, he said.

Dreaming of Hindu-Muslim unity, at the beginning of the non-cooperation movement, the Congress had joined hands with the Khilafat Movement, in 1920-21. Supporting this mediaeval faith, the leaders had hoped to secure Muslim support for the Congress and, together, trounce the British. But it did not take long for pampered religiosity to turn into gross fanaticism. As expected, differences broke out over almost all issues. There was no open cleavage yet, but cracks were visible. Rabindranath wrote two articles on these, *Samasya* (Problem) and *Samadhan* (Solution). Many years have passed since then, two nations have been born but fanaticism and mixing up religion with politics are still with us.

It was not enough that the Hindus and Mussalmans should unite; Tagore insisted they must be equal. The Hindus have need for solidarity just as much as the Mussalmans have. "It is easier for the Muslims to unite than for the Hindus. The Hindus are vast in number, but weak in action. Merely turning the spinning-wheel will not solve the problem. Even if we get rid of the foreigners, the country will have troubles of its own, as in the past; even a nation State may not bring the end of mutual acrimony and mass suffering. The spinning wheels had whirred two hundred years back, the looms had been busy as ever, but the problems have not ceased. Independence is a noble aim, but to think that it can be achieved through trivial means is not based on reality or on one's strength," he said.

By the end of the autumn holidays, in 1923, the poet went out on another tour of Gujarat. Last time he had been to Porbundur. Now he visited many of the native States. With the substantial help received from the rajas, the foundation of a new Kala Bhavan building was laid at Santiniketan.

In the meantime the Chinese Government had sent an invitation, which he accepted. Before leaving for China he delivered, in fulfilment of an agreement, three lectures at Calcutta University.

China had her period of trouble since the establishment of the Republic in 1912. During a short spell of comparative peace the lecturing committee of Peking had invited intellectuals from abroad. The first year it was John Dewey, the next Bert-rand Russell, now it was Rabindranath. The poet was accompanied by Kshitimohan Sen, Nandalal Basu, Leonard Elmhirst and Miss Green and also Professor Kalidas Nag of Calcutta University.

The party left Calcutta on March 21, 1924 halting at Rangoon, Penang, Kuala-Lampur and other places. From Malaya he wrote, "The country does not belong to the people, but has been divided between the British rubber planters and the owners of the tin mines. The labour is supplied by the Chinese and the Indians, the true Malayan is a stranger in his own land and exists like a parasite." Elmhirst noted the beginnings of a political awakening as yet un-aggressive. This was in 1924. Since then the Far East has been in a turmoil.

From Singapore they took a Japanese liner and reached the Chinese mainland. From Canton Sun-Yat-Sen, the Head of the Chinese Republic of the South, sent an emissary, but the poet could not manage to go to Canton, and the two great men never met, for Sun-Yat-Sen died the next year.

On April 12 the party reached Shanghai, a vast cosmopolitan city. The Japanese, the British and Americans held positions of importance and were quite influential.

In a party held in his honour, he met some of the leading citizens. The seekers of truth in Asia, the poet said, had always offered the message of *maitri* (friendship) for a better, a noble world. Today too Asia was waiting for the same type of thinkers. He appealed to the young men of China to help in bringing together India, China and the other Eastern cultures in a closer bond.

"I have come to ask you to re-open the channel of communication which I hope is still there for, though overgrown with needs of oblivion, its lines can still be traced. I shall consider myself fortunate if, through this visit, China comes nearer to India and India to China—for no political or commercial purposes, but for disinterested human love and for nothing else." Towards the beginning of the century the Japanese thinker, Okakura had given out the formula: 'Asia is one'. Rabindranath brought that message of unity to the doors of China.

From Shanghai they went to Hangchow. The address which he gave after returning to Shanghai, at a meeting of its Japanese residents, contained some sharp criticism of the foreign policy of Japan. He advised them not to imitate the primitive mentality behind imperialism. It was the sure road to ruin. Needless to say, the uncalled for sermon did not please the well-to-do Europeans, nor the young westernised Chinese nationalists. The poet's view was sharply criticised in the papers. The English papers were unsparing too.

However, twenty-five organisations gave him a joint reception on the eve of his departure from Shanghai. Floating down the Yang-Tse he reached Nanking, where he addressed the University on the spirit of the new age and Asia's role in it.

Now the party moved towards Peking. From Shantung it was provided with a special train and bodyguards. When Tagore reached Peking on 13th April there was a large crowd waiting at the station; the streets were strewn with flowers, while every now and then ear-splitting squibs rent the air, in the traditional Chinese style. The foreign correspondents were surprised at the reception.

With great eclat the poet's birthday was celebrated in Peking. Hu-Shir, one of the leading intellectuals, presided over the meeting. Rabindranath was awarded the title *Chu-Chen-Tan* which means Cloud-Rumble-Morning. On the occasion *Chitra,* in Chinese, was staged.

On May 9, Tagore delivered the first of his public lectures at Chew Kwang theatre in which he analysed the great movements which had stirred his native land in recent times. During the next three days he spoke successively on 'The Role of the Giant', 'Civilisation and Progress', 'Satyam' and 'Judgment'.

The strain proved too much, and doctors advised him to go to the Western Hills, a beauty spot of China, for rest-cure. After a week he returned to Peking and delivered his address at a meeting organised by the International Institutre of Religions.

The poet and his party left Peking on May 20, and after visiting a few places of interest, came back to Shanghai from where they left for Japan. Kshitimohan wished to make a closer study of Buddhist culture and stayed on for some time.

This was Rabindranath's third visit to Japan. In a Tokyo meeting he again sharply criticised Japan's militant nationalism. Politicians nowhere and at no time have paid the slightest heed to the voice of the poet or to the still small voice. Nor did the Japanese during the hey-day of their power and glory.

In Japan the poet met the Indian revolutionary, Rashbihari Basu. In 1916 at the time of his escape from British India, Basu had adopted the name of a relative of the poet, P. N. Tagore. The poet knew all about the past history of Basu; but to avoid the British intelligence he saw him alone.

His tour of China and Japan had a strange sequel. Within a few months of his return home, the revolutionaries of many nationalities joined forces and started, at Shanghai, an Asiatic Association. From American newspapers it appears that the organisers had openly stated their indebtedness to the poet's exhortations and inspiration.

The four-month tour of China and Japan over, he returned to Calcutta on July 21, 1924. But he had to leave, again, after two months. The Government of Peru had invited him to attend its hundredth Independence Day celebrations. So from China to Peru. The poet was accompanied by his son, daughter-in-law, and their adopted daughter, Nandini, and a teacher of fine arts, Surendranath Kar. These were going on a tour of Europe. A few days before sailing, the poet had an attack of influenza. He boarded the ship in a state of convalescence, at Colombo, yet on the ship's deck he was writing his diary and poems.

From France he took an Argentine-bound ship. Elmhirst now joined him as his secretary. On board the ship he was busy writing either his diary or the series of poems published in *Purabi.* Within a few days of leaving the port, he had a fresh attack of fever, and had to be confined to bed. But the writings continued. Three weeks went by like this. When he reached Buenos Aires he was quite weak; the doctors advised him against the journey to Peru, which was too distant and difficult. So in the end Peru had to be dropped. The poet was offered a house twenty miles from the city in a rural retreat at *Sanasidro.* He was also given to understand that the Peru festival was really a war memorial, there was nothing very idealistic about it. It is not quite clear whether the British Embassy was not involved in this tutoring. During his 1926 visit to Europe, his Russian tour had been cancelled on grounds of ill health perhaps due to similar tutoring.

From the South American tour Bengali literature gained two books—*Jatri* (The Traveller's Diary) and *Purabi* and the poet a friend, Senora Vittoria (i.e. Victoria) Ocampo. *Purabi* was dedicated to her, where she is mentioned as Vijaya (translation of Vittoria;. The poet did not forget her and in his last illness he would often speak of this remarkable woman:

> The sunlight blazes hot
> This lonely midday;
> At the *empty chair* I glance,
> No trace of consolation is there,
> Filling its heart
> Words of despair seem to rise in lament,
> The voice of emptiness laden with compassion
> Whose inmost meaning cannot be grasped.

On his way back he stopped at Genoa. The rest of the party, the European tour over, joined the poet here. At the time Mussolini held absolute sway over Italy. There was a grand reception at Milan. Professor Formichi, a Sanskrit scholar, acted as the poet's interpreter. Invitations began to pour in from many Italian cities. But the poet was far from well and these had to be turned down. At Venice he boarded a ship for India and reached home after an absence of five months in February 1925.

19

Intrigues and Politics

THE POET STAYED on during the summer months at Santiniketan. Gandhiji, who had come to Calcutta on Congress business, visited him there in May 1925. The discussion, around the ethics of *charkha,* went on for two days; but each remained unconverted to the other's point of view,

He had also to write on the political and pressing problem of *Swaraj.* His two essays, *Charkha* (The Spinning Wheel) and *Swarajsadhan* (The Striving for Swaraj) have stood the test of time. Tagore was a realist and he said that *charkha* could never bring political salvation of India, for, after all, even before the advent of the Britishers, *charkha* was not unknown. In *Swarajsadhan* Rabindranath had championed the neutrality of the State towards the religious problem.

Towards the end of 1925 the Italian professor Carlo Formichi came to the Visva Bharati as a Visiting Professor. He was accompanied by young Giusepe Tucci, who was later to become a great Tibetologist. They carried with them a gift of valuable Italian books from Mussolini. Tucci's salary was paid by the Italian Government, the poet felt that his school was becoming a real international institution, but was unable to understand the motive behind the Italian overture. For reasons of his own Mussolini was eager to procure certificates of good conduct from respectable people from all countries. One from Tagore would be welcome. These calculated gestures were meant to cajole the Indian poet, who hardly knew what was happening in Italy and why.

Formichi acted his part well and played up Mussolini's great love of India. The poet,, happy at the gift of books and with Professor Tucci, was taken in and sent a telegram to Mussolini thanking him.

Three days after Formichi's arrival, the Governor of Bengal, Lord Lytton, on his way to a Durbar at Suri, stopped at Santiniketen for a few hours. The heat of non-cooperation had not yet cooled down, and the Governor's visit to Santi-niketan at such a time gave rise to a good deal of speculation. The ill-informed newspaper correspondents probably did not know that the poet had no hand in the matter and could not well say "no" to a visitor, especially the Governor of the Province.

The first All-India Philosophy Congress was being

held in Calcutta on December 19, 1925. The Conference had elected Rabindranath its President. Rabindranath was of course never a philosopher. Yet there must have been some ground for this choice. A few years ago a teacher of philosophy, S. Radhakrishnan, had written a book on *The Philosophy of Rabindranath Tagore* which seemed to imply that Tagore had a philosophy of his own or at least a point of view. In his address Tagore drew the attention of the educated classes to the philosophy of the people, a neglected aspect of folk culture. This was characteristic. No one else would have thought of it.

Lucknow had sent an invitation to the poet for the All-India Music Conference. He was staying at an old palace when news reached him of the death of his eldest brother, Dwijendranath on January 18, 1926. He had to return in a hurry. Dwijendranath's eldest son, Dwipendranath an early resident of Santiniketan, had died a few years earlier. The poet had to look after the affairs of the family and attend to other social duties.

In the meantime Dacca University had requested him and the two Italian professors to deliver some lectures there. The poet was accompanied by some of Santiniketan teachers, as he wished to tour some places in East Bengal which he had not seen for long. A royal reception awaited him at Dacca, where he put up in a houseboat. This was his first visit to East Bengal after the award of the Nobel Prize and his last to Dacca.

The East Bengal tour over, the poet came back to Calcutta in a very happy mood; but a rude shock awaited him. The political situation was fast deteriorating. It was evident that the *Khilafat*—a buttressed love of Hindus and

Mussalmans was not going to last. In April 1926 there was a sudden clash between the two communities. It began with the playing of music before mosque by some Arya Samajists. Paradoxically, ever since Gandhiji's support to the Khilafat, both Hindus and Mussalmans had become more fanatical. To ensure the purity of Islam it had become necessary for the Muslim population to stop, at all costs, music or singing before and near the mosque premises; for the same reason the Hindus found it doubly necessary to be musical, especially in front of mosques. The Government, to suit its own ends, set the two communities by the ear and in cosy corners of exclusive clubs Englishmen laughed over the whole affair.

The poet was staying at the Jorasanko Mansion and saw poor, fear-ridden Muslim families seek shelter in his ancestral house. Embittered, he wrote in a letter, "Frank atheism is much better than this illusive religious fanaticism. .. .If India after making a bonfire of her religiosity can acquire a true religion, even genuine atheism, then she will be truly re-born." A few days later in the poem *Dharma Moha* (Religious Illusion) he wrote :

> He whom falsity captures in the guise of a religion
> That blind man he either kills others or gets killed
> Even the atheist receives the blessings of the Lord
> He makes no show of being religious.

From Calcutta he came back to Santiniketan, where the year ending and New Year's Day were duly observed. On coming to know that the residents of the ashrama were planning to produce a pantomime based on the poem

'Pujarini', he wrote out a playlet, *Natir Puja* (The Worship of the Dancing Girl). This was put on boards on the birthday evening at Santiniketan; Gauri, Nandalal Basu's daughter, appeared in the role of the *prima donna.* This was later staged in Calcutta. Gaud's superb performance won the admiration of the Calcutta connoisseurs, never an easy thing. The educated public could now feel that even the nobler emotions of life could be expressed through dance, which need not be a monopoly of demimondes and professionals As a result, dancing has become popular even in middle-class homes.

At the end of his tour of East Bengal the poet had once again started composing songs. The songs of *Natir Puja* belong to that late afflatus; others under the general title *Vaikali* (Afternoon Melodies), were serially published in *Prabasi* (1926).

20

Europe Again

THE BIRTHDAY CELEBRATIONS over, the poet again went out to Europe, but really it was to Italy. Professor Formichi, after his return, had sent a pressing invitation. But actually it was Mussolini who was playing host. The official invitation came informally and indirectly, and partly due to his passion for travel, partly cajoled by others, he decided to go. Many were surprised and annoyed at rinding the poet accept an invitation from a fascist government.

In all he spent a fortnight in Italy. At his request Benedetto Croce, who had been removed from the University, was brought from Naples to meet him. From Rome via Florence, where he was honoured by the Leonardo da Vinci Society, he reached Turin. From Turin the poet reached Switzerland, going upto Villueneuve, a small village where lived Romain Rolland. It had become a place of pilgrimage for intellectuals. The poet put up in a hotel, in the same room, it is said, in which Victor Hugo had spent some time. Rolland's cottage was a little way off. Rolland had been shocked at the poet's pro-fascist statements in praise of Mussolini. He, however, understood that Rabindranath could not have known the actual situation in Italy. But Rolland showed him coloured reports of his statements, torn from their context, published in the Italian press. The poet was left uneasy, but did not publish any disclaimer at the time. When, after about twelve days he came to Zurich he met some of the victims of Mussolini's fury. The first-hand account of fascist atrocities shocked the poet. At last he was roused.

Once disillusioned about Mussolini, he wanted to undo the wrong. From Vienna, he sent a letter to Andrews in which he expressed his considered views about Italy and Mussolini. This was published in the *Manchester Guardian.* Reading it, Mussolini and his aides were furious and at once began a tireless tirade. It was lucky for the poet that he "was able to get the fact from Rolland and express his disclaimer in time. But already some harm had been done.

Moving through Zurich, Vienna and Paris he reached England. From London he drove straight to Totnes, where the previous year the Elmhirsts had started a school. As Elmhirst writes: "It is some of these same principles that, learnt from the poet, we have been trying out in Devonshire, Darlington Hall, since 1925." From London he left for Central Europe. This was his second visit to the region. With him were Prasantachandra (P.C. Mahalanobis) and his wife, Rani Devi. Rathindranath had been taken ill, and had to stay back. The brunt of the tour fell on the Mahalanobis couple. Mrs. Mahalanobis however managed ably.

Tagore visited Norway which he had missed during his last short trip to Scandinavia. Through Professor Sten Konow who had been a Visiting Professor at Visva Bharati during 1924-25 the poet had come to know Norway more intimately. Professor Konow was keen on getting him there. The poet himself was no less eager. To him it was the land of Ibsen, one of his favourites and even, perhaps, an early influence.

Spending a few days in Sweden and Denmark, the poet once again turned towards Central Europe. Strangely, as he was travelling from place to place, after a blank of four months to him there was a harvest of songs. The first was written during the Baltic crossing:

> Do not call him to thy house, the dreamer,
>   who walks alone by thy path in the night.
> His words are those of a strange land,

and strange is the melody
played by him on his one-stringed lute.
There is no need for thee to spread
a seat for him;
he will depart before day-break.
For in the feast of freedom
he is asked to sing
the praise of the new-born light.

It might as well have been written on the banks of the Padma or the fields of Santiniketan.

Hamburg, Berlin, Munich, Nuremberg, Stuttgart, Dusseldorf, he passed through all as in a pageants Addresses, interviews, continued as before, and yet the songs came. But there were personal worries. Following a serious operation, Rathindranath was lying in a nursing home in Berlin. The poet looked him up and finding him much better left for Czechoslovakia. He stayed at Prague for five days, and received much help from Professor Winternitz and Lesny, both of whom had spent happy months at Santiniketan.

Moving through bankrupt Austria, the poet reached Vienna, once the proud capital of the Austrian Empire. But he had reached the end of his physical endurance. At last the breakdown came and when he reached Hungary, he was forced to take rent in a sanatorium by Lake Balaton. At the request of the people, the poet planted a sapling by the lake, which survives to this day. He wrote a poem for the occasion which was afterwards inscribed in stone near the plant:

When I am no longer on this earth, my tree,
Let the ever-renewed leaves of thy spring
Murmur to the wayfarers,
'The poet did love while he lived.'

At Balaton there were no pressing engagements and, at the insistence of Prasantachandra, he agreed to edit two books of epigrams, *Lekhan* and *Vaikali,* to be printed in facsimile. The first was published during his lifetime, a few copies of the second were printed some years after the poet had passed away.

As soon as he was a little better he left for Yugoslavia, where, at the Belgrade University, he gave two addresses. After a lecture at Sofia, he reached Bucharest where he spent five days. Thanks to lavish hospitality, programmes and dinner parties by artists and intellectuals, there was hardly a moment to call his own.

From Bucharest he took ship at a small Port on the Black Sea. The ship stopped for two days at Istanbul. The University and other institutions sent invitations, but he was too tired to stir out. His companions went on a sight-seeing tour of the city. The poet stayed back. From the Greek port of Piraeus he paid a flying visit to Athens. The Greek Government conferred on him a title of honour. The last song of this period was written at Piraeus on 26 November. At Athens, Professor and Mrs. Mahalanobis parted company from him. They would make a longer tour of Europe. On his way back the poet stopped at Alexandria, from where he drove to Cairo. At one of the receptions, there was a programme of Egyptian music. To the poet the music of Arabia and Persia seemed to present some similarities with the modes of Indian music. He also paid a visit to Cairo's famous museum. King Fuad presented some precious Arabic works to the Visva Bharati library.

The poet returned to Santiniketan on December 18,

1926 on the eve of the Paus festival. He found India torn with debate and dissension. The hope of Hindu-Muslim unity had proved to be a mirage. The dream of 1921 had faded. The Congress was meeting at Gauhati during Christmas; all the leaders were there. Just then Swami Shraddhananda was shot dead by a Muslim in Delhi. Five years earlier in the same city in the Hindu-Muslim unity festival, Shraddhananda had addressed the public from the courtyard of Jumma Masjid. Now his blood stained the roads of Delhi. Such was politics, mightier than religion. A few days before, while the poet had been away, Shraddhananda had paid a short visit to Santiniketan, and endeared himself to the inmates. So they felt the shock all the more 3ceenly.

21

The Brotherhood of Man

EVER SINCE HIS return from china the poet had often played with the idea of renewing India's lost contacts with Greater India, Malaya, Indonesia and Indo-China. He felt that in order to write a true history of Indian culture and its influence abroad, it was necessary to collect data in which these regions abounded. In the old days all these places had been touched by the Hindu and Buddhist faiths. To this day, the area from Burma to Cambodia believes in Buddhism. As researches were being carried out in his institution regarding the relation between China, Tibet and India, he wished to open up similar projects about Greater India. In his eagerness to see these lands and know their cultures, the poet himself travelled to Malaya, Java and Bali. As in the case of the China tour, the Birlas agreed to bear the expenses of the poet and his companions.

There were six of them in the party, including Professor and Mrs. Bake, a Dutch couple, studying Rabindra and oriental music at Santiniketan; the artist Surendranath Kar and his student, Dhirendra Krishna Dev Burman. Ariam Williams (afterwards Aryanayakam) a Sinhalese-Tamil, then a teacher at Santiniketan, had left for Malaya earlier to prepare for the tour. Dr. Suniti Kumar Chatto-padhyaya (i.e. Dr. S. K. Chatterji, who is now a National Professor) who represented the University of Calcutta, was also with the party. Suniti Kumar has left a vivid account of the tour in his interesting *work,Dwipamaya Bharat.*

The poet spent nearly a week at Singapore. It was an endless round of addresses, interviews, invitations and sightseeing. The Indian settlers in Singapore belonged mostly to the working classes. On hearing that a universally respected Indian had come, they all wanted to have a 'darshan'.

From Singapore to the States of Malaya. Most of the people of the peninsula were Muslims, and the area had long been parcelled into a number of small sultanates, all under British control. The real rulers were the British owners of the rubber plantations and in mines. The Indians, Chinese and Malayans were mostly labourers of the plantations and the mines and a handful of clerks at the offices.

The Malayan tour lasted for twenty-six days, in the midst of this crowded programme he was writing a series of letters in one of which he said: "I am dead beat. There are two or three types of programmes in the course of a day. Lectures and invitations at new and strange places, long journeys and little rest; earning a little money and then getting rid of the hard-earned dollars, moving from hotel to hotel, so goes my travel, an exercise for both feet and throat."

The owners of the rubber plantations and tin mines had so far looked upon India as a recruiting ground for cheap 'coolie' labour. That somebody from that land should receive such honour did not please them, and on the sly they started a campaign of calumny. A young South Indian journalist took up the challenge and pricked the bubble: by quoting the original passages he proved how the English papers were garbling the poet's ideas. This silenced everybody and there was no further trouble. The better class of Britishers were ashamed of the conduct of their countrymen and they wrote to the poet letters of apology and appreciation.

From Malaya he left for Bali by way of Java. The Hindu culture and religion at one time had pervaded the entire Eastern Archipelago. Now it was confined to Bali, but beyond recognition. The poet was thinking how best to revive the broken contact. Like his visit to China, the trip to the eastern islands revealed him in the role of a pioneer. From Bali the poet and his party reached fava. Earlier he had broken journey at Batavia (Jakarta); this time he proposed to see the country more closely.

After three weeks in Java, towards the end of September, the poet and the party left for Siam. On board the ship he wrote the well-known poem, *Sagarika,* a beautiful allegory on the ancient bonds between India and the eastern islands, and the poet's keen desire to revive these. In Siam (Thailand) they stayed at Bangkok and were received with courtesy by the king and his family.

Most of the poems written during the journey were included in *Parisesh* (Final), which the poet thought was going to be his last poetic harvest. In this he was mistaken.

Tagore reached Calcutta by the end of October 1927, after an absence of three and a half months.

A direct result of the Java tour was the introduction of 'Batik', an indigenous method of printing cloth. This was first introduced in Kala Bhavan, from where it has now spread nearly throughout the world.

The poet's time was divided between Calcutta and Santiniketan. He was then writing *Yogayog.* In this novel the readers had expected hirn to continue the story of three generations. This had been his own idea too. But he was getting on in years. He had hoped to complete the cycle of the Kumu-dini-Madhusudan tangle, but the leisure for it never came. It is also possible that the heartrending episode he had called up was proving too much for the ageing poet to bear and continue. But *Yogayog* in its present recension is a work of art sufficiently complete in itself.

Talks of a visit to England were again in the air. The Oxford University had invited him to deliver the Hibbert Lectures. Fifty years before a Western scholar (Max Mueller) had initiated these lectures with his essays on 'The Religion of India.' Now for the first time an Indian poet and thinker was invited to speak on the 'Religion of Man.'

He wished to board the ship from Madras. Aryanayakam was going with him. Professor and Mrs. Mahalanobis too were on their way to Europe and they also joined him. But *en route* the poet's health suddenly broke down. In the end it was decided to postpone the English tour.

In 1928 the poet's son, Rathindranath and his wife went to Europe and for a while he was left alone. For some time he put up with Mukul De, the new Principal of the Calcutta Art School. It was a spacious house on Chowringhee where he was well looked after. In the evening would gather some of his young friends and admirers. They would often ask him for an anthology of his love poems, to be used as a presentation at weddings. Rummaging through his old poems, he felt, like adding a few more: the result was *Mahua.* At sixty-eight one could not of course expect the warmth, colour and immediacy of his earlier verse, such as *Kadi O Kamal* and *Manasi.* Yet these new poems had a sense of maturity and fullness not to be found in his more youthful verse.

In Europe the World War had ended some ten years earlier; peace treaties were concluded among nations; but still there was no peace. Secretly or openly every nation was forging newer weapons of destruction. The intellectuals of Europe were worried over the future of the world and had sent an appeal for peace. For the *Golden Book of Peace,* the poet wrote : "In our political ritualism, we still worship the tribal god of our own make and try to appease it with human blood. This fetishism is blindly primitive and angers truth that leads to death-dealing conflicts. To many of us it seems that this blood-stained idolatry is a permanent part of human nature....Let us, today, by the strength of our own faith prove that the homicidal orgies of cannibalistic politics are doomed, in spite of contradictions that seem overwhelmingly formidable."

Back at Santiniketan, the poet had his regular office work to attend to. The Visva Bharati Executive Council had now appointed a Committee for Reconstruction. The institution itself was facing one of its periodical financial crises. So the days went. A life of routine was beginning to pall. An invitation from the National Council of Education in Canada brought the longed for release. The Council used to meet once every three years and discuss educational problems. Rabindranath was asked to speak on 'Education and Leisure', a topic which suited him. This was the first recognition abroad of his work as an educationist. Later, in 1930, Professsor Findlay, of England, dedicated his *Foundations of Education* to Rabindranath.

When he reached Canada, he found Andrews had also managed to be there after his tour of the States. The poet stayed in Canada for ten days. Apart from his talk on the 'Philosophy of Leisure' he had also to speak, naturally, on literature. He met the Governor, Willingdon, who later came to India as Viceroy.

22

A Litterateur's Routine

THE POET RETURNED from Canada in mid-July 1927. But the rain-swept plains of Santiniketan brought him no new message. A strange loneliness was gnawing at his heart. Was he ageing ? He was nearing seventy. A new diversion of strange forms and colours began to fill his leisure hours. This was painting, a new love or 'new mistress', as he called it. But he was ill at ease since for the time he was not able to create anything in literature.

News reached that in Calcutta some young people of the Jorasanko Mansion were thinking of staging his old play, *Raja O Rani.* Tagore had been critical about this, his first drama, and always thought it rather melodramatic and immature. Now that he had a chance, he at once started to rewrite it. The changed version in prose, was no longer *Raja O Rani* but something new, *Tapati.* It was staged at Jorasanko for four nights. Rabindranath himself appeared (at sixty-nine) in the role of King Vikram. The choreography was distinctive, and painted scenes had been dispensed with. The backdrop in realistic theatre he always considered a childish device.

During his stay in Japan the poet had invited a jiu-jutsu or judo expert to come to Visva BharatL He very much wanted the children, especially the girls, to acquire this simple, graceful and effective art of self-defeiice. His own people, however, did not seem to take to it; even the authorities of his school failed to make any permanent provision for the scheme. Had the poet's suggestion been accepted by his countrymen, some at least of the outrages of 1946-47 and after might not have taken place. But who would listen to a poet recommending the Japanese art of self-defence ?

From 1925 Sayaji Rao, the Gaikwad of Baroda had been contributing substantially to Visva Bharati. The Gaikwad who often lived abroad, had returned to India for a while, and he wished to receive the poet at his capital. An invitation for a lecture was duly sent. Somehow the poet did not like the idea. "I have been asked to deliver a lecture at Baroda. I am bound to His Highness' Court by chains of silver. For the sake of Visva Bharati I have staked my all. . . .1 don't like it at all." Yet he had to go.

In 1930 the poet visited Europe for the last time In early March he left for England, accompanied by his son, daughter-in-law and their adopted daughter. This time Ariam acted as his secetary. His son Rathindranath's health suddenly broke down at the last moment and a doctor had to be included in the party. So, with this rather large retinue he left for England.

His destination was Oxford, where he had to deliver the Hibbert Lectures. The invitation had also come earlier, in 1928 but because of illness he could not fulfil the engagement. This time another motive behind the visit was the exhibition of his paintings of the last few years. Original in temper and technique, these had affinities with the European *avant garde,* but there could hardly have been any conscious affiliation or imitation. The poet was, however, eager to know the response of the European art-world.

Rabindranath's paintings have been commented upon variously. All that we shall permit ourselves is that they have a uniqueness and genuineness that cannot be ignored. Disturbing, they will compel even a master to pause. Rabindranath somehow felt that these pictures had to receive the imprimatur of Western connoisseurs first. There had been no exhibition of his pictures in India, and he went straight to Paris, the Mecca of artists. "My last creations I shall leave here," he wrote in a letter from Europe. The poet was a guest of M. Kahn and stayed in a small town near Monte Carlo. The other members of his party went to Switzerland for a change.

From Paris he went to England on May 11, 1930. This time he did not stay in London but went straight to Woodbrooke, a suburb of Birmingham and a Quaker establishment. At the time his former secretary, Amiya Chakravarty, and his wife were staying there. He was sure to get much help from Amiya in the matter of writing and correspondence.

At Woodbrooke the poet was requested to address the Annual Meeting of the Quakers. He spoke of India's hopes and aspirations and the situation in the country. This was followed by a lively debate, as is the custom in such meetings of the Quakers. In the end the poet spoke plainly and asked his audience to judge India only after answering what they would have done had they been in her place. The Indians wanted to serve their own country and sought England's help.

The Hibbert Lectures were read out in May. His theme was the 'Religion of Man'. At the end Sir Michael

Sadler said: "We shall never forget in Oxford the gift you have given us and the inspiration you have brought to us."

From England he arrived in Berlin where he met the Chancellor of the German Reich, Dr. Branting and other members of the cabinet at the Reichstag on July 12,1930. A few days later he met Professor Einstein. This was probably the outstanding intellectual event of the whole tour. There was later another meeting in America between the poet and the scientist.

An exhibition of his paintings was held at Gallery Moller. This was possible largely because of the efforts of Dr. Miss Silig of Berlin. From Berlin he came to Munich where he was taken to the Planetarium and Deutsches Museum. But what impressed him most was the passion play at Oberam-mergau.

Sometime before a cinema director had requested him to write something for the screen. He wrote *The Child* which shows the distinct influence of the Passion Play. This was written in English perhaps his only work of its kind. On his return to India he wrote another version, in Bengali, *Sishutirtha.* In the quest for truth the sceptical men lose faith, at last an unruly mob kills the leader:

> They ask each other in bewilderment,
>   'who will show us the path ?'
> The old man from the East bends his head
>   and says: 'The Victim '!
> 'We refused him in doubt, we killed him in anger
>   now we shall accept him in love'
> for in his death he lives in the life of us all,
>   the great Victim.

The soul of the dead leader guides them from above. After a long and difficult trek they reach a hut where sits the mother with the child on her lap. Here is the object of their age-long search : He who is of old, of today, forever, the Newly-Born, a rather pastoral version of the Incarnation, but impressive.

Amiya Chakravarty who was with Tagore during his tour of Germany wrote: '-We are moving through Germany like an Emperor. All that are good and great in this country are coming to us unbidded. I cannot think Rabindranath is held in greater esteem anywhere else."

From Elsinore by way of Copenhagen he came back to Berlin where Andrews joined him. The party reached Geneva in the middle of August 1930. Geneva was then the headquarters of the League of Nations. During its inception he had described it, rather unkindly, as a 'league of robbers'. At Geneva the Russian tour was finalised. He had wanted to visit that country earlier in 1926 but due to some difficulties this had to be postponed. This time he was determined, and it was not easy to stop him. With Amiya Chakravarty, Dr. Harry Timbers and Ariam in the entourage, the poet left for Moscow in September, 1930. Miss Einstein and Saumyendra-nath Tagore had joined the party from Germany.

At Moscow he was welcomed by Professor Petrov, the President of Cultural Relations. The same evening the writers and artists arranged for a concert in honour of the poet. Here he was introduced to Professor Kogan, President of the Soviet Arts Academy, Professor Pinkevitch, of the Moscow University (II), Madame Litvinov, Vera Inber, the novelist Feodor Gladkov, etc. A few days later he visited a Pioneer Commune where he met the young members. At their request he sang to them his 'Janaganamana'. He also naturally visited collective farms. The curiosity of the Russian peasantry came to him as a pleasant surprise.

An exhibition of his paintings was held in the Moscow State Museum. The Curator of the Art Gallery, Professor Kristi, in his welcome speech said: "It is with special pleasure that we have arranged an exhibition of his works in order to acquaint our intellectuals and our working masses with them—the more we acquaint ourselves with his paintings the more we are struck. We consider these works to be a great manifestation or artistic life and his skill will be, like all high technical achievements, of the greatest use to our country."

His last public address was given on September 24 at the Central Office of the Trade Union. A Soviet poet read a poem addressed to Rabindranath. Goal Perin recited the Russian translation of his poems, while the actor Simonov read out portions from a translation of *Post Office.* Next day he returned to Berlin.

Moscow was a new experience. In a letter written on the way to America he said: "The Russian experience has provided me with much food for thought. I have been able to see clearly how the spirit of accumulation may run counter to man's inherent self-respect." More plainly he wrote: "We have to forget ourselves completely, a greater challenge has presented itself before us." Like Tolstoy, he too was thinking of sparing the poor peasants from supporting him and paying his expenses. "I have thought of this even before. I had often hoped that our property might turn into a people's property and we might act like trustees. But the wheels of the *zamindari* did not take that road." In another letter: "There will be many reversals in the history of our land. In that period of transition all have to suffer, it is idle to suppose that one can avoid the crisis and live at ease." Yet the poet could not give shape to his true faith, there were a thousand and one obstacles within and without.

But *Letters from Russia* was not in the least an uncritical hallelujah. The letters reveal a number of facts carefully collected, as well as close and mature thinking. Even before these were collected in the volume, *Letters from Russia,* in a concluding essay he had analysed the ultimate meaning of individuality and the dangers of dictatorship. Only by reading these letters along with this summing up can one get his total view on the Russian experiment. It is neither an eulogy nor an attack, but a sensitive appraisal.

The Soviet tour over, the poet came to the United States with Ariam and Timbers. Andrews had been sent earlier to prepare the ground for fund-raising. But the depression had set in and charities had to wait. The poet stayed in New York for six weeks in the hope of an interview with Rockefeller. Friends later advised discretion. The times were bad, later on, may be. .. . There was however no end of engagements. A grand dinner was arranged at Baltimore Hotel; five hundred guests welcomed the poet. But who were these men ? As *The Saturday Review* pointed out, in the list of those present the names of business tycoons figured frequently, but there was not one single poet in the crowd, not even a literary figure. The British Ambassador paid courtesy visits and even introduced him to President

Hoover. Butlectures were not on the bill, lest he said anything in favour of Russia or against the British atrocities in India.

An exhibition of his paintings was held in New York City. Ananda Coomarswamy wrote a brief, competent introduction to the booklet published on the occasion. As a fund-raising campaign the American tour had been a complete failure. After three months in the States the poet returned to England by the end of December.

The Round Table Conference was meeting in London. The attempt was to arrive at an all-party agreement over the promised new Constitution for India. Gandhiji had been requested to join the conference, but he could not agree to the conditions imposed by the Secretary of State for India. As a result the Congress view was not represented at all. The poet wrote: "I believe it would have been worthy of Mahatma Gandhi if he could have accepted unhesitatingly the seat offered to him, even though the conditions were not fully acceptable to him. I feel sad that such an opportunity has been lost for the moment, for India and for all the world, for today is the age of co-operation." Afterwards Gandhiji did change his mind and a year later he joined the second Round Table Conference.

The poet came back to India early in 1931. To Europe he had brought his plea and exegesis of the 'Religion of Man'; while the Continent now knew him not merely as a poet but als o as a powerful and significant artist and an original thinker in the sphere of education. The Russian visit had given him new ideas. Inspired by the Russian example, he even dreamt of co-operatives at Santiniketan and of a collective life on the Russian model. But in this he received little or no response from his people and the dream of a commune soon faded.

The poet now stepped into his seventieth year. This was marked by a simple birthday function. In his address the poet said: "I am a poet, nothing but a poet. I am not a metaphysician, theologian, a religious preceptor or a leader of men. I am but the messenger of the *Many."* In a letter he put it more clearly: "I am engaged in diverse activities, I am eager to express myself differently, in varied ways. People feel an inconsistency in all this. I do not. They say that I sing, I write, I paint, I teach, that I gather delight from the plants and trees, the sky and the world of light, from land and water . . . .1 am by nature a believer in totality. I accept the whole . . . .1 believe that gliding through all things my soul can achieve its fulfilment, receive the touch of truth."

After the birthday festival he paid a short visit to Darjeeling. But the cold hillside did not cool the fever of his mind. India was passing through a trying time. The talk of a new administrative setup was in the air, and everyone believed 'something would turn up'.

23

Trying Times

THE POET KNEW that when the British Government transferred power to the Indians, the period of transition would be a trying time. In that last hour the Government would find it necessary to stamp this idea on the Indian people and the world outside that the moment British control was withdrawn, the country would fall a prey to anarchy, that the Indians were unfit to govern themselves. They would also naturally wish to secure an admission from our own people or some of them, that the British regime was an acceptable state of affairs. During that terrible transition mutual hatred would be fanned to fury. How right he was.

Gandhiji had gone to England in October 1931 to attend the Second Round Table Conference, as the sole spokesman of the National Congress. The attempt to arrive at a common solution acceptable to the different sections of Indians had failed. At last, he had come back to India, disappointed, empty-handed.

Lord Willingdon had taken over as the new Viceroy. A former Governor of Madras and Bombay, he was well acquainted with the weaknesses of the Indian people and an expert in the policy of divide and rule. The civil disobedience movement had been called off after a gentleman's agreement between the former Viceroy, Lord Irwin and Gandhiji. On returning to India, Gandhiji heard about violations of that agreement on the part of the Government officials. On the other hand the pro-Government circles were openly blaming the Congress for the trouble in the country. Gandhiji sent a request to Lord Willingdon for further negotiation. The Viceroy's curt 'no' was a clear indication of the change in policy and within seven days of landing at Bombay he was put under arrest on January 4, 1932.

He was detained in the Yarveda Jail, Poona. Within a few days most of the Indian leaders found themselves in prisons all over the country. In fact, India became a vast prison house. In a statement to the Press Rabindranath protested against these measures. He also sent a cable to the British Prime Minister, Ramsay Macdonald: "The sensational policy of indiscriminate repression being followed by the Indian Government starting with the imprisonment of Mahatmaji, is most unfortunate in causing permanent alienation of our people; you are making it extremely difficult for us to co-operate with your representations for peaceful adjustment."

The birthday celebration of the poet in Calcutta was over, the agony and excitement over Gandhiji's imprisonment had passed. The poet wanted to be away for sometime from the city. He moved to Khardah, a suburb of Calcutta, situated on the Ganga and lived quietly in a rented house. His mind was taken up with entirely different issues. Of course he was writing poems, but poems with a difference. Many years before at the time of publishing an anthology of his verse *Chayanika* he had a few illustrations of his poems done by the young artist Nandlal Bose. Now himself turned an artist he was writing poems on his own and other people's pictures. This bunch of poems were printed along with the supporting pictures in *Bichitra,* dedicated to Nandalal on his fiftieth birthday in 1939.

He returned to Santiniketan towards the beginning of February 1932. In his address on the tenth Sriniketan anniversary he reminded his countrymen to patronise 'swadeshi' (home-made) goods, even if this meant some inconvenience; for, he said, this was a good way of knowing the country as one's own.

But he himself had to go out at short notice. An invitation came from the Shahenshah Rezashah Pehlavi of Persia, for a visit to his country. It was too good to be declined. New lands, new people always attracted him. But how to go *to* Persia ? Various alternatives were suggested. There was even a proposal to take him by plane. But would he stand the strain of a flight ? A test flight was arranged, with the poet, the Dutch Consul-General and his wife in the plane. He stood it well. A public reception was held in the mausoleum garden. A huge crowd had turned up. The police force proved quite inadequate and the army had to be called out. Tagore spent some time at Hafiz's grave, and his mind went back to his boyhood days. He distinctly remembered how his father used to recite to him quatrains of Hafiz.

He spent a week at Shiraz, enjoying to the full the delicacy of Persia. On their way to Isfahan the group had to pass by the ruins of Persepolis, the ancient capital of Persia. As it was not possible for the old poet to go round the ruins, Dr. Hartzfelt the German archaeologist, had made a special collection of *objects d'art* to be shown to Rabindranath . . . . In Isfahan the party spent six days and the poet utilised the opportunity to look closely at examples of early Islamic monuments.

Two weeks after reaching Bushire the poet and liis party arrived at Teheran. The journey could have been quicker. But his health might not have stood a quicker journey across the bad roads in the Persia of 1932.

During the two weeks that the party stayed in Teheran there were no less than eighteen functions. The King, Reza Shah Pehlavi, granted him an audience. The poet's birthday was celebrated, an all-day affair in the royal gardens. Deeply touched, Tagore wrote a poem addressing Iran:

> Iran, all the roses in your garden and all the birds have acclaimed the birthday of the poet of a far away shore and mingled their voices in paean of rejoicing.
>
> Iran, your brave sons have brought their priceless gifts of friendship on this birthday of the poet of a far away shore, for they have known him in their hearts as their own.
>
> Iran, crowned with a new glory by the honour from your hand, this birthday of the poet of a far away shore finds its fulfilment.

In the meantime the Iraqi Ambassador brought him an invitation from the king for a visit to his country. He left Teheran for Iraq by car. The route passed by steep hills, whereon were inscribed the Achamanean Darius' Behustan edicts. A little way off were the Sassanian sculptured mausoleums on the hills of Takibustan. The poet had a glance at all these. He was not unfamiliar with the history of Persia, and had no difficulty in following what was shown to him.

The borders of Iraq were still a long way off and he had to spend a night at Kermmensha. Next day from the Iraq border he took a train to Baghdad, the capital. A crowd had collected at the station to have a glimpse of the Indian poet. He was put up at one of the hotels in the city, and later met King Faizal. The King's simple, unostentatious manners made a very favourable impression on the poet.

At Baghdad there were the usual receptions. But the culture of the cities did not satisfy the poet for long and he expressed a desire to meet the Bedouin chiefs in their desert camps. In his excited youth had he not written: 'I wish I had been an Arab Bedouin.'

The Bedouins treated him to lunch in their desert tents and demonstrated their weird, manly, traditional dances. The Bedouin chiefs seemed to be well posted about international affairs and told the poet that the differences between the Hindus and the Muslims in India were a creation of the educated minority. Sometime before, a few Mussalmans from India on their way to the London Conference had come to Baghdad and tried to poison people's minds. The chiefs had refused to accept their invitation.

From Baghdad the poet and Pratima Devi returned to India by a Dutch plane. His companions, Amiya and Kedarnath, stayed back.

Returning from Iran and Iraq, the poet heard the disquieting news that his only grandson (youngest daughter's son), Nitu, was lying seriously ill in Germany. A few years before he had been sent there, with high hopes, to learn printing technology. Tagore at once sent his daughter, Mira Devi, to Germany. News was received that the boy had passed away on August 7. How this affected the old grandfather is difficult to guess. He had always ignored personal sorrows or kept them behind an impenetrable screen. In a poem he however wrote:

> In the days of my sorrows, I tell my poems—do not shame me.
> Do not exhibit before all men the sorrow that is not everyone's.
> Do not hide your face in the dark, nor bolt your doors.
> This is a great world...
> not mine alone,
> It is for the countless many...
> Do not shame me before all folks,
> before them my loss and pain are like a tiny-drop.

He spent some time with Professor Mahala-nobis and his wife at their retreat at Baranagore, near Calcutta. There was no end of worries; his finances were in a bad way and he was forced to accept the professorship of Bengali at the University of Calcutta where he was also invited to deliver the Kamala Lectures. Before he joined, the Syndicate arranged a reception for the poet on August 6.

Coming back to Santiniketan he started a new experiment in technique, prose-poems. He had thought that *Parishesh,* the last collection of his poems, would be what the title indicated, the end of his poetic career. But soon something new came up, *Punascha* (Post-script) experiments in *vers libre.*

The country was agog with politics, the irrational communal and class differences were raging. The Hindus, the Muslims, the Sikhs and the depressed classes (as the scheduled castes and tribes were then called) were all in the fray. The Congress workers were in prison. Suddenly news came from Poona that Gandhiji had undertaken a fast unto death.

The reasons behind Gandhiji's fast have to be explained briefly. Within a week of his landing in India, Gandhiji had been arrested on 4 January, 1932 and kept a prisoner for nearly nine months. The differences between the Hindus and the Muslims had been used by the British Premier, Ramsay Macdonald, to provide for separate electorates; Macdonald announced that even Hindus were not a homogeneous group or 'nation', and that henceforth the caste Hindus and the scheduled castes were to vote separately. India was one; the admission of separate Muslim electrorates had made it two; the new formula would break it up further. From his prison Gandhiji registered his protest and started a fast from September 20, 1932.

Rabindranath sent him a congratulatory telegram. The sacrifice of his valuable life for the cause of Indian unity was quite worthy of him, wired the poet. Gandhiji wrote back that this was the kind of blessing he had expected from Guru-deva, the Master.

The Congress leaders were all in prison. Rabindranath's mind knew no peace. On September 26, with Amia Chakravarty and Surendranath Kar, he left for Poona. The day he reached Poona news was received that Macdonald had agreed to Gandhiji's suggestions. Then Gandhiji broke his fast. The poet was present by his side, and at his request he sang one of his songs:

> When the heart is hard and parched up,
> Come upon me with a shower of mercy.
> When grace is lost from life,
> Come with a burst of song.
>
> When tumultuous work raises its din
> on all sides shutting me from the beyond,
> Come to me, my lord of silence, with
> thy peace and rest.
> When my beggarly heart sits crouched,
> shut up in a corner, break open
> the door, my king, and come with
> the ceremony of king.
>
> When desire blinds the mind with delusion and dust,
> O thou holy one, thou wakeful, come with thy thunder.

From Poona the poet came back to Santiniketan. In the agitation of the last few days all thoughts of poetry had been laid aside. He now wrote a long short story *Dul Bon* (Two Sisters), somewhat in the manner of *Sesher Kabila* (Eng. trans.: *Farewell My Friend).* There was the same lyrical flair, it was full of striking phrases and 'psychology'.

24

Professor Rabindranath Tagore

IN 1933 TAGORE APPEARED in a new role as a University Professor. Of course he did not have to take regular classes. For his Kamala Lectures he chose *Manuser Dharma* or the Religion of Man. Not an abridged version of the Hibbert Lectures, the treatment was at once simple and more intimate.

Madanmohan Malaviya came to meet him at Baranagore at the Mahalanobis house. Vithalbhai Patel who was in Europe on grounds of ill health, had written to Malaviya that, on the eve of new constitutional changes, Europe was being flooded with a campaign of vilification aimed against India. British agents were out to prove the incompetence of Indians to self-rule and that their demand for a larger share in the country's administration could never be entertained. Miss Mayo's infamous book *Mother India* had been translated into most European languages. In a statement Rabindranath expressed his feeling that the tide of British propaganda could hardly be checked by writing a few articles or sending Indians abroad. It would be necessary to establish information centres in the Western capitals.

The summer was passed at Darjeeling. On the reopening of the school and college at Santi-niketan he had a long discussion on the Bengali language and prosody with the staff and students. Most of the discussions centred round the new experiment of prose-poems in which he had taken a more than passing interest and for which he had made rather large claims.

At Santiniketan the staging of some plays before the long vacations was an old practice. Pressed for new plays he wrote two very dissimilar pieces, *Tasher Desk* (Kingdom of Cards) and *Chandalika* (The Untouchable Maid). Way back in 1892 he had written a rather funny story in *Sadhana.* What with its songs and dance, the satire, *Kingdom of Cards,* though an adaptation, was really something new. *Chandalika,* a more genuine and piercing story was adapted from old Buddhist legends, one of his favourite sources.

The delighted response of the Santiniketan audience did not, however, stop the leaky hole of Visva Bharati's finance. Outside performances were necessary. The shows had a larger social value too, educational and aesthetic. So, as usual, he took his troupe to Calcutta. The acting, decor, make-up and conversation in *Tasher Desh,* with Rabindra-nath's direction and the imaginative stage production by Nandalal and Surendranath Kar, created a unique experience such as the audience had never known before. The idea that he was a poet has prevented most people from realising the fact that he was so many other things besides.

That year he did not move out during the autumn holidays. One eason for this was that the ashrama was full of guests and visitors. All kind of odd demands were made upon him, and if he ever declined people took offence. "At seventy-two the headpiece has become a junk, and mistakes are many and frequent, but people like to judge by old standards," he would sometimes say in self-defence.

In Bombay preparations for a Rabindra Week were afoot. An exhibition of his paintings had been arranged, also the staging of his play *Shap-mochan* (Redemption) and *Tasher Desk.* The latter had been translated into Gujarati, but the Bengali version was to be acted.

A large troupe of Santiniketan boys and girls, teachers and artists, left for Bombay. It hardly looked like a fund-raising expedition. At Bombay the usual round of lectures, parties, and receptions followed him everywhere. From there he came over to Waltair, where he had been invited for a lecture at the Andhra University. The subject of his talk was 'Man'.

From there he pushed on to Hyderabad. The President of the Nizam's Executive Council, Sir Krishanprasad, had sent an invitation. It was some five years before, in 1927, that the Nizam had donated one lakh rupees to Visva Bharati for a department of Islamic Studies. This was an opportunity for Tagore to offer his personal thanks to the Nizam. He stayed in Hyderabad as State guest for about a fortnight, met several prominent people, spoke at many meetings. Some subscriptions and donations for Visva-Bharati were received.

After about a month and a half in Central and South India the poet returned to Calcutta, where he delivered the opening and concluding addresses at the Rammohun Centenary Celebrations. His subject was *Bharat-Pathik Rammohan* (Rammohan, an Indian Pilgrim). But this was not the only meeting he addressed; he had to speak at many other functions as well. People did not spare him despite his age. Whether he would have liked to be spared is also doubtful.

On his return to Santiniketan, Sarojini Naidu, the guiding spirit of the Rabindra Week Celebrations in Bombay, paid him a short visit. Two other distinguished visitors of the year were Jawaharlal Nehru and his wife, Kamala Devi. Their only daughter, Indira, was a student at Santiniketan and they had come to see her.

A few days later he came to know that Gandhiji was coming to Calcutta in connection with the Harijan movement. Because of the Poona Pact, the caste Hindus of Bengal were rather annoyed with him, they felt that the numerically stronger Muslim community would soon threaten their very existence. A large section of the Calcutta public had decided not to offer him any reception. Rabindranath advised the public against such calculated discourtesy. He himself bad many differences with Gandhiji. Only a few days before, during the Bihar earthquake, in which many lives and much property had been lost, Gandhiji had declared that the calamity had been due to the sin of untouchability. The poet had sharply contradicted the statement. But no one could deny his great soul and his love of India. So, in the teeth of opposition, Rabindranath spoke out, "I welcome Gandhiji." In May, 1934 at the age of seventy-three the poet ventured with a party to Ceylon. While the party went ahead by rail the poet himself went by a ship from Calcutta port, a novelty. His birthday was spent on the Bay of Bengal. Two years ago on this day he remembered he had been at Teheran.

At Colombo there were the usual lectures and

exhibition of his paintings, and the play, *Shap-mochan*. To the modern Ceylonese Indian dance and music, decor and dress, appeared almost unknown and strange. Due to centuries of Dutch and English rule the people had grown rather westernised,even Buddhists had taken either Dutch or Portuguese names. To the Sinhalese audience Indian dance was a new experience. Some Ceylonese students had come to Santiniketan before; but from now on boys and girls began to come in greater numbers, especially in the Department of Fine Arts, Music and Dancing.

Apart from Colombo he visited Galle, Horana, Kandy, Matara and other places. He stayed at Kandy for a week, and in its quiet surroundings completed the novellete *Char Adhyaya* (Four Chapters). It is strange how in spite of constant movement and excitement the love story of an ill-fated couple, kept running in the poet's mind. From Kandy he left for Anuradhpura where he visited the ancient ruins. From there he moved on to Jaffna, a centre of Tamil culture. At one time the north of Ceylon had been part of the Tamil empire and Tamil settlers had been living there for generations. At Jaffna *Shapmochan* was staged for three nights; there was also a public address by the poet. After travelling from place to place for about six weeks, Tagore returned to India by the end of June, 1934.

After the autumn recess he again visited the South. On his way back from Ceylon he had wished to break journey at Madras for a few days, but he had been in a hurry. Hence this second visit, with the usual troupe. There were several shows, but the local audience appeared to be rather apathetic. From the financial point of view the show was a failure. After twelve days spent in Madras he came back to Calcutta by way of Waltair.

In the meantime he had been invited to deliver the Convocation Address of the Banaras Hindu University. As he was about to set out, news was received about Malaviyaji's illness. The Convocation had been postponed. But once the poet had decided on something it was difficult to hold him back; the trait was growing stronger with age. He went to Banaras all the same, coming back after five or six days on December 4, 1934. The convocation was fixed for early February (1935) and he had to go there again.

The day on which he was leaving for Banaras, February 6, 1935, Sir John Anderson, Governor of Bengal, paid a brief visit to Visva Bharati. Anderson was a Governor to reckon with, he had a brilliant record in Ireland, where he had ruthlessly put down the Irish nationalists. He was now trying to repeat his performance in Bengal by suppressing the revolutionary movement. On the eve of his visit Santiniketan was thick with the police and secret service men. The District Superintendent of Police had informed the poet that, for reasons of safety, the police wanted to detain some students of the college. He said to the police chief in that case they themselves could welcome the Governor, he would be away. However, later on, a way out was found: all the residents were sent away to the annual festival at Sriniketan. The Governor inspected virtually an empty campus.

At Banaras the poet delivered the Convocation Address, the University on its part conferred upon him the D. Litt. degree. From Banaras he went by car to Allahabad. He had to address a few meetings there too, including one of the University Students Union. From there he proceeded to Lahore, again at the invitation of the Students' Union. He was not keeping well and had been advised against such a long journey.

He reached Lahore on February 14, 1935 and stayed as the guest of Dhanram Bhalla. Two weeks were spent in Lahore. Punjab was being swayed by winds of diverse doctrines, the difference between the Hindus and the Muslims was gradually widening. The Sikhs had some time back taken exception to a poem by Tagore on Guru Govind Singh. This was due to a defective translation in Urdu. They felt that the poet had been disrespectful to their Guru. This, of course, was far from the truth. The leaders of the Sikh community held many discussions with the poet and in the end felt convinced of their mistake and of the poet's sincere regard for the Sikh Gurus. The saintly appearance of the poet carried its own authority and his conversation lent additional charm. They later held a reception in his honour at the Gurdwara, a great distinction. It may be mentioned in passing that, both at Shanghai and Vancouver, a similar honour had been shown to the poet by the local Sikh community.

On his way back he spent a couple of days at Lucknow with Professor Nirmalkumar Siddhanta. One of the professors, Dhurjati Prasad Mukherji, a connoisseur of his poetry and music, arranged a musical *jalsa* (soiree). In spite of running a temperature he heard one of the classical maestros till midnight.

When from the North Indian tour he came back to Santiniketan, the Uttarayan house was empty. Rathindranath had left for England to discuss the future of Sriniketan with Eimhirst. The Dartington trust had been making substantial contributions to Sriniketan since 1922. It was not certain if this would be available after 1935, when the new Indian Constitution came into force.

The poet was now taken up with a new hobby, building a mud house. It was to have mud walls and a mud roof. Tagore went into raptures over the idea. Frequent consultations were held with Nandlal and Suren Kar; the poet was hoping that if the experiment succeeded, it might solve the problem of building thatched cottages in the rural areas. The experiment, he liked to believe, had a practical use.

There was a house-warming ceremony on his seventy-fifth birthday. The same evening Rajsekhar Basu's well-known farce, *Birinchi Baba,* a satire on bogus saints, was staged; the poet had made some changes in the script and was present at the performance.

There had been some speculation as to where he would spend the summer, when the poet suddenly took a decision and went to live in his favourite houseboat, now on the Ganga. The Padma was too far away; moreover, she had shifted her course from Shelaidaha. While in Calcutta the Bengali Literary Academy had arranged for a reception on his completing the seventy-fourth year. A little later he had to preside over the Buddha's birthday celebrations in a monastery in Calcutta. In a moving address he said: "The Buddha whom I accept as the greatest of mortals, to him on his birthday on this full moon day of Vaisakh, I wish to offer my salutations." A monograph collecting all his writing on the Buddha has been published by Visva Bharati.

He was floating from place to place on the Ganga. The boat reached the ghats at Chander-nagore. "There in front of the place where we anchored our boat, stood the building where I had spent many long days with Jyotida." For lack of repairs the house was in a dilapidated condition. He wished to rent a house by its side. Now, at seventy-five, old memories trooped back, especially memories of an affectionate sister-in-law, a star that still shone as bright as before, and of an indulgent and loving elder brother.

Boating days over, he returned to Santiniketan. A group of poems had gathered in the meantime, in the old familiar metre, *Vlthika.* After *Parisesh,* which he had often thought would be his last book of verse, had come the amazingly new experiments of *Punascha* (Post-script). Nor was this going to be the last word for soon after came *Sesh Saptak* (Last Note). But even this, as we know, was not to be the last word. There were more poems in the offing, more and new.

The artist in him could not be starved for long. Rehearsals of *Arupratan,* the revised version of *The King of the Dark Chamber* were under way. It was to be staged in Calcutta. The poet left for the city with his troupe: there were two shows at the Empire Theatre on December 11-12, 1935. The play proved to be a success, but the poet had a setback. So much exertion, anxiety and excitement at seventy-five, it was not the body's fault. He had to cancel the Orissa Music Conference programme.

In February 1937 the Education Week and a conference of the New Education Fellowship were being held in Calcutta at the University Senate Hall. The New Education Fellowship was in its origin a European movement; the poet had been present at its 1930 Elsinore sessions. A branch of NEF had been opened at Santiniketan, with the poet as its President and two of the Professors of Visva Bharati as joint secretaries.

Tagore gave two addresses at the Education Week Conference; one of these 'Sikshar Sangikaran' (Education Naturalised) had been included in his book on Education *(Siksha)* .At the end of his address he put forward a suggestion to the Minister for Education for a guided Home Education Course through the medium of Bengali. It was a request on behalf of candidates who could not afford to study in school. Without government support, Tagore knew such a scheme could hardly hope to succeed. Needless to say, nothing was done. Later Rabindranath himself sponsored a scheme of his own, and Visva Bharati started the Loka Siksha Parishad or People's Education Centre, a useful institution now fallen on evil days.

After attending the Education Week the poet returned to Santiniketan. It seemed to him that for a long time his life had lost all touch with poetry and music. He felt like asking his 'daimon' for an explanation. But the regret was short-lived. He was busy turning the lyrical drama of *Chitrangada* into a musical dance drama. He had done this already for *Sishutirtha* and *Shapmochan.* Buttheir dramatic content had been too thin to find an entirely satisfying embodiment as dance-drama. How this adaptation would succeed was not quite clear. But in the new version of *Chitrangada* dance, music and acting blended into a beautiful whole and it has been a favourite ever since.

25

The Diffusion of Culture

IT WAS DECIDED to take the *Chitrangada* troupe on a North Indian tour. Fund-rising for Visva Bharati was apparently the aim of the tour, but diffusion of culture was how Tagore saw it. With a rather huge entourage the poet visited Patna, Allahabad, Lahore, till in the end he reached Delhi.

One evening Gandhiji came to see him. He did not like the idea of the old poet's moving from place to place in search of a little money for Visva Bharati. He inquired about Visva Bharati's deficits. Sixty thousand rupees, he was told. Gandhiji arranged for the amount to be paid to its account and advised the poet to return. But a programme had already been announced at Meerut and the party went there in fulfilment of the contract. Then it returned to Calcutta in April 1936.

Thanks to Gandhiji, Visva Bharati cleared off its old debts. The poet felt relieved. But for how long ? It was a sinking bark with a hundred holes, and he would have to turn to the Mahatma once again, a few years after.

On the literary front, breaking through the metaphysical and rhymeless prose-poems, came bursts of sheer, amusing incoherence, of a mind at ease, free from reason's rigid hold. Also the waking dream of a world of whim, visionary pictures and designs—strange, weird, ceaseless. These are poems of *Khapchhara* (Without Rhyme or Reason). This book of poems was dedicated to Rajshekhar Basu. The poet had himself drawn the illustrations or supplied the verses for the sketches. Earlier the poet had been charmed by Parasuram's* *Gaddalika.* Tagore not only dedicated the book to him, but in the hope of getting him to Santiniketan, had a marble plaque 'Rajshekhar Vijnan Sadan' put on the door of a tin-roofed science laboratory. But he could not be drawn in. Tagore interested him, but not his Visva Bharati, a distinction made by quite a few.

As soon as the life at Santiniketan palled, Rabindranath would run away to Calcutta. This was an old practice. He came to stay at the new house which the Mahalanobises had recently built at Baranagore. There was no distraction of functions and meetings and he hoped that the days would pass pleasantly. But returning to Santiniketan we find him writing: "Tired of the tyranny of the city, I have escaped." People would not let him alone; but the question

* The pseudonym under which Rajshekhar Basu preferred to write.

is, would he have liked to be left alone ?

The autumn holidays were nearing. A new play was called for but there was neither time nor inspiration, so he re-wrote a narrative poem *Pari-shodh* (Retribution) and turned it into a dance-drama.* He went to Calcutta with the boys and girls to stage it in a college hall to feel the reaction of the elite of Calcutta. The reaction was reassuring.

Then came an invitation from the University of Calcutta to deliver its Convocation Address. This was the work of Shyamaprasad Mukherji, its Yice-Chancellor. In the eighty years of its existence the University had not so far invited any non-official. Usually the Viceroy or the Governor addressed the meeting. Rabindranath accepted the invitation and did something that had not happened in the University's history so far. He gave his address in Bengali. So far neither in the University of Calcutta nor in any other university in India had one addressed the graduates in their mother tongue. Rabindranath showed the way, but few have followed his lead, not even the institution of his own making.

In Calcutta the poet usually put up, as we have already seen, with Professor Mahalanobis. One day he went by houseboat to Chandernagore to inaugurate a Literary Conference. On another occasion in Calcutta, he gave an address at an All-Faiths Conference held in connection with the Shri Rama-krishna Paramhamsa Centenary. His theme was the universal essence of religion and the canker

*The dance-rdama referred to is *Shyama.*

of communalism. "Religion which conies to us to offer freedom, turns the greatest enemy of freedom. Of all the bonds the bonds of religiosity are the hardest to break. The most hateful of prisons the one that is invisible, where man's soul is a prisoner of his own deception." Bengal was then full of communal passion. Hence these words, bitter but true.

He came back to Santiniketan after about a month. A few days later, the members of the Sunday Club of Calcutta, numbering about forty, paid him a day's visit. There had not been a gathering like this before. No literary conference, it may be mentioned, was ever held at Santiniketan during the poet's lifetime.

On the Bengali New Year's Day (1937) the Chinese Hall (Cheena Bhavana) was formally inaugurated. Jawaharlal Nehru was expected to come, but at the last moment he had been held back and sent his address through his daughter Indira. In modern times Rabindranath was the first Indian to forge the bonds of unity between India and China as well as with the rest of the world. The study of the Chinese and Tibetan languages and culture had been started much earlier. The opening of the Cheena Bhavana was mainly a fulfilment of years of hope and steady activity. It was the young Chinese scholar, Tan-Yun San, who was responsible for building it up, he had gone to China, collected funds and handed over the money to Visva Bharati. Tagore said in his address: "Friends are here from China with their gifts of friendship and co-operation. The Hall will serve both as nucleus and as a symbol of that larger understanding that is to grow with time . . . .

"Visva Bharati will remain a meeting place for individuals from all countries, East or West, who believe in the unity of mankind, and are prepared to suffer for their faith. I believe in such individuals even though their efforts may appear to be insignificant to be recorded in history."

After the summer break-up the poet felt like going out. With a fairly large group he left for the hills of Almora. He carried with him a box of scientific books and card-sketches by Nandalal.

At Almora he wrote two very dissimilar works, *Visva-Parichaya* and *Chharar Chhabi.* He had at first entrusted the work of writing a book on modern science to a teacher of physics at Visva Bharati, Pramathanath Sengupta. The poet started revising the latter's manuscript but soon he rewrote the whole thing himself. But modern science is not easy to make out and to do the job the poet had to read a good deal and held many discussions with those more knowledgeable. He had long wanted to start a series of easy introductions to subjects of popular interest, like the 'Home University Series' which would be priced cheap and reach a large section of the public. Years before the plan had been announced in the papers but nothing practical had some out of it. Now the series was started with a book on modern science. It was dedicated to Professor Satyen Bose (Satyendranath Bose or S. N. Bose), the well-known Indian scientist. In the dedicatory letter, the poet said that knowledge of science is essential for our people "in order to free the intellect from illusions, to keep it aware of a scientific temper is the first necessity."

Along with work on the science book he was also writing

verses for children. These were later collected in *Chharar Chhabi,* with pictures by Nandalal to help. He found out a tripping measure and simple language to suit. This allowed the tired mind a fresh bath in the ever-fresh waters of the child-mind. He bathed, as it were, once more, in the days that were no more. Many years before, at Almora, he had written a number of children's poems which were collected in his *Shishu* (The Crescent Moon). This time, it was more sophisticated.

Apart from reading and writing, most of his time was spent in painting. The pictures would take shape alongwith the brushwork, nothing was premeditated. The local indigenous colours used by the Kumaoni artists, at times he would experiment with these too.

He came back from Almora after nearly two months in June 1937. The change of place had not improved his health. He could feel that it was fast giving way. May be that was why he paid a short visit to the old *zamindari* at Patisar, as if to look his last on all things lovely.

Coming back to Calcutta he had to speak at a Town Hall meeting on August 2, 1937. It was convened by a section of Calcutta citizens to protest against the inhuman treatment accorded by the Bengal Government, then dominated by the Muslim League, to the deported political prisoners in the Andaman Islands, then a penal settlement, and to express sympathy with their hunger strike. At the end of the meeting the poet sent a telegram to the prisoners assuring them of the country's support but requesting them to desist from fasting.

At last he returned to Santiniketan. The rains had come. For the past few months all his time had been taken up by science writing and paintings. The rains once more released his mind on the wings of song. With a string of these songs he again left for Calcutta with a troupe to stage the *Varshamangal* or the rain festival. Again back in Santiniketan, he was passing a normal round of days and there was nothing outwardly wrong with him. But one evening in the course of conversation with some of the inmates, he suddenly lost his consciousness. Doctors rushed from Calcutta and within a few days he came round. But he felt, rightly, it was nature's danger signal. He woke up to a new supra-consciousness. The poems of *Prantik* are a sombre record of that revelation of a borderland existence.*

> In the heart of the darkness of a world without light the messenger of death came slow and unnoticed;
> and all the subtle dust that had clung, layer after layer, in life's farthest horizon, was cleaned with the acid of bitter suffering.

The opening poem is a prelude, or a summary of the rest.

After his quick recovery he started his usual load of work once again. But he knew that his body was ailing and he went to Calcutta for a check up, staying, as usual, with the Mahalano-bises. At that time Calcutta was wild with excitement. The All India Congress Committee was meeting there. Gandhiji and other leaders were all there.

*In the words of a critic: "The very first line of the first poem strikes an austere note, bringing us straight to the heart of the mystery—the nearness of death and alongwith it, the familiar idea of rebirth through suffering, a dying into life.

Many came to meet the poet. Gandhiji was expected to come one day, but he suddenly fell ill. On hearing of his illness, the old poet himself went to see him.

A controversy was going on in Congress circles over the national song of India. A group favoured 'Bande Mataram'. But Jawaharlal and others felt that the song in its entirety would not be acceptable to all groups in India. Rabindranath sent his own views, supporting Jawaharlal, for which he was severely attacked by the nationalist papers. On majority vote the Congress, in November 1939, decided to accept the first stanza of 'Bande Mataram' as the national song of India. Later, Rabindranath's own 'Janaganamana' was also accepted as a national anthem.

The poet came back to Santiniketan, his mind filled with new ideas. An anthology of Bengali verse was on the anvil while a new edition of *Gitabitan* (his collected songs) was also contemplated. The first edition, rather hurriedly got up, had been arranged more or less chronologically. This time the rearrangement was made according to theme and content; this was no easy task to undertake for an old man of seventy-seven.

Since he had become known, letters came from all over the world from all sorts of men and women, even children. He replied to most of these to the best of his ability. One such letter deserves special mention. It was published as an open letter in England in reply to a question as to what should be the attitude of Indians to the 1935 reforms. He replied that if this kind of independence had been granted to the British they would have scorned even to touch it. He made it clear that so long as Britain wanted to keep

India within her imperial grasp, it was vain to expect either admiration or friendship. The Second World War was yet two years away. From what he had seen and known of the European nations he could see that they were "paving the path for mutual annihilation". As for the future in India he said that we should "ally ourselves with those humane forces in the world, wherever found, which are seeking to end altogether the exploitation of man by man, and nation by nation."

In summer he came to Kalimpong. This was his first visit to the place. Though a health resort, Kalimpong was left out by the fashionable; for them nearby Darjeeling offered many and obvious attractions. He liked Kalimpong more than Darjeeling, which seemed to him too sophisticated and formal. While he was at Kalimpong, All India Radio arranged for a special broadcast on his birthday. The whole country heard the most musical and mature recitation in the poet's own voice.

He spent a month at Kalimpong, busy writing philological essays on the Bengali language: *Banga-bhasa Parichaya.* It was at this time that Maitreyi Devi invited him to Mongpu. Mongpu was a quiet hill town, where her husband was the director of a cinchona research centre. Maitreyi Devi's father, the philosopher, Surendranath Dasgupta, was intimately known to the poet. This was his first visit to Mongpu and also his first close contact with the family. Maitreyi Devi soon became a great favourite; her charming reportage, *The Poet by the Fireside,* gives an intimate portrait of Rabindranath in a relaxed mood.

26

The Restless, Unsettled Phase

AFTER TWO MONTHS in the hills he returned to the plains and to Santiniketan. For many reasons the poet's mind had been quite disturbed. One reason was the Sino-Japanese war. The poet had genuine admiration for both the nations and felt deeply hurt at the Japanese aggression. In spite of his love for Japan he could not but send a strongly-worded note on Japanese foreign policy. This had been flashed in the Chinese papers. In defence of the Japanese policy the poet, Yone Noguchi*, wrote a rejoinder. Rabindranath now joined battle and did not hesitate to compare the Japanese militarists with Timurlane. He put on record his disillusionment about the Japanese whom he had respected as a nation of artists and as a people who believed in moral principles. He expressed his hope that both China and Japan would one day forget their bitterness and meet as friends. Concluding the letter he wrote, out of the bitterness of his heart: "Wishing your people, whom I love, not success, but remorse."

During the Paus festival, Elmhirst came from England, to see how the work of rural reconstruction at Sriniketan was getting on. Andrews also dropped in after a rather long absence. Towards the beginning of 1938 Jawaharlal Nehru came in conflection with the opening of the Hindi Bhavan.

*Noguchi had been welcomed in 1935 by Tagore at Santiniketan.

The Congress President, Subhas Chandra Bose, came to meet Jawaharlal. The two met at the poet's house, but no one knows what transpired between them.

It was a critical period for the Congress though in eight provinces the Congress happened to be in power. The trouble centred round the election of a new President of the Congress. Subhas was an extremist, and Gandhiji and others did not favour his candidature for re-election. But he won.

Returning from Calcutta in January 1939 he wrote, or re-wrote, three new plays, *Parisodh, Chandalika* and *Tasher Desh.* A public performance in Calcutta was the next thing. *Parisodh* was given a still more new look and became *Shyama.* The new edition of *Tasher Desh* was dedicated to Subhas Chandra Bose. In the dedication, the poet wrote, "You have taken upon yourself the sacred task of infusing new life in the nation, in acknowledgement of which I dedicate this book to you."

The poet's days passed in a variety of work, writing, painting, visiting Calcutta now and then. The Orissa Congress Ministry invited the poet to spend the summer at Puri as a State guest. At the Circuit House, rooms were set apart for the poet. He had lived in Puri some fifty years before. But now he was in a reminiscent mood. He had written poems in those days and was wricing poems even now: but as he said, "in today's poems the rush and energy of youthful enthusiasm can never be there." Perhaps what is there is a deep passion of a self-withdrawn mind trying to know and express itself.

He stayed as Puri for three weeks. Under the

chairmanship of the Chief Minister, Biswanath Das, the poet's birthday was celebrated with great pomp. Andrews also came there; this gave him great happiness.

From Puri to Mongpu, from the sea to the hills. Last time at Mongpu he had enjoyed both its natural beauties and the affectionate looking-after by Maitreyi. The little services and delight of a happy, well-to-do family with children about, these he had not known for many years.

He left the hills just before the rains on June 17, 1939. The Indian situation was far from happy. The Congress was divided against itself. In spite of stiff opposition Subhas had been elected Congress President for the second time. Gandhiji did not like this, since his nominee, Pattabhi Sitaramayya had been defeated. In spite of his respect for Mahatmaji, Subhas did not accept the mild and tolerant Gandhian way and the Congress High Command frowned upon him with open disfavour. Matters came to a head after the Tripuri session and Subhas had to resign from the Congress Presidentship; later on he had to leave the organisation itself.

All these worried the sensitive poet. This was the face of politics even before Independence. Rabindranath wrote, "Wherever power concentrates it secretes its own poison. I am afraid the power of the Congress may have become a source of sickness."

Foreign news was even more heart-rending. One day at Mongpu he had cried out; "I do not wish to open the papers, or listen into the radio. The endless history of tyranny is unbearable . . . .I have lost all desire to live any longer. This world has grown unfit for human living. But how long shall I have to witness this brutality, how long ?"

Returning from Mongpu he spent two months at Sriniketan and Santiniketan. At Santiniketan he addressed the workers and explained to them, for the last time, the aims and ideals of the institution.

In the meantime Subhas Bose sent him an invitation to lay the foundation stone of the Mahajati Sadan. During his tenure as President of the Congress he had raised funds towards the building of Congress House. The land was a gift from the Corporation of Calcutta. Rabindranath gave it a beautiful name Mahajati Sadan—the House of the Great Nation(s)—and in the fitness of things had been asked to lay its foundation stone, and he did.

On September 1, 1939, the Second World War was declared. Within two days of the German attack on Poland, England declared war against Germany. Before a fortnight had passed the Russians attacked Poland from the eastern flank. Poland which had been patiently building herself for the last two decades was razed to the ground by heavy bombing.

The poet had come to Calcutta on his way to Mongpu, where he was going to spend the autumn days. In Calcutta he found that the Indian political situation had suddenly become complicated. According to the British view the war was India's war as well. India had been demanding Independence all these years, and the British were making only hypocritical promises. India's obligations to the British Empire were clear and obvious but not *vice versa.* The Indian leaders declared that in order that India could give her free and full cooperation in the defence of democracy, the British Government should first grant Independence to her and create bonds of true and abiding friendship. There were many signatories to this demand. On the top was Rabindranath Tagore.

In Midnapore a Vidyasagar Memorial had been put up. Rabindranath was requested to be the Chief Guest at the opening ceremony.

He returned to Santiniketan before the Paus festival. The Paus address, *Antardevata* (The God Within) was printed and distributed before the service. It was a clear analysis of the causes of the war and the war sitution. On Christmas morning he wrote a new and passionate poem on Christ:

> Those who struck Him once in the name of the rulers, are
> born again in this present age.
> They gather in the prayer halls in a pious garb,
> They call their soldiers 'kill, kill', they shout;
> in their roaring mingles the music of their hymns,
> while the son of man in His agony prays, O God,
> fling, fling far away this cup filled
> with the bitterest of poison.

February 17, 1940. Gandhiji and Kasturba came to see the poet. Both felt that the poet's health was fast deteriorating. Gandhiji stayed on for two days, going round the departments. Before he left, Rabindranath, anxious about the future of Santiniketan, gave him a sealed cover. The poet had written: "Visva Bharati is like a vessel which is carrying the cargo of my life's best treasure, and I hope it may claim special care from my countrymen for its preservation." In his absence he wished to put Gandhiji in sole charge of the institution. Gandhiji in his turn handed it over to Maulana Abul Kalam Azad, then the Minister for Education. After Independence the Indian Government honoured that request in 1951 by accepting the financial responsibility for Visva Bharati and turning it into a Central University, not an unmixed blessing. Both Rabindranath and Gandhiji were gone.

Now his days followed a dull-round. His was a decaying body, defective hearing, failing eyesight, but the vigour of mind still unimpaired. But it was starved of nourishment. In a letter to Amiya Chakravarty he wrote: "The trouble with me is that my body is static but, worse, so is my mind. With you near, the mind begins to stir and flow. People around me do not realise how much I need that strong spur of thought."

His own disabled condition had its comic side and the nonsense rhymes of *Khapachhara* were meant to express this mood as well as to cheer himself up. It was the same with the humourous poems of *Prahasini.* He played with nonsense rhymes and with their aid to forget, if for a while, the darkening universe that was closing stealthily but steadily.

After the New Year and birthday celebrations he again left for the hills to his favourite haunt at Mongpu, where his birthday was observed by the Buddhists of the area.

Next day from Calcutta came news of the death of his nephew, Surendranath. He had been ailing for sometime and the poet was prepared for it. But the sudden death of Kalimohan Ghose was a shock. One by one, tolling reminiscent bells, the old familiar faces were disappearing.

In the country: Congress bickerings, communal riots,

crimes against women; outside: a world-wide war—these were the staple news. To lighten the agony he satirised the whole thing in a ballad:

> Across the seas in death's drama
> strange things are happening,
> And in Bengal in the tamarind grove,
> one hears the policeman sneezing.

At his age what else could he do ? Yet he sent a cable to President Roosevelt expressing his hope that the United States might stand against the universal destruction and establish peace in the world. It drew no response.

But the entire energies of a tired mind were not devoted to brooding over world problems. He also looked within and back. The past stood out vividly in his mind's eye. The setting sun harked back to the early days. In chastened idiom, he put it across to others, such was his late brilliant autobiography, *Chelebela* (My Boyhood Days).

On August 7,1940, the Oxford University conferred upon him the D.Litt. degree (honoris causa) at Santiniketan, Though belated, this was unique, since Oxford had come all the way to Santiniketan. The Chief Justice of the Federal Court of India, Sir Maurice Gwyer represented his University and read the Latin citation, to which the poet replied in stately Sanskrit. Years before there had been a proposal to award him the degree, the year when *Gitanjali* was published. Lord Curzon it is believed, had opposed the move.

The days passed slowly, wearily. The body was getting weaker every day and walking proved to be difficult; he had to be carried about in a wheel-chair; sight had failed, hearing was equally bad. Yet men came and troubled him for all kinds of services, great and small. It was under pressure that he wrote the astonishing story *Laboratory* and after it *Badnam* (Bad Name). Reading these one might think, as with Yeats, that with age the poet was becoming more modern. A critic has noted: "Men grow conservative with age; in the case of Rabindranath it is the opposite that is true."

He was not feeling happy at Santiniketan. The Calcutta doctors had advised him against so much moving about. But once he had made up his mind it was not easy to hold him back. Rathindranath had gone on an inspection of the *zamindari.* Pratima Devi was at Kalimpong. So there was nobody near who could control him. In a letter hastily put together before die journey to Kalimpong, he writes: "For some time past the body has shown signs of decay ; it is a torture to live through the long hours, yet one has to work. There is no place in India where I can go and stay undisturbed. Parts of the mechanism have become junk. 'Doctor Ray (Bidhanchandra) has asked me not to go to Kalimpong. But I am so anxious for rest that I cannot listen to his warning. I am leaving for Kalimpong today."

Within a week news was received that the poet had suddenly lost consciousness. Professor Mahalanobis with a doctor, left by plane. Pratima Devi was alone, but quite by chance Maitreyi Devi happened to be there. Rathindranath was contacted with the help of a radiogram message. Rabindranath was brought down to Calcutta in a state of coma. For one month he was bed-ridden. It was an anxious time yet even during the period of convalescense he used to dictate poems. He came back to Santiniketan on November 18. For the next eight months he had to be under strict regimen. Doctors flitted in and out all the time. Two girontic books written during the period were called, appropriately, *Rogsajyey.* (In the Sick-bed) and *Arogya* (Recovery).

In his long life he had always been chary of receiving personal service. But now he had to leave himself almost entirely at the mercy of his attendants. In one of the poems we hear his sad, bemused admission: "At the evening of my life I now know what happens to a living toy." Elsewhere, in a more feeling tone: "They come crowding in on my life at the early dawn. But those who are near me in the empty hours at this tired twilight's fading light you have brought with you your own lamps to give me the last touch of the lands before the boat leaves the shore. . ."

So the days passed in an arm chair, or in bed. Sleepless nights and restless days full of strange thoughts. But through it all the unceasing stream of poetic creation, sometimes serious, at others light. Some of his best poems belong to this late period and they show a maturity of vision and an awareness of self and society and mystery, rarely to be met in the poet's earlier works. In the hour of parting he feels:

> I know I have failed and my poems
> Have just missed reaching the All.

Such awareness may seem to celebrate a sense of loss, it is really a gain in insight.

Came the Paus festival. His address—*Arogya*

(Recovery)—had been dictated earlier. He could not attend the service in the Mandir. "I am present in the ashrama and yet unable to take my seat at the Paus festival, such a thing has happened for the first time today." On the 26th of January, perhaps anticipating the Republic Day resolution, he reminded the rulers of India and all rulers in a poem that the end of autocracy was at hand.

Britain, involved in a terrible war, was seeking Indian help but how weak, impotent and poor she had kept the Indians at all times ! To ask slaves to help was indeed a mockery.

At the Magh festival too his address had to be read out in the Mandir. In this, his last sermon, he once more paid his tribute to Raja Rammohun Roy.

Another aspect of the poet's mind was revealed in the stories and verses of *Galpa Salpa* (Little Tales). In these there was no touch or trace of a tired mind or the suffering of a sick body. Even at this age he could think of rapid readers for children. The last of the series was written on March 12, 1941. His birthday was observed duly. The address, his last, 'Crisis in Civilisation' was read out from a wheei-chair. He said: "This helpless country has been denied mastery over the machine, by means of which the British have strutted as a world power. I have seen with my own eyes the extent of Japan's prosperity and national uplift. I have witnessed again, in Moscow, the tireless energy with which the Russians have tried to wipe out from their country disease and illiteracy, ignorance, penury, and every outward mark of shame. Free from racial prejudice, the Soviets have projected all over their domain the power of human fellowship. The swift and surprising progress they have attained makes me at once happy and jealous !

"One unusual respect of Soviet life that impressed me in Moscow was that the tie of common interests resulted in a great joint endeavour and prevented communal differences from developing into political conflict."

"The turning of the wheel of fortune," he concluded, "will compel the British one day to give up their Indian Empire. The hour is near when it will be revealed that the insolence of might is fraught with great peril," and he quoted a Sanskrit couplet: "By unrighteousness man prospers, gains what seems desirable, defeats enemies, but perishes at the root."

27

A Romantic is No More

HIS LAST BIRTHDAY (7th may, 1941) was observed in a simple style. In a verse letter the poet worte.

> On this my birthday
> I seek for friends.
> In their last friendly touch

In the earth's final friendliness
I shall carry with me life's final gift
Man's last blessing.

A few days after, a representative of the court of Tripura conferred upon him the title of *Bharat Bhaskar* (Sun of India). In his early days Tripura had sent its congratulation to the young poet. The last honour too came from Tripura. The wheel was coming full circle.

That year it was a terribly hot summer. Professor Buddhadeva Bose visited the poet at Santiniketan and had many lively discussions with him. These were later published in the journals and collected in a booklet, *Sahityer Swamp* (Nature of Literature). Two months before his death, he had once more to engage in polemics, but there was no alternative. The leaders of the National Congress were all rotting behind prison bars for the unpardonable crime that they had asked for a clear statement of British war aims. Such demands revealed the ingratitude of the Indian people—this was the angry comment by Miss Eleanor Rathbone, an Independent member of Parliament. Her article, which was highlighted, contained severe strictures on Jawaharlal. From his sick-bed the eighty-year-old poet drafted a rejoinder. A memorable document, this was his last essay on Indian Independence and human dignity (June 5, 1941), and a grateful nation joined its silent chorus to its ringing utterance.

But the body was failing. He knew it.

The doctors finally decided upon a surgical operation. He was taken to Calcutta on July 25. It was a simple leave-taking, the poet reclining against a heap of pillows in Visva Bharati's only rickety omnibus.

He was operated upon on July 30 at the Jora-sanko Mansion. A little before, a poet to the end, he had dictated:

> Your creation's path you have covered
> With a varied net of wiles, Thou Guileful one.
> False belief's snare you laid with sinful hand in simple lives.
> With this deceit you have left a mark on Greatness ; for him kept no secret night,
> The path that is shown to him by your star is the path of his own heart over lucid,
> Which his simple faith makes eternally shine.

The operation was not a success. His condition quickly deteriorated. He lost consciousness and breathed his last on August 7, 1941 at midday.

> The first day's sun
> has asked
> at the manifestation of new being,
> who are you ?
> He gets no answer
> Year after year went by
> the last sun of the day
> the last question utters
> on the western seashore
> in the silent evening—
> who are you ?
> He gets no answer.

Ages hence the question will echo and re-echo, and receive no answer. The sun had set. □

INDEX